CRYPT

OF THE

GLADIATOR

A James Acton Thriller

Also by J. Robert Kennedy

James Acton Thrillers

The Protocol	*The Thirteenth Legion*	*Embassy of the Empire*
Brass Monkey	*Raging Sun*	*Armageddon*
Broken Dove	*Wages of Sin*	*No Good Deed*
The Templar's Relic	*Wrath of the Gods*	*The Last Soviet*
Flags of Sin	*The Templar's Revenge*	*Lake of Bones*
The Arab Fall	*The Nazi's Engineer*	*Fatal Reunion*
The Circle of Eight	*Atlantis Lost*	*The Resurrection Tablet*
The Venice Code	*The Cylon Curse*	*The Antarctica Incident*
Pompeii's Ghosts	*The Viking Deception*	*The Ghosts of Paris*
Amazon Burning	*Keepers of the Lost Ark*	*No More Secrets*
The Riddle	*The Tomb of Genghis Khan*	*The Curse of Imhotep*
Blood Relics	*The Manila Deception*	*The Heretics Bible*
Sins of the Titanic	*The Fourth Bible*	*The Hunt for the Holy Grail*
Saint Peter's Soldiers		*Crypt of the Gladiator*

Dylan Kane Thrillers

Rogue Operator	*The Agenda*	*The Messenger*
Containment Failure	*Retribution*	*The Defector*
Cold Warriors	*State Sanctioned*	*The Mole*
Death to America	*Extraordinary Rendition*	*The Arsenal*
Black Widow	*Red Eagle*	*The Betrayal*

Just Jack Thrillers

You Don't Know Jack	*Jack Be Nimble*

Templar Detective Thrillers

The Templar Detective	*The Unholy Exorcist*	*The Black Scourge*
The Parisian Adulteress	*The Code Breaker*	*The Lost Children*
The Sergeant's Secret		*The Satanic Whisper*

Kriminalinspektor Wolfgang Vogel Mysteries

The Colonel's Wife	*Sins of the Child*

Delta Force Unleashed Thrillers

Payback	*Forgotten*	*Charlie Foxtrot*
Infidels	*The Cuban Incident*	*A Price Too High*
The Lazarus Moment	*Rampage*	*Righteous Hell*
Kill Chain	*Inside the Wire*	*So They Don't Have To*

Detective Shakespeare Mysteries

Depraved Difference	*Tick Tock*	*The Redeemer*

Zander Varga, Vampire Detective

The Turned

CRYPT

OF THE

GLADIATOR

A James Acton Thriller

J. ROBERT KENNEDY

This is a work of fiction. Names, characters, places, and incidents are products of the author's imagination. Any resemblance to actual persons, living or dead, is entirely coincidental.

Copyright ©2025 J. Robert Kennedy

All rights reserved. No part of this publication may be reproduced, stored in or introduced into a retrieval system, or transmitted in any form, or by any means (electronic, mechanical, photocopying, recording or otherwise) without the prior written permission of the publisher.

ISBN: 9781998005963

First Edition

For Lili Bettez, born March 11, 2025, a little shooting star who, in her mere three hours of life, touched so many hearts.
You were loved and will be missed.

CRYPT

OF THE

GLADIATOR

A James Acton Thriller

"Avē Imperātor, moritūrī tē salūtant!"
"Hail, Emperor, those who are about to die salute you!"

Suetonius, circa AD 121, recounting the events of AD 52 at Lake Fucinus, likely not a phrase routinely uttered before battle by gladiators.

"There is a sufficiency in the world for man's need but not for man's greed."

Mahatma Gandhi

PREFACE

Gladiator fights, forever associated with the decadence of ancient Rome, have been glorified in literature and film, with few things so brutal also considered honorable. Excavations of ancient sites have found tributes to these fierce warriors painted on walls, much like today's sports heroes are memorialized by their supporters with a can of spray paint and graffiti of varying degrees of artistic merit.

But by AD 432, the fights were rare, relegated to the outer fringes of the Roman Empire, to underground arenas, the tastes of Romans changing over the centuries. With Christianity spreading, the Church's influence growing, it was now considered immoral, and was officially banned.

Yet deep down, the people still craved it, still followed their forbidden heroes, still paid to see what their religious and political leaders would deny them.

And in that fateful year, the yearning crowds would be given one more match by their emperor, one more battle, one more chance to see blood spilled on the sands of the mighty Colosseum.

One more opportunity to quench the thirst that all men throughout the ages have suffered.

To see the once mighty vanquished, the once respected shamed, the once superior cut down to nothing.

But what if that man had no intention of giving them what they wanted?

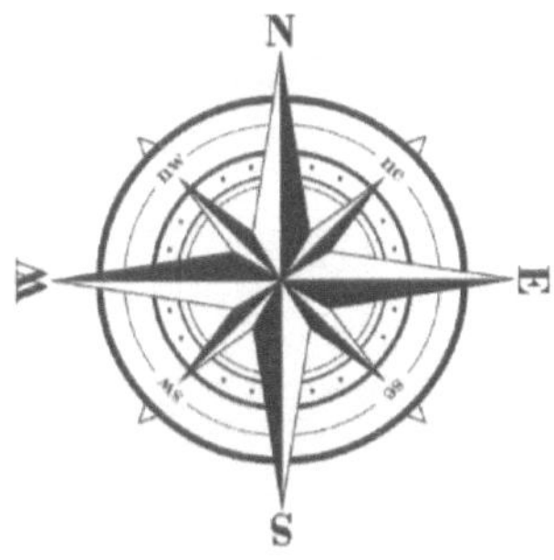

Apostolic Palace of the Lateran

Rome, Italy

Present Day

Mai Trinh smiled as her fiancé, Tommy Granger, inched his way up the ramp. He had a problem with heights, exacerbated by yesterday's near fall off a ladder. He was so cute, and she was so proud of him, his latest example of technological wizardry unbelievable. She had no idea how he did it. She was an academic, determined to follow in the footsteps of her mentors, Professors Acton and Palmer. They had taken her in after her forced exile from Vietnam and had become like her American parents.

She loved them, and she was certain they loved her.

And she definitely loved this man staring at his feet, and not the drop just to his left.

She extended her hand. "You're clear."

He took it, and she hauled him toward safety. She smiled at him and he returned it, her heart melting like it always did when he looked at her.

He leaned in and gave her a quick kiss, and she reached up to make it something a little more when somebody shouted behind her.

A shout of panic.

She spun toward revving engines, and saw a guard drop, then another, spotting two SUVs racing toward the gate, strange popping sounds accompanying the roar of the motors. The flimsy gate was tossed aside as the first vehicle blasted through, and she stood frozen as panic overwhelmed her.

"Oh shit!" Tommy grabbed her hand and hauled her toward the SUV the professors had rented as more of the suppressed gunfire continued around them. Tommy tripped, breaking their grip, and she spun to help him as the first of the attackers' vehicles skidded to a halt, all the doors opening, four men stepping out, dressed in gear as terrifying as anything she had ever seen, in real life or otherwise.

"Run!" screamed Tommy, but she hesitated. She couldn't leave him. "Run! I'll be right behind you!"

She didn't want to leave him, but if she could reach their rental, it was up-armored. She could open the door and save precious seconds. She turned, sprinting toward the safety of the interior. She slammed into the side of it and hauled on the door handle, thanking God it was unlocked, when she spotted one of the attackers raising his weapon, aiming it at Tommy.

"No!"

The man swung his weapon toward her and squeezed the trigger, the popping sound louder this time. She gasped, unsure for a moment what had happened, then a searing pain erupted in her stomach, and she gripped at it as she stared down, crying out at the sight of blood rapidly staining her white shirt. She collapsed to the grass as a curious sensation swept over her, the world slowly going dark, the popping sounds fading in the background, the last thing she heard, the desperate cry of the only man she had ever loved.

"Mai!"

Leptis Magna, Tripolitania

Western Roman Empire

AD 431

"The western gate has fallen!"

Comes Rei Militaris per Africam, Count of Military Affairs for Africa, Decimus Cornelius Vindex, cursed as he spun toward the messenger. "Details, man! I need details!"

The young soldier, covered in sweat and grime, flinched, his eyes bulging. "The gate has been breached, Dominus! Enemy troops have entered the city!"

"Are we holding the line?"

"For the moment, Dominus, the breach has been contained, but—"

Decimus glared. "But?"

"The commander says he can't hold it for much longer without reinforcements."

Decimus turned to his second in command, *Tribunus Laticlavius* Tiberius Aemilius Severus. "Strip every third man from the other gates. Send them to hold the line."

"Yes, Dominus!" Tiberius, a trusted friend of many years, turned, passing on the order, messengers standing nearby sprinting from the rooftop from which they were observing the battle.

Decimus peered over the wall into the courtyard below. "Status?" he shouted.

A soldier turned and peered up. "We're barely three-quarters done! We need more time!"

"You don't have it. Tell the men to redouble their efforts or they answer to the emperor himself, should they survive the Vandal hordes!"

"Yes, Dominus!"

More orders were barked, but they were useless. The men were going as fast as they could. The enemy at the western wall would take the city. It was inevitable. It was why he had been sent here. Rome's influence in this area had been weakening for some time, and he had been dispatched by the emperor to secure the treasury and return it safely to Rome, and evacuate as many of the citizenry as possible.

His mission wasn't to save the city, but to save the gold, the jewels, the valuables—the things that fueled an empire.

The city would fall, but Rome would be back someday. For what reason, he wasn't sure. Much of what he had seen was a wasteland, sand stretching in every direction, little evidence of civilization. Why they were here was beyond him. Yet he didn't care. Someone, somewhere, centuries ago, had decided to take this land, to build cities, including this declining yet still substantial outpost and port.

He had never understood the desire to occupy territory simply for the sake of occupying it. Territory should have strategic importance—wealth, local manpower to mine and farm, to man the navy, to bolster the armies. But there was little of that here. Yet there was a treasury worth a fortune, some of it provided by the empire, some of it stripped from conquered peoples, all of it hastily moved from the capital of Oea to the west, where the Vandal hordes were threatening though had apparently bypassed. It suggested they perhaps were after the treasury, their spies betraying its new location.

When sent here, he expected a few carts full of precious metals and gems. What he had found was far more—and perhaps evidence that his evaluation of this barren land was woefully inaccurate.

He stared out over the city, fire and smoke intensifying in the western half. He had deployed the bulk of their troops to the northwest and southwest, creating a wedge, forcing the enemy through the hills and concentrating them at the western wall.

Most of these men would die here today. Not his concern. While his heart wept at the loss of any soldier serving under his command, they were here to serve their emperor, their empire, and it was their duty to die should it be necessary.

And the emperor had deemed it so.

He sighed, returning to the wall. "Send the transports that are ready to the east gate!"

"Yes, Dominus!"

The order was issued as Decimus returned his attention to the west of the city. He cupped a hand to his ear, tilting his head slightly. He could hear the clash of swords, men crying out in rage and agony. He yearned to be in the fight, to be there with them, parrying blows with a shield, thrusting the tip of his blade and scrambling the innards of those who would dare oppose the Roman Empire.

But that was no longer his job.

He was a leader now. He guided the men from afar, at too safe a distance. It was an honor to do so, a privilege, though it was also the most difficult promotion he had ever accepted. He had been tempted to turn it down, but one doesn't deny the emperor what he wishes.

His sword would likely never draw blood again.

Tiberius returned with a report from another messenger.

"Well?"

His friend frowned. "It's not good news, Dominus. Reports indicate the lines are faltering."

Decimus tensed. "Where?" He peered to the south then spun north. There was no evidence the enemy had broken through their external lines. If he pulled those troops inside the city through the northern and southern gates, they could potentially hold.

But it could ruin a carefully laid plan.

A plan hampered by the emperor.

He had arrived by sea. This was, after all, one of the largest ports on the Mediterranean. However, his orders forbade him from transporting the treasury in the same manner. He had been ordered to return across the desert, where they would use the port in Alexandria, a safer prospect not just militarily, but from a weather perspective. Entire fleets had been wiped out by Mediterranean storms, and the emperor wasn't willing to risk the treasury from suffering a similar fate.

It was the correct choice, though it posed difficulties now that the enemy had engaged.

He had no doubt they were attacking now because they had discovered his arrival with an entire legion of fresh troops and likely feared more were on the way. They had to attack now or risk their own destruction in the future, though he wondered if they had merely discovered they were leaving with the treasury and were motivated by greed. It was possible, though he doubted it. He had fought the uncivilized before. All they cared about was blood.

His men below needed time to empty the treasury. Nothing was to be left behind. The emperor's orders were explicit. Pulling those troops could give them that time.

Horses whinnied below. He peered down into the courtyard to see half a dozen transports underway, heading toward the eastern gate.

Progress.

"Send every second man from the north and south gates to the lines. Order the rest, except lookouts and messengers, to the eastern gate."

"Yes, Dominus."

Tiberius stepped away to execute the orders, and Decimus once again stared out across the city as the sun slowly dipped in the west, long shadows cast that could soon hide a greatly determined enemy. He didn't fear death. As a soldier in the Roman Empire, he had expected to die young. But his skill on the battlefield had kept him alive, and as he rose through the ranks, forced him farther back from the front, eventually directing men into battles in which he once fought.

Though he didn't fear death, he did fear what would become of his family—his wife, his children. He hadn't been born a citizen. He had earned that right. His position granted him significant wealth, providing his family a comfortable life in Rome, within the estates outside the city. If he were to die, what would become of them? If he died in the good graces of the emperor, they should be fine, but Roman politics were fickle. Winners were always backed—assuming those winners didn't become overly ambitious and threaten the political elite.

He had shown no interest in politics. None whatsoever. Frankly, it disgusted him. He was a soldier. He would execute his orders but had no desire to become part of the government that controlled the daily lives of the citizens he served.

He sighed.

Should I fail to secure the treasury, it will be my head.

He closed his burning eyes.

And those of my family.

Apostolic Palace of the Lateran

Rome, Italy

Present Day, Three Days Earlier

"Isn't this exciting?"

Inspector General Mario Giasson of the *Corpo della Gendarmeria dello Stato della Città del Vaticano*, or the Corps of Gendarmerie of Vatican City State, gave Father Esposito a look. "From my perspective, this is nothing but a security nightmare."

The Vatican's chief archaeologist regarded him. "I suppose from your perspective, it is. But for me, as an academic?" He shrugged. "It's a dream."

Giasson folded his arms and sighed heavily as he assessed the excavation unfolding in front of them. To his left was the Lateran Palace—Church property—which meant it was his responsibility to protect it. The Pope often spent time here, so security was paramount, and his expert eye had already counted 32 people scrambling around that he had no clue about. Who were they? Would they pass a background check? Were they threats?

Anything was possible. Even if they were here as part of their job, it didn't mean one of them didn't harbor ill will toward the leader of the Roman Catholic Church. On any given day, they might be a law-abiding citizen, but then, when an opportunity presented itself, they could snap and take advantage.

No, this wasn't exciting at all.

"We're not sure what we've found. When they were digging the subway extension, they stumbled upon what we think is an ancient burial crypt."

"How ancient?"

"Hard to say at this point. We'll need to examine things more closely, do some carbon dating. From the little bit I've seen? At least fifteen hundred years. There are indicators here that it's from before the collapse of Rome."

This piqued Giasson's interest. Though he was Swiss, ancient Roman history always fascinated him. "So, what does this mean? When they found that burial chamber under New York City, they cleared it out and continued tunneling. Something tells me that's not what's going to happen here."

Esposito chuckled. "No. What they found in New York was a curiosity that could be explained. A hoax. Elaborate, but a hoax. Not really a piece of history. But this"—Esposito gestured toward the excavation—"there's no doubt this is real, and it's ancient."

Giasson chewed his cheek, knowing full well he wasn't going to like the answer to his next question. "So…"

"So, I'm afraid they're going to have to find a new route for their subway."

Giasson sighed. "And let me guess. We're going to have to get used to having people on our property."

"Absolutely." Esposito indicated an excavator already at a segment of the wall that once surrounded the centuries-old residence. "There's no doubt they're going to be asking to start digging on the other side of the wall before the day is out."

Giasson growled. "As long as they don't knock it down."

Esposito dismissed the concern. "They shouldn't need to. They'll just go under, shore it up. But if I were you, I'd be preparing for this to be a months-long problem, not weeks-long."

"Months?"

"If not years."

Giasson cursed. "Years?"

Esposito eyed Giasson with a wry smile. "With the amount of time you've spent with Professors Acton and Palmer, I would have thought you'd become a little more familiar with how archaeological digs work, especially something this size."

"I'm usually too busy ducking from bullets and grenades."

Esposito's face clouded over, no doubt with the recollection of what had just recently happened with the discovery of the Heretics Bible. "They do attract trouble."

Giasson inhaled deeply. "They either cause it or find it." He tilted his head forward and scratched his forehead, closing his eyes. "We're going to have to set up an interior security perimeter. Station personnel here 24/7. Just how deep into our property do you think this is going to go?"

Esposito shook his head. "No idea. It could go a few meters. It could go all the way under the palace."

Giasson's jaw dropped. "Under the palace? That won't do."

"They'll follow the dig to wherever it goes. Don't worry, like I said, they'll shore things up, make certain the structural integrity of any of the buildings here will be maintained."

"Do you have any experience in these things?"

"Some, but not enough. Not if we're getting underneath something as important as the palace. But don't worry. The Italians certainly do."

Giasson chewed his cheek for a moment, then muttered a curse. "That may be, but I don't know them."

Acton/Palmer Residence

Overlook Village Gated Community

St. Paul, Maryland

"Did you guys hear about what they found in Rome earlier today?" asked Mai Trinh as she sipped on a glass of Chalk Hill Chardonnay.

Archaeology Professor James Acton drained the last of his Corona. "Does the Pope shit in the woods? Is a bear Catholic?"

The Vietnamese exile and new American citizen stared at him. "Huh?"

Archaeology Professor Laura Palmer swatted her husband. "James, keep it polite."

He cocked an eyebrow at her, extending a hand. "Hi, Jim Acton. Have we met?"

The hand was batted away. "You're terrible sometimes."

He grinned. "You married me."

"Yes, I'm wondering about that now." Laura turned her attention to the young woman they both thought of as a daughter. "Yes, we have heard of it, in case you weren't able to interpret my husband's idiocy."

Tommy Granger, Mai's fiancé and a tech whiz kid, downed his own beer. "I got it."

"Yet you didn't laugh," observed Interpol Agent Hugh Reading, nursing a bottle of ice-cold water, still recovering from his heart attack, though finally well enough to travel.

Tommy shrugged. "It wasn't that funny."

Acton reached into a nearby cooler, extracting another *cerveza*. He positioned the bottle cap at the rim of the table and slammed down on it with the palm of his hand, popping the top off.

"James! You're going to ruin the table doing that!" admonished Laura.

"It adds character."

"Bollocks! You just don't like the table."

"How can you say that? I chose it."

She gave him the stink eye. "*You* chose it? Name one thing in this backyard that you chose?" He opened his mouth, and she cut him off with a raised finger. "Besides the barbecue."

His mouth snapped shut.

"That's what I thought." She faced Mai. "Like I was saying, yes, we heard about the discovery. Very exciting."

"I'd love to go." Acton shoved a lime wedge through the top of the bottle then jammed his thumb over the opening, tipping it upside down and watching the slice slowly rise to the bottom. "I love ancient Roman history. And a fresh dig? There's nothing like it."

"Why don't you go?" asked Reading. "It's not like you two can't afford it."

Acton dismissed the idea. "You don't just drop in on other people's digs. It's considered rude, and I have no doubt they're getting swamped with requests. If they want us, they'll ask."

"You should ask, Mr. Professor. You're a very important man," said Rose, their domestic, who was becoming part of the family and was now Reading's temporary caregiver.

"I knew there was a reason I liked you, Rose. Yes, I *am* a very important man."

Laura rolled her eyes. "Oh God, now you've got him going."

Teeth were flashed, a shoulder swatted again.

Tommy looked up from his phone. "Part of it is on Church land."

Acton's eyebrows shot up. "It is? Since when?"

Tommy wagged his phone. "I don't know. I just Googled it, and they said excavations have begun"—he peered at the phone again—"At the Lateran Palace." He looked up. "What's the Lateran Palace?"

"It's a lot of things, not the least of which is the official church of the Pope," replied Laura. "Thanks to the Lateran Treaty, it's considered Vatican soil."

"Well, there's your in." Reading crushed his now empty water bottle and screwed the cap back on, the vacuum created holding it in its now compacted form.

Rose leaped to her feet and took the bottle, retrieving a fresh one from a cooler nearby. Reading smiled gratefully as she cracked the seal and handed it to him.

"You're so good to me."

She beamed a smile, and his broadened.

"She's paid to be," noted Tommy, and everyone glared at him. "What?" he asked as he shrank into his chair.

Mai leaned in and whispered in his ear, explaining things to him.

"Oh." His eyes shot wide. "Oh!"

Reading's cheeks were already red, and Rose stared at her hands as she sat back down.

It had occurred to Acton during the Grail incident that Reading and Rose could be the perfect match. They were both single—chronically single, from what he could tell of Rose's history they had managed to glean. They were both attractive, similar in age, and could hit it off if given the chance. Hiring her to take care of Reading while he was here was a stroke of genius, if he did say so himself. Perhaps the Florence Nightingale effect might take shape here, and two people could come out of this happy. And if his good friend was happy? He didn't care if manipulation was involved.

Acton quickly changed the subject, jerking his chin toward Tommy's phone. "So, they're saying it's on Church property now?"

"Yeah," replied a still flustered Tommy. He tapped at his display, and Acton's phone beeped. "I just forwarded you the article."

Acton pulled it up on his tablet sitting on the patio table and quickly skimmed the first few paragraphs, then tapped on a photo.

"That's Mario!" exclaimed Laura, excited at seeing their friend. "You don't think—"

Acton finished her sentence. "That we should give him a call? Terrific idea." He glanced at his watch and cursed. "Maybe we should wait until it's not after midnight there."

"Good thinking." Laura pulled out her phone.

"Who are you calling?"

"Mary."

Acton's eyebrow cocked at the mention of their travel and former British Secret Service agent. "A little presumptuous of you, don't you think?"

She eyed him. "Do you really think he's going to deny us?"

Acton eyeballed her. "Me? Abso-freakin'-lutely. You? He'd never say no to you."

"Pish-posh. He's a married man."

"Right," he grunted. "Since when did that matter?"

"True."

"Bat your eyes at him, flash those pearly white, show him your tits. Whatever you need to do to get us on that dig."

Laura tilted her head toward her husband. "Show him my tits?"

Acton held both hands up in defense. "Hey, I didn't say let him touch them. But let's put those girls to use."

Rose giggled. "Men are the same everywhere. They can't think when there are boobs in the room."

Acton noticed Reading stealing a glance at Rose's chest, and he grinned at him. His friend blushed and jerked his head in the opposite direction.

"Bollocks," he muttered.

"Is everything all right?" asked Rose.

"Uh, yes. It's nothing." Reading jerked his chin toward Laura. "Better make it a video call. Listening to boobs just isn't the same."

Tommy chortled. "He's right about that!"

Acton roared with laughter, and Rose joined in, swatting Reading playfully. "You're as bad as Mr. Professor!"

Reading grinned and shrugged.

Mai swatted Tommy hard, and he rubbed his shoulder. "Hey, I didn't start this!"

She cupped her breasts. "Show some respect, or all you'll be doing is listening to these things."

Tommy quickly leaned over, placing his head on her shoulder, and batted his eyes up at her. "I'm sorry. Please let me see the twins."

She snickered. "Fine. You're forgiven."

"Good." He sat up, staring expectantly. "Well?"

She eyed him. "Well what?"

"I thought I was going to get to see the girls."

"Not here!"

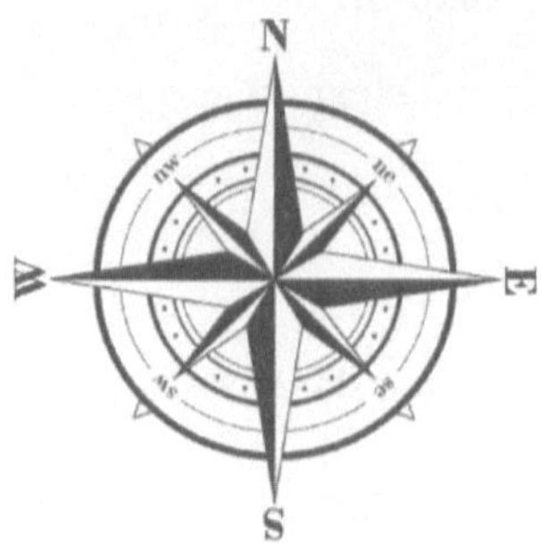

Leptis Magna, Tripolitania

Western Roman Empire

AD 431

"The last transport is away!"

Cheers erupted around him. Decimus didn't allow himself any signs of celebration. It had taken far too long. The enemy had breached the western gate. His forces were fighting bravely but losing against the overwhelming odds. His men were better trained, better equipped, and fighting from a fortified position, yet their foe seemed to have unlimited numbers.

Fires burned throughout the western half of the city, uncomfortably close to the administrative buildings at the center.

He turned to Tiberius. "The citizenry?"

"Those with Roman citizenship who have chosen to evacuate have already left."

Decimus exhaled loudly. "Why anyone would remain is beyond me. They'll be slaughtered."

"Everything they have, everything they own, is here. For many, this is the only home they've ever known. Would you leave Rome if it were to fall?"

Decimus grunted. "Rome will never fall."

Tiberius smirked. "Hypothetically."

"You've made your point." Decimus sighed. "Give the order to fall back in an orderly manner. Delay the enemy as long as they can. We'll need the convoy to clear the city and reach the gorge before sunrise."

"I still don't understand why the emperor wants us to go overland. It's far slower."

"Ours is not to question why." He faced the north and its silted harbor. This had once been a great city of almost 100,000 souls, a Roman jewel on the north coast of the continent. But now, it was a shadow of its former self—barely 20,000 currently calling it home, its dominance and importance usurped by Oea to the west.

"Incoming!" shouted someone to his left.

The warning yanked Decimus from his thoughts. His personal guard swarmed into position, and he and Tiberius took knees as shields rose, protecting them. Several thuds followed, most of the arrows clattering harmlessly onto the stone roof.

Decimus turned to Tiberius. "I do believe we're no longer welcome here."

Tiberius smirked. "What was your first clue?"

Decimus rose. "Time to leave, gentlemen."

His guard rose, shields still held in formation, and they retreated to the stairs.

He descended to the ground floor, Tiberius and the head of his personal guard, *Centurio Protector* Gaius Julius Varro, flanking him. His guard tightened their circle as they headed for the courtyard. If he had the troops, he would hold the city—but he didn't. And that wasn't the mission.

Save the treasury. Get out as many citizens as you can.

To both sides of him were local slaves lining the walls, their hands clasped in front of them, their heads bowed. He wondered what would happen to them. He had no doubt the moment the last Roman soldier left the compound, they would shed their Roman garb and disappear into the city. Life here had been good—even for the slaves.

Far better than what awaited them once the city fell.

Rome, wherever it went, brought peace, stability, prosperity. A better way of life, a better quality of life. Why people refused to recognize this, insisted on resisting, was beyond him. Perhaps it was human nature to resist the oppressor.

But that was politics, and he was a military man. His duty was to execute his orders, not question them. When he reached Rome, he would ask the emperor for several legions to come back and reclaim the territory, though he had the distinct impression from their last meeting that this option wasn't on the table.

Rome had lost interest in this region.

The lack of interest had emboldened the barbarian king Geiseric to lead his Germani tribe south, across the Strait of Gades, where Europe and Africa almost touched. Rebellions weren't tolerated. Just look at what had happened to the Jews—few remained in their so-called Holy Land. But this wasn't a rebellion, it was an invasion, and he feared it would go unpunished unless someone in Rome believed a lack of retribution might embolden others on the fringes of the empire.

They emerged into the late evening, the sun low on the western horizon, and mounted their horses. Decimus signaled the final exit with a heavy heart. Scores of soldiers marched rapidly toward the main gate, a wary eye kept out for stray arrows. The banners were lowered as they passed through the gate, and they headed down the central road toward the eastern wall of the city.

Screams and shouts of soldiers still fighting behind him had his jaw clenching. He felt like a coward. Yet he had his orders. Dying on his feet served no purpose. If he died, the treasury would fall into enemy hands, and that would mean disgrace for him, his men, and the empire.

No. He had no choice. He had to lead what was left of Rome out of this lost territory.

Horns blared, announcing the retreat, and the sounds of battle changed behind him as he cleared the eastern gates. The convoy, heading to safer Roman territory, stretched out for miles ahead—carts laden with treasure, with supplies, with civilians, with the wounded.

Carts moving far too slowly.

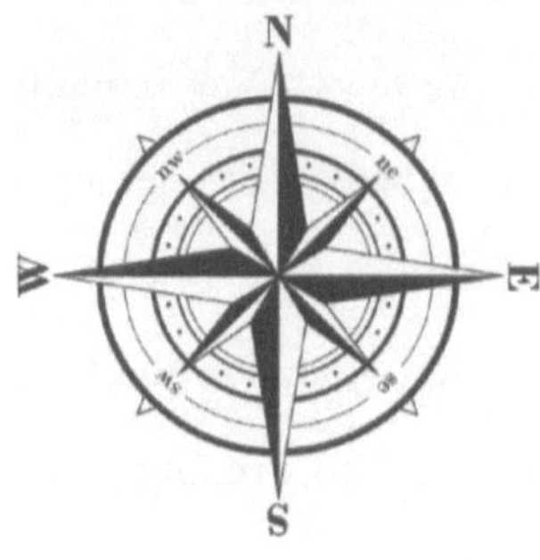

Giasson's Office

The Vatican

Present Day

"I highly recommend His Holiness not visit the palace grounds until this is done."

Monsignor Luca Ferraro, the Pope's personal aide, frowned. "He's not going to like that."

"That may be, but it's necessary."

Ferraro leaned back in his chair and folded his arms. "Is it, or are you just being paranoid like you usually are?"

Giasson eyed him. "With everything that's happened over the past few years, I think paranoia is a good starting position for anything security related."

Ferraro batted a hand. "That was before my time."

"Clearly."

Ferraro regarded him. "No need to be rude, Inspector General."

Giasson held up a hand in apology. "I'm sorry. No offense was intended. But you're right, you weren't here. We've had murders, we've had kidnappings, we've had attacks. No one respects hallowed ground anymore. They certainly won't respect the palace grounds. Will you pass on my recommendation?"

"Of course. Even if I don't agree with you sometimes, His Holiness always hears your position. He respects you tremendously."

Giasson bowed his head. "That's good to hear, and I appreciate it. Your job is to keep His Holiness happy. Mine is to keep him safe. Those don't have to be opposing positions. In this case, I suggest we err on the side of caution and recommend he not set foot there until we can at least establish proper security. And even when that's been accomplished, he should only go there if it's absolutely necessary."

Ferraro gave a curt nod. "Agreed."

Giasson turned to Father Esposito. "What can you tell us about the dig?"

"It's progressing faster than you would expect. They're in a hurry, for obvious reasons. They're excavating around the perimeter, starting at the initial discovery site."

"When will they have established what the perimeter actually is?"

"It's hard to say. It depends on the size. They're heading in both directions from the original discovery, and already it's encompassing a pretty decent area. As we know, they've already crossed the wall at one point, and obviously, they'll cross back over eventually. The good news from our standpoint is that, so far, it looks like it's beginning to bend back toward the wall, so, unless there is a surprise, we might be able to avoid going under the palace itself."

Giasson exhaled audibly. "Thank God for that."

"Indeed."

"Have you requested a personnel list from the Italians?"

"I have. I've been promised it by the end of the day."

"The sooner the better. I want everyone vetted. Full security clearances."

"Of course. I was thinking about your concerns about who we could trust on our property."

Giasson tapped his chin. "And?"

"Like I said, my team doesn't have the experience in something of this scale. But there are a pair of archaeologists that do, and I think we can all agree we can trust them."

Giasson smiled. "I was thinking the same thing."

Ferraro regarded them both. "Do you two care to share?"

Giasson smirked. "You *are* new, aren't you? Professors James Acton and Laura Palmer. They are the best in the business. His Holiness knows them and likes them. And they can be trusted to have our best interests at heart."

Ferraro's head slowly bobbed. "Yes, I've read the reports on them. But if we involve them, doesn't that mean we can also expect trouble?"

Giasson and Esposito both snorted. "You *have* read their files," said Giasson. "Do you honestly think this is one of those situations?"

Ferraro threw up his hands. "How should I know? I'm new here, remember?"

"I think we can rest assured that in this situation, all we're dealing with is a simple dig, and nothing anyone should be interested in causing trouble over."

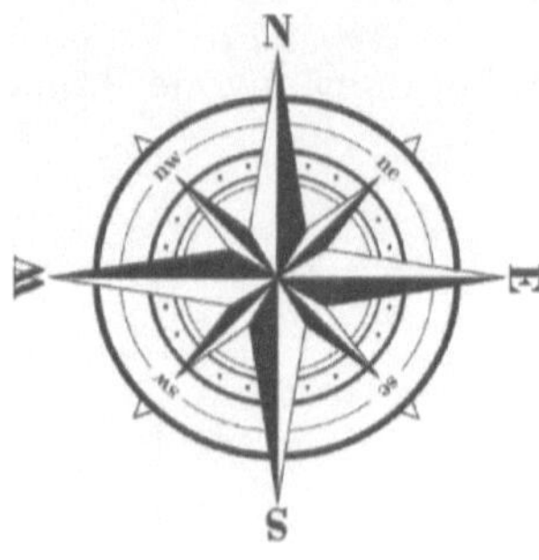

East of Leptis Magna, Tripolitania

Western Roman Empire

AD 431

"Just how stupid are you?"

The man Decimus addressed stared back at him, puzzled. "I'm sorry, Dominus, I don't understand the question."

Decimus stabbed a finger at the cart loaded high with furniture and personal belongings. "We are fleeing for our lives, yet your wagon is loaded as if you were merely moving to another city."

He pointed at the poor beast struggling to pull the load, slowing the entire procession down, forcing others in the convoy, desperate to escape the barbarian horde behind them, to leave the hardened trail to pass this idiot.

"This is everything we have, everything we own! You can't expect us—"

Decimus glared at him. "Be very careful how you finish that sentence."

The man's jaw snapped shut, wisely choosing silence rather than guessing at what response might be satisfactory. Decimus turned in his saddle and beckoned several soldiers. "Empty the cart. Empty them all. Food, water, shelter. That's it. We don't have time to waste on bullshit like this!"

"But—!"

Decimus drew his *spatha*, bringing the tip of the long, tempered blade to the man's throat. "You were about to say?"

The man's eyes shot wide, and his wife gasped. He said nothing.

"That's what I thought."

Decimus sheathed his blade then continued forward, repeating the order. The surviving soldiers descended upon the carts of the civilians, chairs, tables, rugs, clothing—tossed aside into the desert sands as he continued to the front of the column where the carts carrying the treasury continued forward, each pulled by two powerful horses. He could redistribute some of the treasure into the lightened carts, but not here, not now. They had to reach the protection of the gorge, then he had to figure out a way to save them all from what no doubt would be a substantial force, hell-bent on revenge.

He could only hope the enemy would waste its time raping and pillaging its way through what remained of the once great Roman city. All intelligence reports suggested they were undisciplined. What had turned them against the power of Rome was a question for those back in the capital to determine, though he had his suspicions. You could only rule an area with an iron fist for so long before the people rebelled. The key to maintaining power was to make life so much better than it was before, that the people willingly submitted, and over time—over generations—knew nothing but the good life that Roman civilization brought.

In time, many of the local population would actually side with their occupiers against an enemy determined to bring them back to their old, barbaric ways. Why live in mud and straw huts, wearing nothing but animal skins, usually starving, when you could live in a modern Roman city with amenities most of the world could only imagine?

Clothes and shelter with a full belly.

Yet here, in the harshness of the desert, even Roman civilization had difficulty improving the life of the locals.

He had traveled across the empire, witnessed firsthand the cities modern methods could create. But nothing was like Rome. How he missed it. Even with the empire's extensive road system, travel anywhere took months. And here, where roads hadn't been carved into the landscape, things were even slower. How much of his life had he spent in the saddle or, when he was younger, on foot, moving from one place to the next, never long enough to lay down roots?

He had met his wife years ago in Rome. An arranged meeting. His commander had wanted his second-in-command to be respectable. That meant family, children. So, he arranged the introduction with his sister-in-law's niece. She had been sweet, shy, and beautiful. But most importantly, she had laughed at his jokes, and her wit had proven just as quick as his.

It had been a match made in the heavens.

He sighed as he reached the head of the column.

What I would give to hold you in my arms right now.

He closed his eyes for a moment, allowing himself a brief respite from the harsh reality, then opened them as hoofbeats pounded on the ground behind him. He turned to see a messenger approaching and halted.

"Dominus! I bring word from Leptis Magna."

"Report."

"The city has fallen. The last of our soldiers fell defending the eastern gate approximately an hour ago."

Decimus cursed, though the news was expected. The men had done their jobs. They had served the empire and the emperor. Their deaths were honorable and, unfortunately, necessary. Every moment bought was another step gained toward safety. "Understood. And the enemy?"

"Holding for now within the city limits. It appears they're going door to door, looking for anyone who remained behind."

Decimus cursed, shaking his head. "Exactly as I warned. Any sign of pursuit?"

"Yes, sir. A patrol did depart the city. However, our rear guard captured them."

"Good. Interrogate them, then execute them. Hide the bodies and distribute the horses and any supplies they might have had on them. Have the rear guard continue their excellent work. The patrol won't be missed for some time, but eventually, their commander will begin to wonder where they are and send others."

"Yes, Dominus."

Decimus dismissed the messenger with a wave of his hand, and the man turned his horse and raced back into the dark, the sun gone. The convoy now traveled with nothing but the moon and the stars to light their way.

A light flared. A torch lit. And he cursed in rage at the violation of his orders. He urged his horse forward, the trusted steed quickly at a gallop. "Douse that flame!" he shouted, though his words went unheard. "Douse that flame!"

This time, the order was repeated, passed down the column. There was a shout, then the torch flew through the air, hitting the sand. Someone extinguished the beacon with a kick of their boot.

He reached the offender, pulling up on the reins. "You fool! I told everyone, no fire!"

"But we're cold, and we can barely see!"

"You idiot! A light in the dark doesn't let you see farther ahead. It merely lets you see your immediate surroundings better. It also can be seen for miles with no other lights around. You better pray no one saw that, for if we're found, the enemy won't be slitting your throat, I will be." He turned to his soldiers. "Make it clear once again to the civilians that there will be no fire of any kind, for any purpose, unless I personally give the order. Anyone who violates it will be immediately executed."

"Yes, Dominus!" echoed his men.

The column resumed, and with satisfaction, he noted they had picked up speed, many carts now loaded with civilians previously on foot, now that their heavy loads had been lightened. They had to reach the gorge. And he had to come up with a plan.

Though they were moving faster, they would never move fast enough.

35

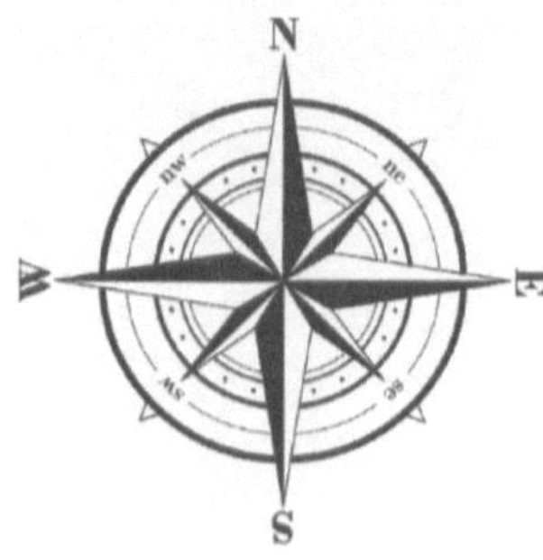

James/Moore Residence, Abbotts Park Apartments

Fayetteville, North Carolina

Present Day

"I'll have another one of those fruity drinks." Sergeant Carl "Niner" Sung caught his best friend, Sergeant Leon "Atlas" James, eyeballing him. "What?"

"You can't say that."

"You can't say what?"

"Fruity."

"Why the hell not?"

"It's not politically correct."

Niner's girlfriend, Angela Henwood, began mixing another piña colada for her boyfriend. "Is it? It's got fruit in it."

Niner threw a hand toward his girlfriend. "Exactly! It's got fruit in it, therefore it's a fruity drink. Besides, when the hell did drinks start to have separate locker rooms?"

Atlas' girlfriend, Vanessa Moore, snorted, the first sign of life out of her since they had arrived. "He's right, you know. This whole thing has been taken too far. I understand the desire for equality, for using different words like humankind instead of mankind, but why the hell should somebody get offended if you say mankind?"

Niner held up his freshly delivered drink. "Or call a drink fruity? Words don't hurt by default. It's context and meaning that do. If I say this is something only fruits enjoy, therefore it's a fruity drink, that's offensive. If I just call it a fruity drink because it's a drink with fruit, that's not offensive. Or at least it shouldn't be."

"Agreed." Vanessa's shoulders slumped. "I can't believe they stole it."

Angela dropped onto the couch beside her and wrapped an arm over her friend's shoulders. "Neither can I. I'm so sorry."

"It hasn't even been a month, and things were going so well."

Niner set his drink aside, the concoction no longer appealing, as Vanessa and Atlas both suffered. His best friend had leveraged every penny he had to help the woman he loved open a food truck. It was her first step toward her dream of having her own restaurant. She was an exceptional chef, and with her training complete, her entrepreneurial spirit strong, Atlas had bankrolled her endeavor. He would do anything for her.

Niner was happy for them. His friend was a changed man since he met her, and Niner was thrilled to hear him making long-term plans, like starting a business together, getting married, having a family.

He glanced at Angela. Things were going great with her. This was the first real long-term relationship he had ever been in, and he was happy. Thrilled. He could see himself marrying this woman, having children of their own.

Vanessa leaned forward, clasped her hands over her face, and sobbed, her shoulders shaking. Someone had stolen the food truck overnight, and it turned out the storage lot where she had been keeping it was unbonded and unlicensed, all the paperwork she had been shown, forgeries. The insurance company had already indicated they likely wouldn't be paying out because a clause in her contract required the truck be stored during non-working hours in a secure, licensed facility. "I thought I did everything right."

Atlas reached out with a massive paw and squeezed her hand. "You *did* do everything right. It was that bastard at the storage lot that didn't."

"I should have checked his license. I should have checked his paperwork."

Atlas had said the same thing to Niner when he had called with the news. His friend was angry. If the insurance didn't pay out, he was on the hook. He wasn't really blaming Vanessa. By default, people assumed the best of their fellow human beings. But in reality, far too often, people were pieces of shit.

Niner had already talked his friend down from heading over there and delivering justice, though as far as he was concerned, it was still on the table. If it had happened to Angela, he would certainly want to tune the guy up. Not kill him, just deliver a good beating. Maybe torch everything he owned.

"I wish there was something we could do to help," Angela sighed. "Maybe we can go looking for it."

Vanessa sat up straight and sniffed hard. "The police said it's probably long gone. It just isn't fair!" she cried, staring at Atlas, her eyes red. "I'm so sorry!"

"It's not your fault, babe."

"We both know it is. And your money!"

"Don't worry about the money. If I couldn't afford to lose it, I wouldn't have given it to you."

She gave him a look. "You and I both know that's BS. Nobody can afford to lose that much money."

Niner grunted. "Certainly not on a sergeant's salary."

Daggers were shot at him by both Atlas and Angela.

He held up his hands in mock surrender. "Hey, don't shoot the messenger. But listen"—he leaned forward—"if you need some help, I've got a little set aside."

Atlas vehemently dismissed the suggestion. "Hell no! Never lend or borrow money from friends, family, or neighbors."

"Listen, we're not family, we don't live near each other, and I can't stand you." Niner grinned. "So, the offer's still on the table."

Atlas laughed. "It's appreciated, brother, but we'll get through this on our own."

"What are you going to do?" asked Angela. "Are you going to reopen?"

"How?" Vanessa's shoulders slumped. "It was everything we had to open this one. If the insurance doesn't pay out, that's it. It's done. The dream is over."

Niner opened his mouth to say something about lottery tickets when he thought better of it. "You know what you need? Something to take your mind off things."

Vanessa looked up at him as she reached forward and grabbed a tissue from a box sitting on the living room table. "What do you mean?"

"My first inclination is to get some weapons and shoot up this parking lot guy's home, but I know Angela won't let me."

"Vanessa won't let me either," Atlas growled.

"They're such killjoys, aren't they?"

"Indeed."

Angela gave him the stink eye. "You were saying?"

He flashed some teeth. "Let's get away. We're both on two weeks' leave, and I've got a shitload of points. And I know Angela does too. How about we buy some plane tickets, go somewhere, and sit on a beach, sipping fruity drinks? Forget about our problems for a while."

Vanessa blew her nose. "You know, that's not such a bad idea. I've got a bunch of points as well. Should be enough for round-trip tickets and a few nights in a hotel."

Atlas chewed his cheek for a moment, the only one in the room really out a lot of money. He sighed. "Maybe that's not a bad idea. Where did you want to go?"

"I've always wanted to see Italy." Angela shrugged. "There's so much history there, so much to see and do."

Vanessa bounced with excitement, her problems, at least for the moment, forgotten. "I like that idea. It's better than a beach. A beach just means I'm going to lie there thinking about what happened. But if we go somewhere like Italy, maybe I can forget about all our problems, at least for a few days."

Atlas sucked in a deep breath, his massive chest expanding. "If my baby wants to go to Italy, my baby's going to Italy. But where in Italy?"

Angela whipped out her phone. "Well, we have to see the Colosseum."

"The Vatican. That would be cool," added Vanessa.

"Been there," said Niner.

"Done that," added Atlas.

"When?" asked Vanessa.

Atlas looked away. "Classified."

"At the Vatican? Are you kidding me?"

"Don't ask, babe."

"Fine, fine. Venice?"

Angela cooed. "Ooh, I'd love to see Venice. Gondola ride!"

Niner cocked an eyebrow. "Gondola ride? Can you imagine the big guy here? As soon as he got in, one end would be pointed skyward."

Atlas flipped him the bird. "I'll sit in the middle."

"Uh-huh. Then you'll just sink."

"Leaning Tower of Pisa," Vanessa gushed. "Oh, I think that would be hilarious. We have to do one of those staged photos where it looks like you're pushing the tower straight."

Niner took another sip of his drink. "Or we could just have the big man actually push it straight."

Atlas flexed, kissing each bicep. "Challenge accepted."

"There's so much." Angela sighed. "It would take a month to see it properly."

"Something tells me the colonel won't be okay with that," replied Atlas.

Niner's eyes widened with a thought. "I've got an idea."

"What?"

"Well, there's so much to see and do, and we have no clue how to prioritize. Why don't we ask the Doc? He would know. He could tell us what's worth seeing, what's not. Hell, he might be able to get us into a few places the public wouldn't normally see."

Atlas leaned back, wagging a finger at him. "That's not a bad idea."

"I have been known to have some good ones from time to time."

"It's rare." Atlas pulled out his phone.

"Do you have the Doc's number?"

"No. I'm just marking it in the calendar."

"Marking what?"

Atlas' meaty thumbs worked the touch screen's keypad. "Niner…had…a good…idea."

Angela giggled, and Niner gave her a dirty look. "Et tu?"

She slapped several fingers over her lips. "Sorry."

"Uh-huh. You'll pay for that tonight."

She grinned. "Can't wait."

Niner placed his drink down. "So, who's calling the Doc?"

"Not you," replied Atlas.

"Why not?"

"Because you're always hitting on his wife."

Angela cocked an eyebrow. "Excuse me?"

"Way before your time," stammered Niner. "Way before I met you." He glared at Atlas, who grinned innocently. "You know you're the only woman for me."

"I better be."

"You are."

"This is true," said Atlas.

Niner smiled at his friend. "Thank you."

"Yes, he hardly ever hits on women now that he's dating you."

Vanessa swatted her boyfriend, who recoiled in exaggerated pain. Nothing hurt the big man. She stared at him. "Apologize."

"To him? Or to Angela?"

"Both."

"Okay." He leaned forward. "Sorry, just joking. For as long as I've known him, my man's been a one-woman kind of guy." He eyed Niner. "Or one-man kind of guy, for that matter."

Angela eyeballed Niner. "Oh?"

Niner squirmed. "A few jokes and suddenly you're labeled."

"Speaking of labels." Angela gestured toward his now empty drink. "Want another fruity drink?"

"Yes. Huh, I wonder what made you think of that?"

Atlas snorted. "See? I told you it had connotations, even if it is subliminally."

Niner rolled his eyes and shook his head at Angela. "You realize I'll never hear the end of this now. It's going to be 'fruity' this, 'fruity' that."

"If the adjective fits," Atlas teased.

Niner folded his arms. "I don't think I want to do a gondola ride with you anymore."

Atlas stared at him. "Dude. There was never going to be a gondola ride with you. It's for couples."

Niner leaped from his chair, dropping into Atlas' lap, wrapping his arms around the big man's thick neck. "You know you secretly want to be alone on the water with me."

Atlas picked him up to throw him when Vanessa yelled, "Don't you dare! You're liable to break something, and we can't afford to replace it anymore!"

Atlas tilted his head, looking up at Niner held high above his head. "You're lucky I'm broke, little man, or I'd be breaking something with you right now."

Niner grinned and reached out, squeezing a bulging tricep. "Ooh, muscles!"

Atlas looked longingly at his girlfriend.

Vanessa sighed. "Fine. We just won't eat this week."

Atlas grinned up at Niner, who squeezed his eyes shut. "It's gonna hurt!"

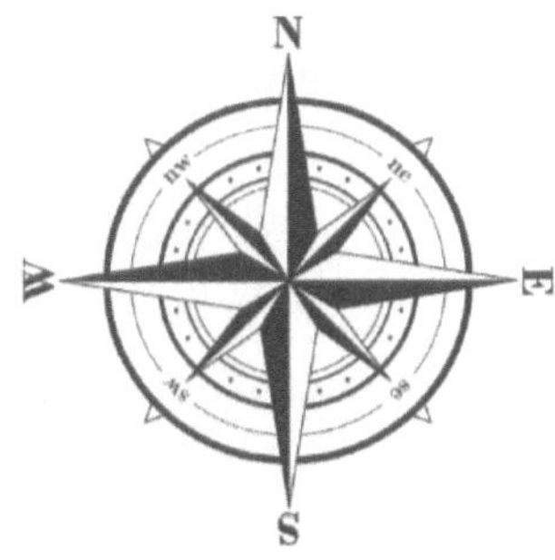

Acton/Palmer Residence

Overlook Village Gated Community

St. Paul, Maryland

"The sink's acting up again."

Acton stepped into the bathroom to find Laura brushing her teeth. He gave the twins a grin, then glanced at the sink, half-filled with water. "Reading said his is doing the same thing."

Laura gently pushed him aside then leaned in and spat. She turned on the tap, rinsing off her toothbrush. "Can you take a look at it?"

He stared at her in the mirror and delivered his best Bones impression. "Damn it, Laura, I'm an archaeologist, not a plumber." He grinned. "Don't get confused just because last night I was expertly laying pi—"

She held up a finger. "Finish that sentence and you won't be laying anything for a while."

He snapped his jaw shut with an audible clunk of his teeth.

"Good boy."

"Why don't I call a plumber?"

"That's an idea. Outsource the work. But you better do it this morning. If I know Hugh, he's going to be trying to fix it himself."

Acton patted her on the cheek—one of the southern ones. "I'll get right on it."

"You do that, and you might just see some action tonight."

Acton hopped on his toes. "Ooh, incentive! You definitely know how to motivate your students."

"I was always a popular teacher."

Acton paused mid-turn.

She batted a hand at him. "Not that popular."

"I'll take your word for it."

She headed for the bedroom, and Acton followed her. "Did you ever, you know, sleep with a student?"

Acton sat in a chair in the corner as Laura dressed. "No. Not that I haven't had offers."

"Oh?" Laura slipped on a bra, much to Acton's disappointment. "What was her name?"

"Jeremy. He was a nice guy, good looking, but not my type."

Laura snorted. "You're terrible."

"That's not what he called me. I think he called me Doctor Love."

"Let me guess. He thought your love gun was worth a deuce?"

Acton slapped both hands over his heart. "Oh my God. Two KISS song titles in one joke. I want to marry you all over again."

She pulled on a pair of shorts. "How about we get to ten years before we talk about renewing our vows?"

"I say forget ten years. Let's just hop in that bed and relive our wedding night." He licked his lips, then barked.

She pulled on a white top with a large Union Jack emblazoned across the front. "Fix the sinks, and your wish just might come true."

Acton opened up his browser, searching for local plumbers as Laura left the bedroom. They headed down the stairs to find Reading sitting at the breakfast nook with their domestic, Rose, both already finished with their morning meal.

"You two are up early," said Acton.

Reading held up his watch and tapped it. "It's almost noon. Nobody considers this early. And I'm still on UK time. It's almost dinner for me."

"Considering we didn't get in until almost three, I think we're doing pretty good."

Reading grunted. "Excuses, excuses."

Rose stood, heading for the kitchen. "I arrived at my usual time."

"Oh, you didn't spend the night?" Acton smirked at Reading, whose mouth fell agape.

Rose gasped. "Mr. Professor!"

Laura swatted him, and he rubbed his shoulder.

"You know, I'm going to grow a callus there eventually."

"Only if you keep saying stupid things."

Rose moved the HexClad pot onto a burner, turning the knob to a medium-low heat. "I have your usual here."

Acton patted his stomach as he sat beside Reading. "Yum."

Laura headed for the fridge and pulled out the orange juice when Rose shooed her away with both hands.

"Sit, Mrs. Professor, sit. I'll take care of it."

Laura didn't bother protesting. This was the usual routine. "Fine, Rose, you take too good care of us."

"It's my job. Now sit."

Laura joined the others as Rose stirred the pot of oatmeal.

"How was your party?" asked Reading.

Acton groaned. "Too long. There's nothing more boring than an alumni fundraiser." He checked his phone. "Mario should be done lunch by now." Reading eyed him. "Okay, fine, getting ready for dinner. I think I'll give him a shout."

Laura held up her tablet. "Check your email."

"Huh?" Acton tapped the icon and his eyes narrowed at an email from Giasson. He opened it and chuckled. "Well, I guess you won't have to flash your tatas after all."

"Why?" asked Reading.

"Mario's asking if we can come and help them on the dig."

"Interesting. I wonder why."

Acton struck a Superman pose with his fists pressed against his hips. "Because we're the best."

Laura giggled. "Call the man before the Avengers book up your calendar."

"Is that the right franchise?"

"And I would know this how?"

"That's right. *I'm* the uberdork." Acton pulled up Giasson's number, then placed the call on speaker, setting the phone on the table. It rang twice before their friend answered.

"Jim, mon ami, thanks for getting back to me."

"No problem. You're here on speaker with Laura, Hugh, and Rose."

"Rose? Don't tell me Hugh has finally found himself someone to keep him honest."

Reading's eyes bulged, and Acton noticed Rose appeared slightly flustered, though didn't protest. His friend stammered for words and Acton laughed. It was clear he didn't want to say anything to offend Rose—and more importantly, hurt her—by claiming it was nothing of the sort, not a possibility, never going to happen, or any one of a number of things someone might say in a moment like this. Reading let it go, which wasn't a surprise. The man had fallen for Kinti in the Amazon. He had a type, apparently.

"No wedding plans yet." Acton received another swat. "So, you need our help," he said before Reading could mount a defense.

"I assume you've heard about the discovery."

"Yeah, we saw the reports yesterday. Sounds interesting. And I understand part of it's on the Lateran Palace property?"

"Yes, and that's our concern. Father Esposito says they don't have the expertise for something like this, and, of course, your names were proposed. Do you have the time?"

"We have *some* time." Laura leaned closer. "I read your email and I don't think you need us to actually run the show. The Italians have lots of experts. But I understand your desire to have someone acting on your behalf, and we're more than happy to help."

Acton squeezed her leg. "How about we fly out tomorrow? We'll go over things, coordinate with the locals, make sure everything's set up to protect your interests, then we can advise from afar if necessary. Father Esposito is more than capable of handling this, I'm sure."

"I'm sure you're right," agreed Giasson. "Though he seems to have less confidence in his abilities than you do."

Acton struck a pose. "Most do. But the ego I have makes me confident in everything I put my mind to."

Laura rolled her eyes. "He tried to bake cookies the other day. It was a freaking disaster."

"It was a *bloody* disaster," corrected Reading.

Acton slapped a hand against his chest. "You guys said they were good."

Reading winced. "I think you mixed up the sugar and the salt."

"Tasted fine to me."

"I think your ego affects your taste buds."

"This is totally possible."

"We'll keep you away from the kitchen," said Giasson. "You'll send me your itinerary?"

"We will. Is it okay if we bring a few friends?"

"That's fine. Just send me the details so I can have all their passes ready for when you get here."

"Will do. We'll see you soon, Mario."

"Adieu."

Acton ended the call then leaned back as Rose brought them bowls of steaming oatmeal. He smiled and leaned in, sniffing. "Smells awesome, like usual. Fruit of the day?"

"Peaches."

"Hmm. Georgia?"

"Of course."

Acton stuck his spoon into the thick mixture and stirred. Rose returned to the kitchen to retrieve their drinks. He took a bite, savoring the texture, then swallowed. "I don't think I'll ever get tired of this."

"Me neither," agreed Laura.

Acton glanced over at Reading. "So, you want to come with us?"

Reading eyeballed him. "I hardly think so. My doctors are pissed enough that I flew here. The only reason they agreed was because you arranged a medical flight."

"Now who's blowing things out of proportion? You were on a perfectly normal Learjet, with a doctor and a nurse on board, who from my understanding, did nothing but sleep."

"And flirt."

"They were flirting with you, Mr. Hugh?" asked Rose.

Reading scoffed. "I'm hardly the type that anyone flirts with. Those years are long behind me." He pointed at his face. "This is *not* a handsome man."

Rose looked away. "I think you're handsome."

Acton raised a hand in the air for a high five, but Hugh glared at him, and Laura worked on the callous.

"Thank you, Rose. That's probably the nicest thing anyone's said to me in a very long time." Reading leaned over and bumped her shoulder with his. "And I think you're very beautiful."

Acton flashed pearly whites, and his wife, rather than giving him another smack, instead was rubbing a knuckle in the corner of her eye. It was a prime opportunity for a wisecrack, but there was no way in hell he was going to do or say anything that might screw up what he had set in motion in Brazil.

"Yeah, I suppose it's best if you stay here. Traipsing around a dig site probably isn't wise."

Reading faced him, but Acton noted he kept his shoulder pressed against Rose's.

Laura agreed. "Probably for the best. But I don't want you here alone. Rose, do you think you could take care of this old man for us? Maybe spend a few nights while we're away?"

She nodded, though kept her eyes diverted. "I'll wait on him hand and foot."

"I like the sound of that," said Reading, and Rose turned toward him, smiling though saying nothing.

Acton smacked his hands together. "Then it's settled. We'll head to Rome in search of fame and glory, and you two stay here and relax." He turned to Laura. "Why don't you ask Tommy and Mai, see if they want to come? I'm sure they will."

"Good idea."

Acton's phone rang, and his eyebrows narrowed at the call display. "Does anyone know a Carl Sung?"

James/Moore Residence, Abbotts Park Apartments

Fayetteville, North Carolina

"Hello?"

Niner leaned closer to the phone sitting on the table, the speaker activated. "Hiya, Doc. It's Niner."

Acton laughed. "Niner! I was wondering who the hell Carl Sung was. I don't think I've ever heard your real name."

"Keep that one under your hat. There are people who'd kill for that information."

"Yeah, mostly women," rumbled Atlas.

"Is that Atlas?" asked Laura.

"Yes, it is. Good to hear your voice, ma'am."

"My God, don't call me ma'am. I feel old enough as it is."

Niner thought better of complimenting the woman, what with Angela sitting within striking distance. "You're on speaker with me, Atlas, Vanessa, and Angela."

"And you're on with me, Laura, Hugh, and Rose," replied Acton.

"Rose?" mouthed Atlas.

Niner shrugged. "Is there a new significant other in Agent Reading's life?"

Acton laughed again. "Careful, we don't want to put too much pressure on these two. So, to what do we owe the pleasure?"

"Well, we're thinking of getting away. We've had a bit of bad news here."

"Oh no!" gasped Laura. "Is everyone all right?"

"Yes, nothing like that. I don't know if you're aware of this, but Vanessa recently opened a food truck."

"Oh, that's wonderful!"

"Yes, a little too wonderful, apparently," grumbled Atlas. "Somebody stole the truck overnight."

"Sonofabitch," cursed Acton. "Do they know who did it?"

"No. And unfortunately, it looks like our insurance isn't going to cover it because the lot we were storing it at was bullshit. The owner lied about being licensed and bonded."

"That's terrible. Is there anything we can do to help?"

"I'm afraid not. We'll figure our way out of this. We just need to get away."

Niner's heart ached as Vanessa wiped more tears away. "Listen, we were thinking of using some of our points and popping over to Italy for maybe a week. But we're not exactly sure where we should go, what we should see. So, I figured you guys were the ones who would know."

"We figured the Colosseum for sure," said Angela. "The Vatican. But there's just so much. Do we go to Pisa? Florence? Venice? Just stay in Rome?"

Acton chuckled. "Yeah, there's a lot of history jam-packed in one country. Listen, we're flying to Italy tomorrow. There's a new dig site just discovered in Rome that the Vatican's asked us to help out with. If you guys can manage, why don't you join us on our jet? Get your butts here tomorrow morning. We'll send you the details. You can fly with us, save your points, and you can see a real live dig. And we'll give you an itinerary for while you're there. Maybe arrange some private tours, let you see some stuff that the masses don't normally get to see."

Vanessa brightened at that. "That sounds wonderful!"

Angela agreed. "It does! Did you say jet?"

Niner confirmed it. "Did I happen to mention that the docs are filthy rich?"

"But I thought they were professors."

"They're professors on the take."

Laura giggled. "Somebody hit Niner for me."

Atlas leaned forward, raising a fist. "With pleasure."

Niner scurried out of the way. "So, you'll send us the details?"

"Yes, I'll have our travel agent Mary contact you. She's going to need your passport information. She'll take care of all the details."

"But what about a hotel?" asked Angela. "We haven't had a chance to make any reservations."

"Don't worry about it. Mary will take care of everything for you."

"So, we'll see you guys tomorrow," said Acton. "On your best behavior."

Niner grinned. "You'll see us tomorrow. No promises on the other thing."

"Good. But just remember, it's a private jet, so, if I want, I can open the door and boot you out."

"Wouldn't be the first time."

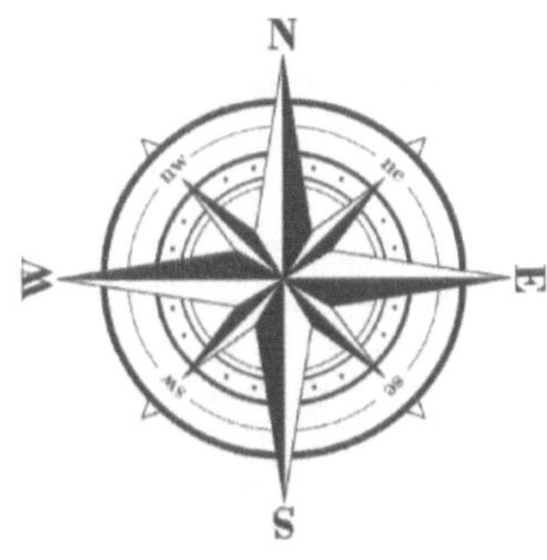

East of Leptis Magna, Tripolitania

Western Roman Empire

AD 431

"Why have we stopped?" Decimus demanded of those around him and, of course, received no response. Everyone here was as in the dark as he was, literally and figuratively. He turned to one of his men. "Go on ahead. Find out what's going on."

"Yes, Dominus!"

The soldier galloped off, heading toward the front of the column. They had made it to the gorge and the protection it afforded them, though it could prove to be their doom. They could defend the entrance, but should the enemy come in numbers, they could round the mass of stone outcroppings and cut them off at the other end.

There was hope the last remnants of the Roman Empire in this region could escape through the gorge and out the other side before that could happen. A small force might hold the enemy at bay long enough for them to give up and return to easier prey. The farther they could get from the city, the more likely those pursuing them would eventually decide it was simply easier to go back and loot what they knew was there, rather than what might be in the carts.

However, if they were aware the treasury was with them, there would be no stopping them. It was unimaginable wealth. His orders were to save the treasury and the citizens of Rome. The implied priority had been the treasury, though the emperor hadn't explicitly said so. In Decimus' mind, people were more important than gold, but it had been his experience that those in power, who made life and death decisions every day, weren't of the same opinion. Most in power had been born into it. They never faced life-and-death situations. They didn't understand what it was like to swing a sword in battle, to see your friends screaming in agony, to witness your comrades fall on the battlefield.

He continued forward at a more measured pace, the column ground to a halt, cursing to himself the entire time.

They didn't have time for this.

The soldier sent ahead returned. "Dominus! There's been a landslide. There are rocks blocking the way."

Decimus cursed again. The scouts sent here just this morning had reported it clear. "How bad is it?"

"Luckily, not too bad. Muscle and willpower will clear it."

"Then get it done. Take whatever soldiers and civilians you need. Hammers, picks, whatever. We need that cleared, otherwise we're dead."

"Yes, Dominus!"

Orders were issued, and soldiers were dispatched to the front of the column, shouts going out for tools and able-bodied men to join them.

Young men leaped to the ground, and it made him proud. These were Romans. This was why the empire was so strong. It was the determination of their citizens, the skill of its men and women, their willingness to sacrifice, that had made the empire what it was. He witnessed it every time he was on the frontier, but rarely in Rome itself. The closer he got to the capital, the softer the population became. They were too comfortable. The opulence, the debauchery, the immorality—disgusting. It was why things were faltering and would continue to do so should there not be a major change.

How do you tell a population, where slaves did all the hard work and the citizens lounged while fed grapes, that they might have to fight to keep what they had? Rome was absolute. Nothing could challenge it. That's what they had been told since the day they were born. And those safely ensconced within the city itself could never imagine anything different. It was a sad state the empire found itself in, but there was nothing he could do about it right here, right now.

He had a job to do.

And the citizens here, accustomed to a difficult life, weren't complaining. They were leaping into action, and he had no doubt the roadblock ahead would be cleared swiftly.

He continued forward, eying their surroundings. This blockage could take hours to clear and might not be the only one. He turned to one of his men. "Scout ahead. See if there's anything else that might delay us."

"At once, Dominus!" The soldier charged ahead as Decimus continued to eye the gorge walls, and it was clear some of it had been chiseled out over the centuries, making it wide enough for carts to pass through. Most of it was fairly wide, allowing carts to pass easily, though some was barely wide enough for a single transport.

A rider approached behind him, and he turned in his saddle.

"Dominus, the last of the convoy has entered the gorge."

"Excellent. Leave sentries to report back should the enemy arrive, but don't engage. Fall back two hundred paces, then set up a defensive line." He pointed at the walls. "And have your men keep their eyes out for any loose rocks. See if you can dislodge them. Anything we can do to slow them down. If you can block the passage, continue to fall back. Let's use the landscape rather than flesh and blood to defend us whenever possible."

"Yes, Dominus!" The messenger turned his horse around and headed back to the gorge entrance.

Decimus continued forward, reassuring the civilians, and eventually reached the carts carrying the treasury when he spotted a curious shadow ascending to his left. He stopped and stared up. It appeared to be a narrow pathway—perhaps natural, perhaps man-made in parts—climbing into the darkness. He dismounted and stepped over to the stone face, confirming it wasn't his eyes playing tricks on him.

He began ascending the path. If men had carved it, it had been long ago. Any evidence of sharp corners from steps honed by human hands had long since eroded away. It could be completely natural, but he couldn't be sure. And did it really matter? He continued to climb, spotting the entrance of what could be a cave ahead. He picked up a loose stone and tossed it inside. The echo suggested it was large and deep.

He stepped to the edge and leaned over. "Bring me a torch!"

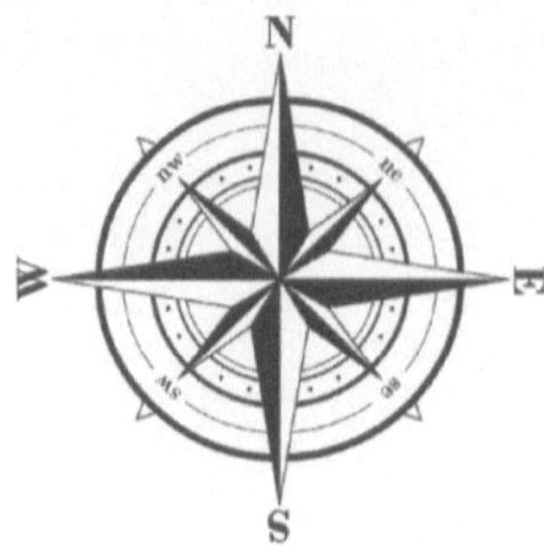

Rome Cavalieri Hotel

Rome, Italy

Present Day

"Oh my God, this is unbelievable!" gushed Vanessa.

Angela had to agree. She had never seen a hotel like this outside of the movies. "There's no way we can afford this," she whispered to Niner, apparently not quietly enough.

Laura turned. "Don't worry about that. Everything's on us."

Angela refused. "No, no, no, this is too much. The private jet was one thing—you were flying here regardless."

Acton held up a hand, cutting her off. "Nonsense. The number of times Niner and Atlas have saved our bacon—a thousand and one nights in a hotel like this could never repay them."

"You've saved our bacon plenty of times too," replied Atlas. "We should be repaying you."

"Damn straight," agreed Niner. "But if we tried to repay you, it'd be a thousand and one nights in a pup tent."

Acton snickered and slapped Angela's boyfriend on the shoulder as several staff members approached.

"Professor Acton, Professor Palmer, so good to have you with us again."

"Happy to be here, Ricardo." Acton turned. "These are our good friends, Mr. James, Ms. Moore, Mr. Sung, and Ms. Henwood. Treat them like you would treat us. Anything they want goes on our bill."

Angela again opened her mouth to refuse, but Acton beat her to the punch.

"Anything. Laura and I have an appointment to go to shortly. You kids do whatever the heck you want. If you're looking for places to see, just ask Ricardo. He knows the city like nobody does."

There was a commotion at the door, and everyone turned to see Tommy and Mai coming through, a porter with a cart filled with gear—sensitive gear, as Tommy had described it—being constantly reminded by their nervous friend, "Be careful, be careful!"

They came to a halt near the group. Tommy quickly double-checked that everything was stable while Mai rolled her eyes. "You're going to give yourself a heart attack one of these days."

Tommy gave her a look. "If one of these falls, it *will* give me a heart attack."

Another eye roll. "Don't be so dramatic. These cases were specifically designed to hold your equipment. If they can't take a three-foot fall, then you wasted your money."

Acton grinned. "She's got a point."

Tommy's shoulders slumped. "You're right." He inhaled deeply, then sighed. "I'm so stressed out."

"You're too young to be that stressed out." Laura turned to Ricardo. "I think we'll all be needing massages later tonight."

Vanessa squealed. "I've never had a professional massage!"

Atlas held up a finger. "Just make sure it's a chick. I don't think I want to see some dude rubbing his hands all over my lady."

Vanessa eyeballed him. "And make sure his is a dude. I don't think I could stand to see a woman rubbing her hands all over my man."

Atlas opened his mouth to protest when Niner snorted. "She's got you there!" He began humming the Final Jeopardy theme, adding some words to the tune. "How does Atlas *get* himself out of this?"

Angela giggled. Niner was hilarious. He always had her laughing. It was one of his most attractive qualities. Yes, he was a damn sexy man in incredible shape, but he was just so funny. Even alone, he made her smile, though he was quite different—a little calmer. She found when he was around his buddies, especially more than just Atlas, he found it necessary to put on a show. She hadn't found the nerve yet to ask him why. She was afraid he might not be ready to open up yet, despite the fact they had been dating for some time.

She was still insecure about the relationship. She loved him more than she had ever loved anybody, and she could see herself spending the rest of her life with him and starting a family, having children. However, they were waiting—with his encouragement. She was about to start nursing college. She had always wanted to be a nurse and had been saving every penny she could for the tuition, and she had more than enough.

She didn't want to be a clerk at the Exchange for the rest of her life, and while training to be a chef with Vanessa, decided she just didn't have the passion for it—that was her mother's. It wasn't her calling. But nursing—that was an honorable profession. Not as honorable as that of her boyfriend, though some might beg to differ. She would be helping people, perhaps saving lives.

When they had their hopes-and-dreams conversation in bed one night, she had revealed her desire to him and he had wholeheartedly embraced the idea, encouraging her to pursue it. The next day, she had applied online and would start courses soon after they returned from this trip, the first real adult travel she had ever taken. Heading to the beach in a bikini and thong wasn't adulting.

There was a difference between vacationing and traveling. This was travel. Holy crap, was it ever. Private jet. Five-star hotel. There was no way she could ever top this. Perhaps that was a bad thing. Every trip from now on would be a disappointment. They could never live up to this.

Acton saved Atlas from the corner he had painted himself into by changing the subject. "Have our rentals arrived?"

"Yes, Professor. Two SUVs exactly to your specifications arrived about an hour ago. I'll have them brought around."

"Are they identical?" asked Laura.

"Yes, ma'am."

"Good. Bring one of them around for us. We're going to be heading out shortly." She turned to their guests. "Do you guys want to relax in your suite for a while, or head out now?"

Angela exchanged a glance with Vanessa. "I think we'll relax for a little bit, don't you?"

Vanessa agreed. "Yes, I'm bushed after that flight, and I've been running on adrenaline for almost twenty-four hours. I'm so excited. Let's relax a bit, then we'll head out."

Laura smiled. "Good. When you're ready to go out, just see Ricardo here. He'll give you the keys for the SUV we rented you."

Vanessa gripped her forehead. "Oh no, you guys have done too much. We can't possibly have you pay for a rental as well."

Acton flashed a grin. "Don't worry. It was rent-one-get-one-free." His face became serious, and he jabbed a finger at them. "Just make sure you return it with a full tank of gas."

Vanessa's eyes bulged. "Yes, sir."

Atlas snickered. "He's joking, babe."

Acton laughed, jerking a thumb at Niner. "I would have figured, spending as much time with him as I assume you do, you'd be on guard for pretty much everything being a joke."

Vanessa grunted. "You'd think."

Acton held out a hand toward the elevators. "How about we get settled in?" He gestured toward Tommy's gear. "If you could have someone load that into the back of our SUV, I'd appreciate it."

Tommy held up both hands. "Whoa, whoa, whoa, the only person who's going to be doing any loading here is me."

"Suit yourself, drama queen. We'll be upstairs."

Mai sighed. "If I don't stay with him, I'll never hear the end of it."

Ricardo stepped forward, handing Mai two key cards. "Suite 1002. If you need anything, just call the front desk and ask for me personally."

"Thank you." Mai took both cards, handing one to her boyfriend.

They seemed like a cute couple, apparently engaged, and very close with the professors. There was a parent-child dynamic about them she found sweet. Niner had told her that Laura had been shot and was unable to have children. It must have been devastating. She couldn't imagine not being able.

Acton smacked his hands together. "So, let's get this show on the road. Mario's expecting us, and despite him being a friend, he doesn't like to be kept waiting."

"You know very well it's because the Pope wants to see us before we head to the dig site," said Laura.

"You're seeing the Pope?" exclaimed Vanessa. "That's amazing!"

Acton turned to her. "Do you want me to see if I can get you guys invited?"

To Angela's surprise, Niner refused. "Too many bad memories with that place, and with that position."

Angela's eyes narrowed as she stared at her boyfriend. "What do you mean?"

Both Niner and Atlas echoed, "Classified."

She groaned. "I really wish if you couldn't tell me something that you wouldn't drop a teaser out there, then claim 'classified' when I ask you what the hell you're talking about."

"Better get used to it," said Vanessa. "I'm terrified that when Leon and I get married and the priest asks him if he'll take me, instead of saying 'I do,' this big lug is going to say 'classified.'"

Acton snorted. "I'd pay good money to see that."

Niner agreed. "You definitely have to do that, dude. Definitely."

Atlas held up both hands. "I'll leave that to you. I know damn well if I were to say that, even as a joke, it'd be the last words to ever come out of my mouth."

"You mean besides 'holy shit, what are you doing with a gun at a wedding?'"

Vanessa patted Atlas on the chest. "And my answer would be, 'because I thought Niner was going to do something stupid.'"

Acton smirked. "That's why *I'd* bring a gun to a wedding." He headed for the elevators. "Let's get going. We're on a schedule."

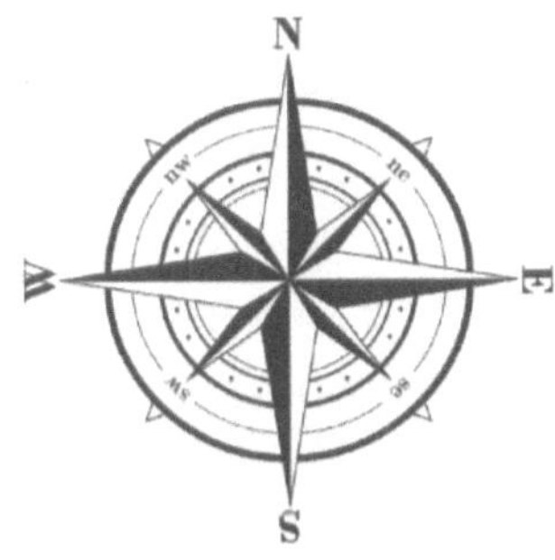

En route to the Lateran Palace

Rome, Italy

"His Holiness is looking well," said Laura as they drove from the Vatican toward the dig site.

"Indeed," agreed Giasson, sitting in the passenger seat as Laura drove. "He gave us quite the scare, but he's tough. He's a strong man, and God didn't feel it was his time."

Acton, sitting in the back seat behind Giasson, said nothing. The man had appeared better than expected, though was clearly unwell, which was understandable—he was, after all, only human. To him, the Pope was just a man who had won an election to become the head of the Church. It didn't mean he was a bad man—having conversed with him on multiple occasions, he was definitely better than most. Though while he believed in something, perhaps even God, he felt all churches were creations of man. The Roman Catholic Church was the ultimate example of this. "It was good to see him again," he finally said. "He seemed genuinely excited by the dig."

"He's always been interested in history from what I understand." Giasson twisted to face him. "But I think it's his association with you two that's truly piqued his interest."

"I have been known to inspire."

"Inspired me," said Tommy.

"And me," added Mai.

Laura gave them both a look in the rear-view mirror. "You two stop feeding his ego."

Giasson laughed. "I missed you two." He faced forward again, pointing ahead. "Take the next left. They've got a bunch of streets closed off, so you won't be able to take the normal route."

Laura turned on her signal light, following Giasson's directions, and they were soon clearing security at the Lateran Palace, then parking near the dig.

Acton whistled at the bustle of activity in front of them—an impressive amount of progress made in just a few days. "Someone's in a hurry."

"Funny. That's exactly what Father Esposito said. Too fast."

Acton opened his door and stepped out. "Well, let's just go see for ourselves, shall we?"

Father Esposito rushed over with a broad smile, his hand extended in front of him. "Professor Acton, Professor Palmer, so good to see you again!"

Acton shook the man's hand. "Good to see you too, Father."

Laura returned the man's handshake. "Good to see you again."

Esposito smiled at Tommy and Mai. "Good to see you two as well."

Tommy glanced around, slightly nervous. "Yes, good to see you too."

"Worried about something?"

"Just looking for protesters."

Esposito chuckled. "We should be safe. Nothing religious about this discovery. Fifth century."

"That's been confirmed?" asked Acton.

"Yes, fourth and fifth century actually. The artifacts match the era. Plus, we found several inscriptions with dates. It's a crypt that's been remarkably well preserved. An incredible find."

"I'm going to check on the security situation," interjected Giasson. "I'll join you again shortly."

Acton acknowledged the man with a nod, returning his attention to the dig nearby. "How goes the cooperation with the Italians?"

"Oh, no problem there," replied Esposito. "We work with them all the time, though usually on their territory. I thought it was best that we have some sort of independent liaison with extensive experience in these things."

"We're happy to help," said Laura. "Though I suspect we're not really needed. You've done this before."

"Only once on this scale. Most of our discoveries are pretty small, and we're never the primaries. This happens to be partially on our soil. And with it being the Lateran Palace..." Esposito hesitated and Acton smirked.

"You wanted someone else to blame if something goes wrong."

Esposito tossed his head back and laughed. "Exactly!"

Acton extended a hand toward the dig. "Shall we? Why not give us the fifty-cent tour?"

"Professor?"

Acton turned to see Tommy standing at the rear of the SUV. He had an uncertain look on his face. "Oh yes, that's right. Tommy and Mai would like to conduct an experiment. They've got some extremely high-resolution cameras that they want to set up around the dig to record everything in real time. In theory, if everything works the way we think it will, we should have a virtual reality version of the dig that we can actually walk through. It could prove to be an incredible learning tool for students in the future. Any objections?"

Esposito shook his head. "Absolutely not. It sounds incredible."

Acton turned to Tommy. "Better hop to it. Just stick to this side of the wall until we clear it with the Italians as well."

Tommy grinned eagerly, then opened the rear of the SUV as Acton and Laura followed Esposito toward the dig. He descended a ladder and Acton followed, then Laura. He helped her down the final few rungs, then turned, taking in the bustle of activity.

"I love this."

Laura agreed. "There's nothing like a fresh dig. Everything's new. Everything's exciting. You never know what you're going to find."

Acton recognized several members of the Vatican's archaeological team, friendly waves exchanged.

"It's not too big an area." Laura indicated the far wall, not even 200 feet from where they stood. "Are we sure that's the perimeter?"

"So far, yes." Esposito gestured to their right, where the remains of the wall that once surrounded the Lateran Palace stood, the ground open beneath it, jacks placed as temporary supports to hold it up. "You can see the heavy equipment's been pulled away. They scraped off the surface after using ground-penetrating radar to make sure they weren't going to damage anything at this level. I've been assured by the Italian team that they're confident this is the extent of it. Everyone has agreed to focus on this side of the wall, then move to the Italian side." He indicated the remnants of a wall nearby, slowly arcing inward. "We found bits and pieces of this around the entire area. It looks like it was a dome structure. Circular. As far as we can tell, this entire area was actually constructed underground with a dome built overtop it."

"Interesting."

Something was shouted in Italian, and everyone turned to see one of the archaeologists pointing up the ladder, urgently waving his hands. Acton looked up to see Tommy struggling at the top with one of his cases.

"Use the equipment elevator!" shouted Esposito, who then pointed to Tommy's right.

The young man stopped and looked, then cursed. "Thank you!" Tommy squared himself with the ladder and began climbing back up, but his foot slipped. He fell several rungs before catching one with his hand. Mai screamed and Tommy yelped as he lost his hold of the case.

Acton cursed and sprinted forward, catching it just before it hit the ground.

"You got it?"

Acton held it up. "Yeah, I got it. *You* got it?"

Tommy didn't appear too certain as he gripped the ladder for dear life. "Yeah, I got it. I just forgot I hate heights." He began his way back up and Acton didn't relax until the young man disappeared over the top. He placed the case next to the ladder, then returned his attention to his surroundings.

"So, you've confirmed it's a crypt?"

"Yes. We've identified over twenty possible separate individuals so far." Esposito led them deeper inside, skeletal remains everywhere, most fairly intact.

"It doesn't look like this was looted," observed Laura.

"Not at all. And we haven't found an entrance. We think it was walled in and domed over, then perhaps forgotten."

"Could be." Acton folded his arms and scratched his chin. "It's odd, though, something like this to not have been looted."

"I wonder if they buried it," suggested Laura. "To protect it."

Acton considered her idea. "We've definitely seen it before, and it would certainly explain why it hadn't been looted. Have you figured out who these people were? What they had in common?"

Esposito grinned. "You're gonna love this." His excitement was contagious.

"What?"

"We believe they're all gladiators."

Goosebumps rippled across Acton's body. "Gladiators?"

"Yes."

"Cool!" Acton's head whipped around. "Weapons?"

"So far, almost every set of remains we've found has been buried with their weapons."

Somebody yelped, and Acton turned to see a reporter on her ass, having tripped over something, her cameraman—the glowing red light indicating he was recording—reaching out a hand to haul her to her feet. She laughed, brushing herself off as she continued to talk into her microphone.

"Looks like your secret is out," commented Laura.

Esposito groaned. "Don't get me started. There's been so much press all over this place, it's ridiculous. Fortunately, we haven't found anything really worth looting, though there is one thing you need to see."

"What's that?"

Esposito gestured toward where the reporter was now standing, the camera trained on a set of remains that appeared different than the others Acton had seen so far. "There's one set of remains that doesn't appear to belong here."

They picked their way to the site, and the reporter's eyes bulged as she recognized them. "Professor Acton!" she exclaimed, switching to English. "Do you care to make a comment on what's been discovered here?"

He didn't care to, though he was here on a job on behalf of the Church. Best behavior. "I just arrived here along with Professor Palmer, so we haven't had much time to see much of what's been found so far. However, it appears quite exciting. My preliminary briefing suggests a crypt with at least twenty souls dating from the fourth and fifth centuries.

As we discover more, we'll have more to say to the press, but for now, we have a lot of work to do. Thank you."

"Of course, Professor. Thank you very much for your time." She returned to Italian, no doubt summarizing what he had just said, then waved a hand in front of her throat, the cameraman lowering his equipment. She smiled. "Thank you again, Professor."

"No problem."

The TV crew headed to the Italian side, leaving Esposito to share his find, and now that their view wasn't blocked, Acton could see why the man had insisted they see it.

"He's got a breastplate," said Laura.

Acton took a knee. "Yeah. If he was a gladiator, he shouldn't have that."

"No, he shouldn't," agreed Esposito.

"Any idea who he is?"

Esposito kneeled, indicating a shattered piece of stone. "We're still excavating. We have managed to piece together that part of his name could be Decimus."

Acton shot to his feet, his heart racing. "Decimus?"

"Yes. Does that mean something to you?"

"It could." Acton glanced over his shoulder to find the TV camera trained on him again, having noticed his excitement. He turned his back to them, lowering his voice. "I think we might need to increase security around here."

"Why's that?"

"Because if this is who I think it is, every whack job treasure hunter out there is going to be heading here before the end of the day."

300 Meters Shooting Range

Minsk, Belarus

Alexie Tankov, retired Spetsnaz, squeezed the trigger, the recoil of the Heckler & Koch HK416 assault rifle jerking his shoulder back. He loved that feeling. He loved everything about guns. The feel in his hands, the sound of the bullets blasting from the barrel, the chime of the spent shell casing ejecting, the smell of gun oil, of the ignited gunpowder.

A well-serviced weapon was power, respect, and a means to an end.

He was tired. Life in Spetsnaz—the Russian Special Forces—had been tough but rewarding. After leaving, he had recruited a group of men, all of whom had served, to provide themselves with the retirement the Russian Federation wasn't capable of. Comfortable, luxurious, decadent. And it had worked. But their lifestyle was expensive, and the bank accounts constantly needed feeding. It meant endless missions and little rest.

He had had enough. He wanted to retire, to lie on a beach somewhere, soak up the sun the doctors said he shouldn't, and just enjoy himself for however many years he had left.

Unfortunately, several of his missions had gone south recently, leaving his bank account thirsty and his retirement account nearly depleted.

It's because you show too much mercy.

He sighed as he fired again, emptying a mag into the target at the far end of the range with rapid single shots, tearing apart the notorious British sports car he had driven into the center of the range himself. It was a gift from a disgruntled client. An insult for failing to deliver on a package a few months ago. Message received. He would send the asshole a photo when those at the range were finished with it.

He ejected the empty magazine, slapped in a fresh one, then paused, contemplating that last thought. He had never been one to show mercy before. Spetsnaz wasn't known for it. They were more of a shoot-first-no-need-to-ask-questions-later type of organization. In his new chosen profession, massacring innocent people simply made you more of a target. Police forces around the world didn't care too much about art thieves. But art thieves who killed a bunch of innocent people? Those were mass murderers. They warranted a different level of attention. But sometimes you had to eliminate a problem, an annoyance, a thorn in your side.

For some reason, he kept allowing his two biggest thorns to live—Professors Acton and Palmer. He liked Acton. There was just something about him. The man had balls. And his wife, holy shit, she was exactly his type.

Unfortunately, he was definitely not hers.

"If you get in my way again…" He opened fire, this time on full auto, just for fun. He removed the spent mag, then cleared the weapon.

Someone coughed behind him, and he turned to see his second-in-command and best friend, Arseny Utkin, with a tablet and a smile.

"I might have something."

Utkin was their finder. He had alerts set up and crawlers configured to find anything that might be of interest to them, searching news sites, discussion boards, the dark web—wherever valuables that might interest their clients were discussed.

"What have you got?"

"Did you hear about what they found in Rome a couple of days ago?"

"Yeah, some crypt, if I'm not mistaken."

"Good. So, you do read the summaries I send you."

"They're riveting. Why wouldn't I?" he deadpanned.

"Now I know you're lying to me. Well, even if you had read them, you wouldn't know this because this is fresh. They think gladiators were buried there."

Tankov cocked an eyebrow, beckoning an attendant then jerking his thumb at the weapon he was now finished with. The attendant rushed over, retrieving the HK, then taking it away to be properly serviced for next time. He and the others kept a private stash here at the firing range rather than at their primary residence, just in case the authorities grew some balls and paid them a visit. They would find weapons, but not the big stuff—not the truly illegal stuff that couldn't be ignored.

"Gladiators? Interesting, but if I remember correctly, gladiators were mostly slaves, so they'd have nothing of value. Why do we care?"

"Because of this." Utkin held out his tablet. Tankov took it, a smile immediately spreading at the sight of Laura Palmer.

"Well, you've piqued my interest."

"Stop thinking with your dick and check out what she's looking at."

He tore his eyes away to see a skeleton, its body armor still visible, well-preserved. "Interesting. I'm sure some of our clients would like to add this to their collection, but this is nothing—not even six figures. I told you, don't waste my time with anything under eight figures."

"And I heard you, and I'm not."

Tankov stopped, squinting as he stared at the image closer. "What am I missing?"

"Zoom out and look at the other remains."

He did. He shook his head. "I'm growing impatient."

"You should be studying your history a little more if you're going to be an art thief."

"That's why I pay you."

"What does this one guy have that none of the others do?"

"He looks like he has body armor."

"Exactly. Gladiators didn't wear body armor. They were given a weapon and a loincloth. That breastplate that guy is wearing means he's not a gladiator."

Tankov zoomed back in. "All right, so what?"

Utkin took the tablet back and tapped at it a few times. "Watch this, and listen carefully."

Tankov watched as the two professors and another man spoke, pointing at some broken stone on the ground at the foot of the armor-clad warrior, but he couldn't make out the words. He replayed it and held the tablet to his ear, still unable to make out anything. "Wait a minute. Decimus? Is that what he said?"

"Exactly." Utkin beamed.

But Tankov was still lost. "Decimus? Is that supposed to mean something to me?"

"No. It wouldn't mean much to anybody unless you're a true student of history, and even then it's fairly obscure history."

"What am I missing?" asked Tankov as he climbed into his Porsche Panamera.

Utkin joined him, closing the passenger side door. "Here's the history as recorded: Decimus was sent in 431 AD to retrieve the African treasury of the Roman Empire before it was overrun by the Vandals, in what's now modern-day Libya."

"Treasury, huh? Now I'm getting a little more interested."

"You should be. History records that he successfully retrieved it before the city fell. But here's what I think will clinch your interest."

"What?"

"He returned to Rome without the treasure."

Tankov shifted the car back in park and twisted in his seat. "Wait a minute, you're telling me that the entire Roman treasury for Africa is out there somewhere?"

"Yes. He apparently hid it where no one could find it, then led the civilians out of the region, saving all their lives."

"I'm gonna guess that the emperor wasn't too pleased."

"No, he wasn't. He was also a thirteen-year-old boy."

"Oh God. All right, what did they do to him?"

"When he returned to Rome, he was sentenced to death, stripped of his citizenship"—Utkin tapped the photo of the downed warrior—"and made to fight in the games."

Tankov's eyes widened slightly. "So, what you're saying is this could be that Decimus?"

"Exactly."

"But what good does that do us? He died, never revealing the location."

"That means the treasure's still there. Otherwise, we would have heard about it."

"Agreed. Again, how does knowing where his body is tell us where the treasure is?"

"Because there's one bit of history that's considered legend and can't be verified."

"What's that?"

"When he died, his trusted slave was with him, and as the gladiators moved in to kill them both, Decimus, when asked to reveal where the treasure was to save his life, slapped his hand against his chest and said, 'The secret dies with me.'"

"So? Sounds like something a Roman general would say, just to piss off the emperor who ordered him killed."

"You don't get it. Everyone always assumed he was slapping his bare chest as a Roman salute." Utkin again pointed at the image. "But if he was wearing his breastplate…"

Tankov's jaw dropped. "Holy shit! We've got to get to Rome, now!"

East of Leptis Magna, Tripolitania

Western Roman Empire

AD 431

It was the solution Decimus had been seeking. No, it wasn't perfect. The cave had revealed an extensive network of tunnels and chambers, sliced through the solid rock by an ancient underground waterway over the eons. His explorations hadn't gone on long before he found what he was searching for—a large enough chamber to hold the treasure, with what appeared to be a loose ceiling at its entrance.

He stood to the side as his men transferred the contents of the carts carrying the treasury into the chamber. Abandoning this vast wealth definitely went against the intent of the emperor's orders, though he could reasonably claim he had not disobeyed the spirit of them.

"Save the treasury and the citizens."

The only way to save the people was to unburden themselves of the treasury. They could come back for it later, in force—a year at most. As long as they completed the transfer under cover of darkness and held the barbarians at the entrance to the gorge, they could make their escape.

It was a desperate plan, but he could see no other choice. If they didn't leave the massive wealth behind, the horde pursuing them would overtake them. They would all be slaughtered, and Rome's property would be lost regardless. At least this way, they stood a chance. The people might be saved, and the massive wealth could be recovered.

It was backbreaking work, and the torches lining the way revealed the exhaustion of his men. There were fresh troops that could be used, but he was limiting the numbers involved. A substantial portion of the force had been sent ahead, along with the civilians. The gorge was wide enough to allow the ragtag group of refugees to pass with their heavily laden carts before the transfer began. They had no idea what was now happening. The rest of his troops, not involved in the effort, had been sent to the entrance of the gorge to hold back the enemy—with orders to fight to the last man.

They would do it. They were his men. He had trained them well, and their commanders would rather die than fail their emperor.

And him.

So many dead. Why did Rome bother with an outpost in such a place? How much was enough?

Tiberius, his second in command, approached, a frown creasing his face. "Sir, we may have a problem."

Tiberius had served Decimus for over a decade. He knew him as well as any man knew his own brother. Something was wrong. Decimus said nothing, instead heading deeper into the underground network, grabbing a torch before the darkness swallowed them up. He led them deep enough that no one should overhear them. "What is it?"

"I overheard several of the men talking. They didn't know I was there."

"What was said?"

"There was talk of returning and taking some of the treasure for themselves."

Decimus bristled. "In jest?"

"Difficult to say. Certainly, a couple of them laughed off the suggestion, but two others pressed the idea. How, when we reached Alexandria and safety, they could sneak away, provision themselves, and come back."

Decimus cursed, his worst fears confirmed. A hoard this size, the bulk of which was meant to pay the bills of the empire in this region, meant it was in convenient denominations of coins and bars. That meant it was easily transportable. Saddlebags and a single cart could carry enough for a man to live out the rest of his life like a king.

The temptation was simply too great for men who had known nothing but poverty.

"I feared as much."

"Do you have a plan?"

Decimus frowned. "Unfortunately, there is only one option I can think of."

Tiberius sighed. "As can I." He leaned against the smooth rock, folding his arms. "All of them?"

Decimus reluctantly nodded. "Everyone."

"Even Gaius and his men?"

Decimus couldn't believe Gaius and his personal guard would betray him, betray the empire. He was tempted to grant them a reprieve.

Footsteps echoed from deeper in the cave system. The flicker of a torch became visible, and Tiberius pushed off the wall, gripping the hilt of his sword. Decimus waved him off as Gaius came into sight. The formidable warrior halted in front of them and bowed.

"If I may offer my opinion?"

Decimus cocked an eyebrow. "You heard our conversation?"

"Every word. Voices carry remarkably well in this passage."

Decimus gave a curt nod. "Very well."

"No one can be left but yourself."

"And me, of course," Tiberius added.

Gaius regarded the man for a moment before returning his stare to Decimus, saying nothing. It was clear the head of his personal guard disagreed with Tiberius' addendum.

"That would include you, my friend," Decimus said to the proud warrior.

Gaius smacked his fist against his heart. "To die serving the empire has always been my dream."

SantoPalato Restaurant

Rome, Italy

Present Day

"So, what do you think of Rome so far?" asked Laura of their guests as they all sat around a table at the SantoPalato Restaurant, renowned for the chef's modern interpretations of Roman classics, specifically chosen for everyone to feel comfortable, and get a taste of history rather than transplanted foreign cuisine.

"It's everything I always dreamed it would be," gushed Angela. "There's just so much history. You can't walk ten feet without there being something that's older than America."

Acton sipped his wine. "Forget older than America. That's only a couple of centuries. Try older than anything since Columbus. It's an amazing wealth of history, there's no doubt."

Vanessa agreed. "I just wish I understood what I was looking at. There's just so much here that's incredible. I could spend months here and never see it all."

Laura smiled. "Years. What did you see today?"

"The Colosseum," rumbled Atlas.

Niner jerked a thumb at him. "Yeah, my big man here wanted to see what it felt like to be a gladiator."

Acton eyed the massively muscled man. "You'd have been a popular one."

Atlas slapped both biceps. "Undefeated, I'm sure."

"Until they sent in the lions," said Tommy.

Niner smirked. "Don't be so sure."

"So, what did you guys get up to?" asked Angela. "Did you see the Pope?"

Laura nodded. "Yes, we did. He's looking well, all things considered."

"That's so cool! You guys live such exciting lives."

Acton jerked his chin at the two Delta operators. "Something tells me their lives are a hell of a lot more exciting."

Vanessa frowned at Atlas. "That may be, but they're not allowed to talk about it, but you guys are. What's he like?"

Tommy shrugged. "He's just an old man that wears a lot of white with a friendly smile."

Mai swatted him. "Show some respect."

"Hey, you're not even Catholic. You're not even Christian."

"That doesn't mean I can't show respect." She turned to the others. "He's one of the nicest men you'll ever meet. He seems to genuinely care about those he's meeting with."

"That's sweet," said Vanessa. "I guess it's what I would expect."

"So, what's the Vatican like?" asked Angela.

Acton leaned back as his glass was refilled. "You want to see well-preserved history, that's the place to go. We'll take you on a private tour in a few days."

Laura pushed her glass toward the waiter. "And go to a mass on Sunday in the square. It's something to experience, even if you're not Catholic."

"That's definitely on my list," said Angela. "But forget all that. What happened at your dig site?"

Acton leaned forward eagerly, still excited by the potential find. "We might have found the final resting place of Decimus Cornelius Vindex."

"Decimus Cor…" Angela struggled to remember the rest of the name, then gave up. "Let's just go with Decimus. Who's he?"

"A Roman general, for lack of a better term. Very powerful at the time. Well respected, well liked, a lot of victories under his belt. In the early fifth-century, the Vandals were challenging Roman power in North Africa—"

"Vandals? You mean like criminals?"

Laura smiled. "No, though that's where the word comes from. The Vandals were a Germanic tribe, probably originating in modern-day eastern Germany, western Poland. They were slowly forced westward, then south into Spain, and eventually were invited over by a disgruntled Roman general into North Africa, where they promptly betrayed him and established a kingdom of their own."

"They weren't simply soldiers," continued Acton. "They were families as well. This was an entire tribe of tens of thousands traveling together. They crossed what's now known as the Strait of Gibraltar into

North Africa, then essentially marauded their way eastward, taking territory held by Rome at the time. With the Western Roman Empire in decline, there wasn't enough manpower to oppose them, so Decimus was sent in to retrieve the Roman treasury, which was substantial."

"Ooh, gold and jewels. You should send me in, Doc," said Niner. "I did, after all, find Atlantis."

Angela's eyes shot up as her head whipped around toward her boyfriend. "What?"

Acton laughed. "Is that classified?"

Niner shrugged. "I don't think so. What happened made the news."

"True enough."

"Okay, forget Atlantis," said Angela, "but you *will* be telling me everything later."

"Absolutely, babe."

"So, this Decimus guy is sent to Africa to get the treasure. Then what?"

"He retrieves it, rescues thousands of the Roman citizens living there, and leads them across the desert to what's now Egypt. But between what's now known as Libya and Egypt, the treasury is hidden somewhere. He returns to Rome, and the emperor sentences him to death for failing to return the treasury. He dies without ever revealing where it was hidden."

Atlas leaned back and folded his massive arms. "So, what you're saying is somewhere between Libya and Egypt, there's a massive hoard of gold just waiting to be found."

"Yep."

"Sounds simple enough," said Atlas sarcastically.

"Exactly. It's never been found because it was well hidden. Legend says he had his soldiers bury the treasure, then killed them all."

"Single-handedly?" laughed Niner. "Impressive."

"Probably not. Remember, this is 1600-year-old history."

"So, now that you've found him—"

"*If* we've found him," corrected Laura.

Niner held up a hand, conceding the point. "*If* you've found him, does that mean you can find the treasure?"

Acton dismissed the idea. "No, it's just a piece of the puzzle that's now answered—where was he buried, and how? The fact his body's intact, and he was buried with his armor and weapons, indicates there was some honor shown toward him in the end. But unless he wrote down the location and had it on his body when he was buried, this is just a curiosity for people like us to get excited over."

"Unfortunately, if word gets out," said Laura, "we could be looking at all kinds of treasure hunters coming in and bollocksing things up."

Niner snickered. "Bollocks. I love that one. So, what's next?"

Acton leaned back. "Well, tomorrow we're going to go back to the dig site, and you're welcome to join us if you'd like. Get a tour, see how things really run. You guys might get a kick out of some of the weapons. We'll be there all day, but I've arranged for a private guide to take you to some of the lesser-known places tomorrow afternoon. When you get back to the hotel, just go see Ricardo."

Angela and Vanessa exchanged excited grins. "That sounds like fun," said Vanessa. "This is exactly what I needed."

Laura grimaced. "Any word on your food truck?"

Vanessa's shoulders slumped. "No. I got an email this morning, and my insurance agent is saying it's not looking good. It was my responsibility to make sure the lot it was being parked at was secure and properly licensed and bonded." Tears filled her eyes, and Laura reached out, squeezing her hand.

"It's all right. Things always have a way of working out."

Vanessa gave her a weak smile, then wiped away her tears with a knuckle. "I suppose, though I don't see how."

Atlas wrapped an arm around his girlfriend's shoulders. "Don't worry, babe. We'll get through this. Who knows? Maybe we'll find that treasure, slip a few bars of gold out for ourselves."

Acton tossed his head back and laughed. "I'll tell you what, if we do find it, I promise to look the other way."

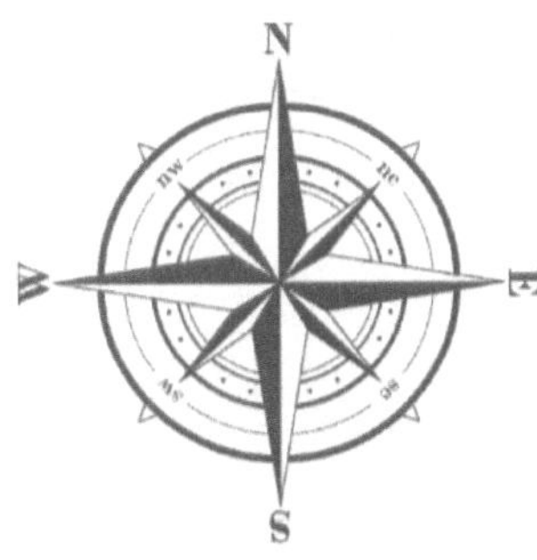

East of Leptis Magna, Tripolitania

Western Roman Empire

AD 431

"That's the last of it, Dominus."

Decimus acknowledged the report from Tiberius with a nod of his head. "Gather all involved in the chamber."

Tiberius frowned. "Yes, Dominus." He shouted, his voice echoing down the narrow passageway, someone at the entrance repeating the order to those below in the gorge where some of the men had sent the now-unburdened horses and their carriages ahead, unmanned, with a smack on the flank. Should any of those guarding the entrance to the gorge survive, they couldn't find empty carts below the entrance of a cave—it might invite exploration and certainly would invite questions. Nor could the horde that would no doubt eventually pour through be allowed to have their suspicions raised.

Secrecy was of the utmost importance here.

A young officer jogged up, out of breath, and saluted. "Dominus, the last of the transports has been sent. I took the liberty of sweeping away our footprints with some boughs from nearby bushes. When the enemy passes, they should see nothing but the tracks of our carts as if we never stopped."

Decimus smiled at the young man—a man who, under different circumstances, would have had a bright future serving Rome and its emperor. "Excellent work." He gestured toward the cavern. The lieutenant smacked his fist against his breastplate once again, then hurried inside with the others.

Gaius approached with the six men of Decimus' personal guard behind him.

"Is that everyone?" Tiberius asked.

"Yes, sir," Gaius confirmed.

Decimus inhaled deeply, holding his breath as his heart ached. These were good men, loyal men who had served him well. He had never heard a complaint, never had to deal with a disciplinary problem. They were the best Rome had to offer—its fathers, its sons, its brothers, its uncles, its nephews.

They had done nothing wrong but be selected for a mission that now necessitated their doom.

He stepped into the entrance of the chamber. Those inside fell silent.

Twenty men.

Twenty exhausted men.

All with expectant looks, many with satisfied airs about them, like men who had completed a difficult task and were taking satisfaction in their work. He loved that look. He loved that feeling. There was nothing like completing an assignment, especially a difficult one. Whether it was physical or mental or strategic, it didn't matter.

"Men."

They straightened to attention.

"I know you're tired. I know I'm exhausted just having watched you." He smirked. The torches still burned, allowing them to see the expression and enjoy the brief moment of levity. Laughter rippled through the chamber, the sound bouncing off the stone walls. "While this task is done, the mission isn't over, and unfortunately, it necessitates one last sacrifice on behalf of your empire and your emperor."

His heart raced, his stomach churned. Sending men into battle, certain to die, was one thing. But murdering them? Without the chance to fight? That was something entirely different.

"The secrecy of what we have done here today is paramount. No one can ever know what we did. And unfortunately, there are those among you who, by their own words, have demonstrated they cannot be trusted to keep this secret."

The young officer's eyes flared. "Who? Name him! Name them, and I shall personally slit their throats!"

"It is irrelevant. They know who they are. But unfortunately, their words have sealed the fate of everyone here." Decimus smacked his fist against his breastplate, the sound echoing through the cavern. "It has been an honor, and your sacrifice for Rome will not be forgotten."

Several men made to move forward as they realized what was about to happen, but the officer had already turned on them, drawing his dagger. "Who among you betrayed us? Who among you condemned us?"

A finger jabbed toward a man cowering in the back. "I heard him talking about it!"

"That's not true! I swear, I was only joking!"

The officer surged forward as Decimus retreated. Several of Gaius' men, equipped with spears, jabbed at the ceiling overhead. Loose stone began collapsing as those inside turned on each other. Decimus closed his eyes as the ceiling fell in, blocking the entrance completely. He covered his mouth with a scarf as dust billowed through the passage, the battle raging behind the pile of stone falling silent.

"At least they died fighting," Tiberius murmured.

Decimus took no comfort in his second-in-command's words, for nothing but shame would be suffered for years to come.

Lateran Palace Dig Site

Rome, Italy

Present Day

This is going to be so freaking awesome!

Tommy could barely contain his excitement as he held his tablet, dragging his finger over the screen. Overnight, the software he had designed had pulled in all the video from the high-resolution cameras he had set up yesterday throughout the dig, the Italians eager to participate in his experiment. His program had then stitched together the data from the 360-degree views, and he now had a virtual environment you could walk through and zoom in on to minute detail.

He couldn't wait to get his VR headset on and truly test it out.

"Can I see?" asked Mai, the excitement in her voice betraying her eagerness. She was incredible. Tech wasn't her area of expertise or interest. She was more like the professors—an academic. But she knew how important this was to him, and she supported him in everything he did.

God, I love that woman.

He handed her the tablet, and her eyes widened as she dragged her finger. She looked up at him, shaking her head in awe. "This is amazing! I can't wait to get the headset on and try it out."

He grinned. "That's exactly what I was thinking. Do you want to go check it out? They're in the car."

Her head bobbed furiously, and they headed for the ramp installed late yesterday, allowing easier access to the site than the ladder he had almost fallen off.

"Bored already?" asked Acton.

Tommy waved. "No, we're just going to go and check out the system with the VR gear. We'll be back in a few minutes."

"When you're done playing with it yourselves, bring the headsets down. I want to see it too."

"So do I," added Laura. "How's it look?"

Mai wagged the tablet. "Incredible. My man is a genius."

Tommy's cheeks flushed, then a rush of emotions swept over him as the professors smiled up at him.

"He definitely is," agreed Laura.

It was as if his own parents were proud of him—pride something he couldn't say he remembered them expressing. He was at least speaking with his father again, though he wasn't sure that relationship could ever be salvaged, and he wasn't sure he cared. Mai was all he needed in his life, though the professors filled a void left by the estrangement with his parents over a decade ago. They were his surrogate family now, and he couldn't imagine his life any better than it was at this moment.

He had a great job, a fiancée not only beautiful but intelligent, funny, and supportive, and two mentors who treated both of them with caring and generosity. They were searching for a house, with a down payment provided by these new parental figures in his life, and got to travel the world, seeing and doing incredible things thanks to their wealth. Yes, sometimes it was dangerous, sometimes they had nearly died. But he wouldn't trade it for anything. His life was exciting, interesting, happy.

And it was all thanks to this woman ahead of him.

If he hadn't had the balls to ask her out in the computer lab that day, who knew where his life would have led?

Mai crested the top and disappeared as he continued up, his eyes glued to the metal ramp, his fear of heights exacerbated by yesterday's near fall.

"You're clear."

He looked up to see Mai extending a hand toward him. He reached out and took it, and she gently tugged him away from the excavation pit. She flashed him a smile, and he returned it, leaning in and giving her a peck.

Somebody shouted to the left, and they both turned to see one of the guards dropping, followed by another as two SUVs blasted through the security gate—a temporary barrier never meant to prevent anyone from getting in.

"Oh shit!" Tommy grabbed Mai by the hand, racing toward their SUV, well aware that the professors' standing orders of all rentals being up-armored whenever possible had been met on this supposedly peaceful assignment.

More gunfire—suppressed—erupted from the windows of the two intruders racing toward the dig. Tommy tripped over something and hit the ground hard as the first SUV skidded to a halt, all four doors opening. Four heavily armed men, dressed head to toe in black, their faces covered, their body armor like something out of Call of Duty, emerged from inside and surged forward, their weapons raised high, disciplined bursts belching from their rifles.

Mai turned to help him when he shook his head and pointed. "Run!"

She hesitated.

"Run! I'll be right behind you!"

She turned and sprinted toward safety as the second vehicle came to a halt, four more men emerging. Tommy pushed to his feet and a weapon swung toward him. He raised his hands and squeezed his eyes shut when Mai—now opening the door of the SUV—screamed, "No!"

A suppressed weapon popped to his right from the new arrivals. He opened his eyes, surprised he wasn't hit—then cried out when he saw Mai lying in a heap on the ground, her white t-shirt rapidly turning red. "Mai!" he screamed, sprinting toward her.

One of the new arrivals blocked his path. He swung a fist, but the man leaned out of the way, raising his rifle butt. The cold, hard polymer made contact with his jaw and knocked him out cold.

Acton stood behind a table of artifacts already processed by the team. He indicated one of the items. "This is a gladius, a type of short sword. The gladiators would have used this in combat, sometimes with or without a shield."

Niner reached to pick it up when Angela slapped his hand.

"Look, don't touch!"

Acton chuckled. "It's okay. You can touch it. Just don't swing it at anybody."

Niner eagerly picked it up and gripped it in his hands. "Shorter than I would have thought."

Atlas regarded him. "Yet on you it seems to be the perfect size." He picked up another matching sword. "This is almost like a butter knife."

Acton snorted, then picked up another weapon, holding it out for the massive Delta operator. "This might be more your size. It's a francisca. A type of throwing ax."

Atlas returned the sword to the table, then gripped the handle with the massive curved blade on the end. "I like this. I feel like I'm in Lord of the Rings."

Niner eyed him. "Yeah, you do kind of look like an orc."

An odd series of pops came from behind him and Acton turned, staring up the ramp. "What the hell is that?"

Apparently, Atlas and Niner already knew.

"Everybody take cover!" shouted Atlas in his impossibly deep voice.

But his warning fell on deaf ears, everyone merely turning to stare at him.

A woman screamed.

"That's Mai!" exclaimed Laura as Acton turned and rushed toward the ramp.

"Doc, no!" warned Niner, but the warning went unheeded.

"Mai!" screamed Tommy from out of sight, the horror in his voice heart-wrenching.

Something was horribly wrong.

Acton reached the ramp and began sprinting up, Laura on his heels when a figure in black appeared at the top, a weapon raised. Acton froze, spreading himself out as wide as he could to provide a human shield for Laura.

"No mercy this time, Professor." The voice was heavily accented. Russian. It had to be Tankov's crew.

He took a step back, his hands high. "No need for anybody to get hurt here."

"I have my orders, Professor."

The finger squeezed then the man gasped, his eyes widening from behind his goggles, and Acton grimaced at the battle ax embedded in the man's side where there was limited body armor to protect him.

"Get down here!" shouted Atlas.

Acton spun, grabbing Laura, and they rushed down the ramp as more pops followed—pops he now recognized as suppressed gunfire. Screams erupted as the members of the dig, unaccustomed to being under fire, panicked, scurrying in all directions.

Acton, still gripping Laura's hand, rushed away from the ramp at a crouch, stealing a glance over his shoulder to find half a dozen men in pursuit, randomly peppering the area with lead.

"Over here!" It was Niner, beckoning them from behind the excavated wall of the crypt. Laura leaped over the stone, Acton following, and they both hit the ground hard.

"You guys okay?" asked Niner.

"Yeah." Acton poked his head up, staring toward the ramp. "But I think something's happened to Tommy and Mai."

Atlas gripped a sword. "We'll worry about them later."

"Who do you think it is?" asked Niner.

Acton frowned. "The guy had a Russian accent."

Laura glanced at him. "Tankov's team?"

"Wouldn't surprise me. But this is a hell of a lot more violent than anything I've seen them do before."

"What did he say to you?"

It was seared in Acton's memory. "'No mercy this time, Professor.'"

Atlas grunted. "So, he knew who you were."

"Yeah, it would appear so."

The hostiles swept through the camp, shooting only at the guards, thankfully leaving those cowering in fear unscathed.

"Let's just keep our heads down. We'll get through this," said Acton, struggling to control his breathing.

"He's right." Niner wrapped an arm around Angela's shoulders. "Just keep your head down. Do whatever they say. They're here for something, not us. Let's just stay out of their way."

Acton raised his head slightly, peering over the wall, and muttered a curse.

"What is it?" asked Laura.

"It looks like they're collecting everything they can around the remains of Decimus."

"You called it, Doc," said Niner.

"I was suspecting retirees with metal detectors, not former Russian Special Forces with automatic weapons." Acton winced as the remains were swept unceremoniously into a large duffel bag, the disrespect shown for the dead disgusting, infuriating. If he had a weapon, he would open fire on them, but all he had was a spear found lying on the ground that, even if he knew how to throw it, would only take out one of the thieves.

Something was said in Russian, and three of the men raced toward the ramp with their heavily laden cargo.

"Professor Acton, show yourself!"

"Tankov," hissed Laura.

But he didn't need her to recognize the voice. He would know it anywhere.

"Now, Professor!"

Tankov raised his weapon, aiming it toward Father Esposito, cowering behind an overturned table. Acton rose, and Tankov faced him, aiming his assault rifle directly at him. "We meet again."

Acton raised his hands. "I wish I could say it was a pleasure."

Tankov chuckled. "Someone here killed one of my men, and I suspect they're with you. Everybody behind that wall stand up or I kill the professor."

"They're not involved in this. This is between you and me."

"On the count of three."

Niner cursed and stood, followed by Atlas and the others.

"Well, well. I recognize you two." Tankov stepped closer, flanked by two of his men. "America's finest. What the hell are you doing here?"

"We're on vacation," rumbled Atlas.

Tankov turned to one of his men, laughing. "On vacation. I love it!" He returned his attention to the group, eyeballing Niner. "Something tells me you weren't the one who threw that ax."

"Don't let my height fool you."

Tankov stood in front of Atlas. "You threw it."

"And I'd do it again."

"I have no doubt." Tankov raised his weapon and pressed the muzzle against Atlas' massive chest. "I should kill you. That man was a friend of mine."

"Everyone you've killed here today has friends."

"This is true, but I don't know them. I knew him."

"Do what you've gotta do. Or be a man, drop that weapon, and let's go hand-to-hand."

Vanessa whimpered, and Tankov's eyes flitted over to the terrified woman. "He's your boyfriend, isn't he?"

"Don't answer him," said Atlas.

Tankov pressed the muzzle a little harder against Atlas' chest. "Answer me."

"Y-yes, he is."

Tankov stepped back. "Unfortunately, if I kill you two, I'll have the American government after me for the rest of my days. I can't have that." His hand darted forward and he grabbed Vanessa by the shirt, hauling her over the wall. Atlas lunged forward, but Tankov's men stepped closer, their weapons raised.

"No, Leon!" begged Vanessa. She was whipped toward one of Tankov's people who grabbed her.

Tankov raised his weapon at Angela. "With your friend. Now."

Angela turned to Niner, tears flowing down her cheeks, her entire body trembling, and Niner gave her a hug. "It'll be all right. Just do everything they say."

She shook out a nod and stepped over the wall, joining Vanessa as Tankov sauntered toward Laura. "There she is. If I had teachers like you in school, I might have just stuck around and got my degree rather than join the forces."

"The academic world's loss, I'm sure," sneered Laura, Acton suppressing a smile and admiring the courage in her voice.

"You'll be coming with me, Professor."

Acton held out an arm, blocking her path. "Why?"

"I need an archaeologist."

"Then take me."

"Sorry, you're not my type. Don't worry, Professor. As long as you stay out of our way, no one else gets hurt. Come after us, and all three of them die."

Atlas growled. "If you hurt a hair on any of them, you'll have all of Delta coming down on you."

"I don't think so. But then again, we won't need to worry about that now, will we? We're taking them with us. They're our security. Once we no longer need them, they'll be set free and there'll be no reason for you to come after us. Leave that to the police."

Tankov held out a hand for Laura, but she refused it, instead stepping over the wall herself and joining the others.

"We'll be leaving you now," said Tankov as sirens wailed in the distance, the locals alerted. They headed toward the ramp, weapons trained on them the entire way. "Remember what I said. Pursue us, and they die."

Tankov was the last to disappear at the top. Atlas sprinted forward, Niner on his heels. The big man grabbed the dead man's weapon and tossed it to Niner, along with a couple of spare mags, then pulled a handgun from its holster.

Acton rushed toward the ramp. "Everybody stay down! Just stay where you are!" he shouted, not getting any disagreement from the academics. He pushed up the steel plates, cringing at the loud echoes of his footsteps. Two engines roared to life as he reached the top. Gunfire sprayed toward him and he hit the deck.

"Remember what I said!" shouted Tankov from inside one of the SUVs as he shot out the tires of their rental. Acton stayed down and peered up to see Tankov and his men escape through the main gate, then he spotted Tommy, prone on the ground, unmoving.

"Oh my God!"

Tommy groaned as someone called his name, the voice barely cutting through the high-pitched whine dominating his ears. It was like it was coming from behind his eyes. It wasn't a sound, it was a sensation, slowly replaced by a horrible pain in his jaw.

"Tommy, wake up!"

It was Acton. What was going on? Where was he? What had happened?

Mai!

He bolted upright, his eyes wide, to find Acton kneeling beside him. "They shot Mai!"

"What?" Acton's head spun around and he gasped, leaping to his feet and rushing away. Tommy pushed to his knees, his head still swimming. "Niner!" shouted Acton, his voice a distant echo.

Somebody rushed past him as more of the world came into focus—screams, crying, sirens.

And then it all came rushing back to him.

The two SUVs.

The men in special ops gear.

The gunfire.

Mai.

He struggled to his feet and stumbled toward their rental. Acton had the rear opened, retrieving a large red duffel bag with a white cross on it. Niner was on his knees, leaning over Mai, who lay prone on the grass as Atlas stood nearby, a weapon in his hands, covering them.

What had happened here? How long had he been unconscious? He stumbled toward his fiancée, his head pounding, his jaw aching, pushing through the pain, the confusion. "Is she all right?"

Acton dropped to his knees, tearing open the first aid kit—standard issue for any rental now arranged by Mary.

"She's lost a lot of blood," reported Niner, yanking supplies from the kit. "But she's still alive."

Tommy took a knee and gripped Mai's limp hand, then nearly passed out when Niner sliced open his girlfriend with a scalpel then jammed his fingers inside of the most important person in his life. "What's happening?"

"She took a round to her side. She's bleeding internally. I need to find the source…" Niner had a determined expression and appeared to be searching around blindly.

Tommy stared, flabbergasted. "Do you know what you're doing?"

Atlas glanced over his shoulder at him. "Don't worry, kid. He's the best damn medic in the Unit."

Police cars burst through the gate, soon followed by two more, officers swarming the scene.

"We need an ambulance over here!" shouted Acton at the new arrivals. An officer raised a radio to his lips as Atlas lowered his weapon to the ground.

"Who speaks English?" asked the big man.

"Pretty much everyone." One of them approached. "What happened here?"

"We were attacked by a group of professional art thieves led by a man named Alexie Tankov. Former Russian Spetsnaz. They stole some artifacts and shot quite a few people. They left less than five minutes ago in two black SUVs—Toyota Land Cruisers. I wasn't able to get their plates." Atlas turned. "Doc, did you see the plates?"

Acton shook his head. "No. I was too busy ducking."

An ambulance roared through the entrance to the palace grounds and came to a halt. Two paramedics jumped out, one rushing over as the other grabbed their gear.

Niner looked up at the woman. "English?"

"Yes."

"She took one round to her left side. The round is still in there. I think it missed her major organs, but it clipped an artery. I'm pinching it now. If I take my hand away, I might not find it again."

A wave of nausea took over and Tommy started fading again. A hand gripped his shoulder. It was Acton.

"You okay?"

Tommy lost control. "No, of course I'm not okay! I can't lose her! She's all I have in this world! She's everything!" He turned to the paramedics. "You have to save her!"

Niner, still with several fingers in Mai's innards, glanced at Acton. "You gotta get him outta here, Doc. He shouldn't be seeing this."

Acton gripped Tommy by the shoulders to lift him to his feet, but he wrenched free. "No! I'm not leaving her!"

"I understand. I wouldn't want to either. But just step back. Let them do their work."

Tommy sniffed. Acton was right. He was in the way. He kissed Mai's hand. "I love you. Just fight, okay? You fight." He let go of her hand and rose, Acton leading him away as Atlas approached.

"Did you tell them what happened?" asked Acton.

The big man nodded. "Yes. But I don't think it's going to help. This was too well coordinated. They came in, guns blazing. That means they knew there'd be a massive police response and that their vehicles would be spotted."

"What are you saying?"

"If I were them, I'd have already switched rides, and I'd have my way planned out of here. These guys are pros, remember. Same type of training we have. There's no way the locals are finding them unless they get lucky."

Acton cursed. "Then I think we have to call in some favors."

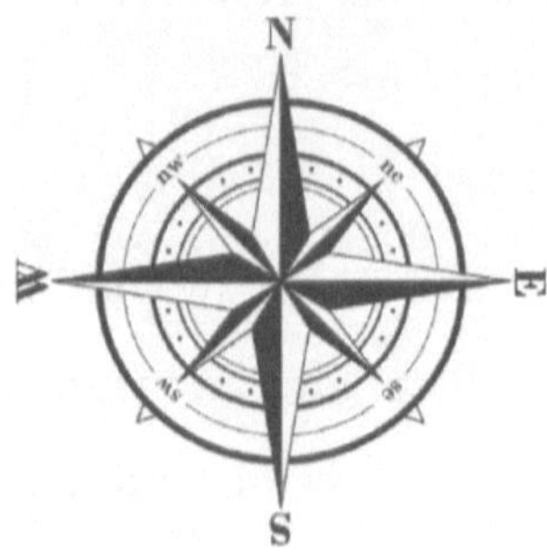

North of the Lateran Palace

Rome, Italy

"If she doesn't shut up, I'm going to shoot her," growled Tankov from the passenger seat.

Laura wrapped her arms around an inconsolable Angela, who kept screaming for Niner. "You have to calm down."

Angela stared at her blankly as she continued to scream. This was getting them nowhere, and if the poor girl didn't shut up, Tankov just might shoot them all. The Russians had shown no concern this time about who they killed. She was pretty sure Mai was dead. She had only caught a glimpse of her lying on the ground near their rental, and she appeared to have a stomach wound and was bleeding heavily. Part of her wanted to scream out as well, to attack Tankov, to reach forward and grab the steering wheel and cause an accident.

She might have lost Mai, and she would mourn for that sweet, sweet girl later, but now she had two other lives she was responsible for. These were her guests, and entirely out of their element, despite whom they might be dating.

She tried a Hail Mary. "Suck on your thumb."

Vanessa's eyes shot wide at the suggestion, and even Angela appeared surprised.

"What?"

"Suck on your thumb." Laura grabbed the woman by the hand, yanking her thumb up and sticking it in the panicked mouth. It had the immediate desired effect. The action—primal—dragging her back to another time when she felt protected. Comforted.

Tankov snickered as they pulled off the road. "I'll have to remember that one."

Laura had struggled to keep track of where they were, at least in general terms. The distraction that was Angela had her pretty much lost, though she was fairly sure they had been traveling north, and not for long. The car came to a halt behind a building, an industrial warehouse from the looks of it.

"Let's go," ordered Tankov.

The doors opened. Vanessa climbed out first, helping Angela down to the ground. Laura followed, and they were led into the back of a large Mercedes Sprinter, its windows heavily tinted. Laura stared up at the sky for as long as she could. If she knew her husband, he would be calling their friend Dylan Kane and enlisting the help of the CIA. She wanted a good shot of her face should a satellite happen to be crossing overhead. She wanted no doubt as to who had transferred to the new ride.

The doors at the back slammed shut, and she sat with the others on the bench lining the driver's side. Angela continued to suck on her thumb and appeared to have calmed down dramatically. Laura took the opportunity to assess the situation as they pulled away. She counted seven of the enemy, all now removing their gear, faces revealed, some of whom she recognized from previous encounters, including Tankov, sitting directly across from her.

Atlas had taken out one of them, which was great, but not much help. There was no way she could single-handedly eliminate seven hostiles. And Angela and Vanessa would likely be useless in any fight.

She had to think her way out of this.

"Why are we here?"

Tankov shrugged out of his body armor, tossing it onto the floor. "I need an archaeologist."

"What for?"

He gestured at several duffel bags. "To examine what we took."

Laura eyed the bags loaded with the remains of Decimus. "You stole a bunch of bones. Congratulations. What's that worth on the black market? A few thousand?"

"You really don't know what you found, do you?"

Laura glared at him. "Enlighten me."

"Do you know who this is?"

"I know who we think he *could* be."

"Who?"

"Decimus Cornelius Vindex."

"Exactly. And you know who he is?"

"I know who he was."

"And what's he most famous for?"

"He had a long career. Why don't you narrow it down for me and save us all some time?"

Tankov laughed, and he elbowed the man beside him. "You can see why I'm madly in love with her."

The word sickened Laura, and her stomach protested. These were seven men. They were three women. What did they have planned? They had already proven they were willing to kill—to murder. Would they stop at rape? Tankov had always shown an interest in her. A disturbing interest. She had to keep the man talking.

"Let me get you started. You think somehow his body is going to lead you to the lost Tripolitanian treasury."

"Very good, Professor."

"And just how do you think a bunch of bones are going to tell you that?"

"Do you know the legend of how he died?"

"I'm familiar with it, yes."

"How familiar?"

"Fairly. I read up on it last night after we realized who we might have."

"So, what did it say happened in his final moments?"

"Prosper of Aquitaine, who claimed to be in the front row due to his status, also claimed to have heard everything."

"Go on."

"He claimed the Black gladiator, who had betrayed the emperor and fought at Decimus' side, pleaded with him to reveal the location of the treasury in order to save his life, but Decimus refused, and instead slapped his chest in salute, saying, 'The secret dies with us.'"

"You know your history well, Professor."

"I did just read it last night."

"That's when I read about it as well." Tankov nudged the man beside him. "To my friend's credit, he already was aware of the history, which is why he spotted the inconsistency in your discovery."

"What's that?"

The man beside him grabbed one of the duffel bags and unzipped it. He reached inside and yanked out the breastplate, still attached to Decimus' ribcage. She frowned at the desecration. "What do you make of this?"

"He was wearing a breastplate. So what?"

"Most gladiators wouldn't."

"True, however, he was a respected Roman general. It shouldn't really be a surprise that he was granted a few liberties. "Perhaps they wanted the fight to be a little more sporting."

"Perhaps. But if he slapped his chest, like the description says—perhaps he was sending a message, and not saluting at all."

Acton/Palmer Residence

Overlook Village Gated Community

St. Paul, Maryland

Reading held up the remote control and pressed *Stop*, ending the movie he had just finished streaming with Rose. He placed the remote on the table and turned on the couch toward her as she twisted to face him.

"So, what did you think?"

He tipped his head to the side for a moment. "Actually, I liked it."

"I told you that you would. I did it because English is my second language, so it helped me follow along. But all my American friends, when I get them to try it, they like it too."

"Well, I never would have thought I'd enjoy watching an English movie with English subtitles. God knows I hate watching foreign films. But this was good. It's amazing how many things you miss when you're just using your ears. I've seen that movie before, and I know I definitely misheard some things the first time and totally missed others."

"So, you don't mind watching like that?"

"Definitely not. Especially with you."

She turned away. "Mister Hugh…" Her voice was barely a murmur.

"Hugh…"

She wrung her hands in her lap. "Is there…?" She hesitated, and his stomach immediately twisted into knots.

"Is there what?"

Her shoulders slumped. "Nothing."

He reached out and took her hand, and she turned, staring into his eyes. "Is there what?"

"I can't say it. It's not appropriate. I'm just an employee."

"You're Jim and Laura's employee, not mine, so ask what you want to ask." She turned away again, and he reached out, placing a finger on her chin, gently turning her face back toward him. "I think I know what you want to ask. And the answer is yes."

She smiled, and his heart melted. "Then you're all right with chicken enchiladas for dinner tonight?"

It was like a gut punch, and he recoiled, aghast at having read something into her innocent question. His jaw dropped. "Umm, yes?"

She giggled. "I'm just joking." She lunged forward, and her lips pressed against his. He was caught off guard and didn't respond for a moment, the experience reminding him of the first time he had kissed a girl when he was nine years old. They just pressed their lips together and did nothing, then wondered what all the fuss was about.

He let himself go, wrapping his arms around her, holding her tight, his lips finally responding, his pulse pounding with the excitement of a first kiss.

And he pushed away, clasping a hand over his heart.

"We better slow down. I don't think my doctors have cleared me for this yet."

She giggled again. "At least you would die with a smile."

He laughed as he steadied his breathing. "Totally worth it." He leaned back in, but was interrupted by his phone ringing on the table.

Rose leaned over to read the call display. "It's Mr. Professor."

"Let it go to voicemail."

Their lips met again.

To hell with the doctors.

It was just kissing. There was no way he needed medical clearance for that, no matter how exciting it was. He was fully aware of what Acton had been doing—creating situations for the two of them to be together, to be alone—and he had to confess, he was glad his friend was interfering. He had always liked Rose, always found her cute, and never would have had the courage to take the initiative.

It wasn't his style.

It never was. Never had been. Even his ex-wife had asked him out. He considered himself a man. A man's man. Tough as nails. But when it came to women, he just didn't understand them and found himself fumbling for words.

But here, now, he didn't need words.

He just had to make sure the bean dip she had made as a snack for them didn't repeat on him.

Oh shit, what if I fart?

The phone rang again, and their lips parted.

"You better get that."

He sighed heavily. "Yeah. I guess I better." He picked up the phone and swiped his thumb. "Hey, Jim. You're kind of interrupting something here." He winked at Rose, and she blew him a kiss.

"Mai's been shot and Laura has been kidnapped along with Vanessa and Angela!"

He bolted upright. "What?" He made a handwriting motion, and Rose leaped to her feet, rushing over to the kitchen counter, grabbing a pad and pen. She returned, handing them both over. "All right, slow down. From the beginning. Is Mai being tended to?"

"Yes, they just loaded her into the ambulance. We're heading to the hospital now."

"Good. Who took Laura and the others?"

"It was that Russian bastard, Tankov."

Reading cursed as he wrote down the name. "That guy really needs to die."

"Trust me. You'll have to get in line."

"Are the police involved yet?"

"The locals are, and I just spoke with Mario. He's already on scene. There's a lot of people dead and wounded. I don't know how many. They just came in shooting. They didn't have to. The guards here were unarmed. Atlas managed to kill one of them with an old battle ax, but there was no way we could stop them. There were too many and they were too heavily armed."

"Do you have a description of the vehicles?"

"Yes. We told the police everything we saw, but Atlas seems to think they would have switched vehicles already."

"They probably did. I'm going to hang up now. I'm going to call Michelle. Get Interpol involved. It's time you called in favors. Reach out to Dylan."

"I will as soon as I get off the phone with you."

"Do you know why they were there? What they wanted?"

"Looks like they were interested in a body. A Roman general named Decimus Cornelius Vindex. They must think there's evidence on him as to where a rumored lost treasure is hidden."

"Good. That means they probably took Laura because they need her, and they'll use the other two as leverage over her. Right now, they're probably safe, but for how long, who knows. I'm going to call Michelle now. You call Dylan."

"Okay. I'm going to do that right now."

"Do that. I'll talk to you soon." The call ended, and Reading continued to scribble down more notes.

"What's going on?" asked Rose, her concern obvious.

"There was an attack at the dig site in Rome. Some Russians we've dealt with before. Mai's been shot and is on the way to the hospital. Laura, Angela, and Vanessa were taken by the Russians. We don't know what's happened to them."

Rose headed back to the kitchen, grabbing the landline. "I'm going to call Dean Milton. Those are my instructions should anything like this happen."

"Do it. I'm going to call my partner." He tapped Michelle Humphrey's name in his contact list, then pressed the phone to his ear.

"Hugh, you cranky old bastard. You're not dead yet?"

Reading grunted at his much younger partner's joke. "No. But the world seems to be conspiring against me to make it happen."

She recognized his serious tone. "What's happened?"

"It'll probably be coming across the wire soon. Apparently, there was an attack at an archaeological dig site in Rome. A lot of people dead and wounded."

A keyboard clacked in the background. "I've got it here. There's word of the attack, but no details. Why are you calling me?" She stopped and cursed. "Let me guess. The professors?"

"Yeah. Jim and Laura were there along with Tommy and Mai plus some friends. Mai's been shot and is en route to the hospital. I don't know her condition, but Jim sounded pretty upset. Laura and the partners of two of their special friends, shall we say, were taken by the Russians."

"Russians? You don't mean Tankov and his crew?"

"Exactly. The locals are involved, but it's only been minutes. We need Interpol involved right away. The longer we delay, the more likely it is they'll escape."

"I'll go talk to the boss, but you know what she's going to say. There's nothing we can do until the Italians ask for our help."

"Then have her reach out and make them ask. This is Laura." His voice cracked. Jim and Laura were two of his best friends. In fact, they *were* his best friends, and he thought of Laura like the daughter he never had. "I have to save her," he murmured.

"No, you don't. You have to take care of yourself. You have to calm down, otherwise you're going to give yourself another heart attack. I'm on it. I'll keep you informed as to what's going on. Do you have somebody there with you?"

He reached out and took Rose's hand, her call with Milton already finished. "Yeah. Someone's here."

"Good. I don't want you to be alone. Now just try to calm down and we'll work the problem from this end."

"All right. Just let me know as soon as you hear anything."

"I will."

Reading ended the call then turned to Rose as she sat beside him. "What did Greg say?"

"He said he's going to contact the State Department to find out what's going on and to see what can be done."

Reading held a hand to his chest, his heart pounding. He reached out and grabbed the pulse oximeter sitting on the table and stuck it on his finger, his eyes closed as he counted to ten. He opened them and didn't like what he saw.

And neither did Rose.

She shuffled closer and rubbed his back. "You need to calm down. Steady your breathing. There's nothing you can do."

His eyes welled up with tears, and he slumped back on the couch. "And that's just it. There *is* nothing I can do. Not anymore." He bit his lip. "What kind of man have I become, when I can't even help my best friends?"

"You're a man that had a heart attack. Nobody blames you for that, and you shouldn't blame yourself. If this were a year ago, or a year from now, you would be helping. The best thing you can do for them now, you've already done. Let your partner help them. You need to relax, remain calm, and use your brain, not your muscles."

He huffed, then wiped the tears away that threatened to escape and shatter any illusions of manhood he had left. "You're right," he sighed. "Let's just hope Dylan and his people can help."

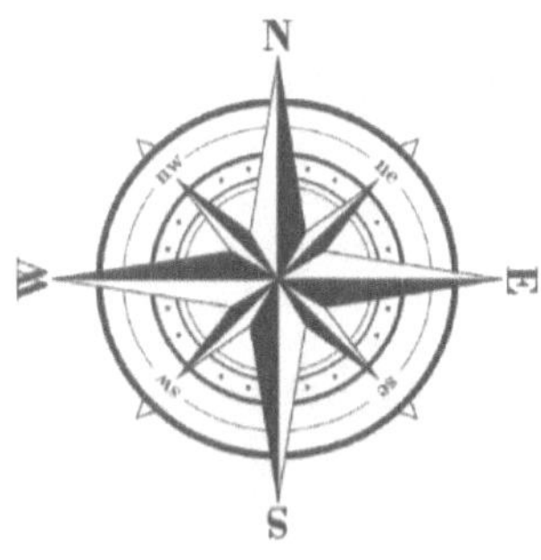

Hôtel de Paris Monte-Carlo

Monte-Carlo, Monaco

"Is that a Glock in your pocket, or are you just happy to see me?"

CIA Operations Officer Dylan Kane pulled back from the woman he was kissing and stared into her eyes with a smirk. "Both."

She grinned. "Glad to see I still excite you. I was beginning to wonder."

Kane ran his fingers through her hair. He was in a committed relationship with the amazing Lee Fang, but he was also a spy, and sometimes his cover demanded he do things he would rather not do. Before Fang, he considered this one of the perks of the job—fooling around with women, usually gorgeous, making love, making them fall in love.

Getting them to spill their secrets.

But now he always felt guilty. Fang was fully aware that what might be about to happen could happen. Their agreement was it wasn't cheating as long as it was part of the job. She just didn't want to hear about it, and he didn't blame her. The guilt had torn him apart for a while until she finally forced him to admit to what was going on. It had made him feel better, and the guilt wasn't as bad as it once was, though it was still there.

And what was happening down below was in no way a commentary on the state of his relationship with Fang. It was merely biological.

He was, after all, a man.

And this was a beautiful woman that had information he needed.

His source dropped to her knees and pulled at his belt. He closed his eyes, picturing Fang. This was going a little further than he had originally planned, yet he had a history with this woman. He had quite literally pumped her for information several times over the years, and it would appear she expected no different.

His fly was unzipped, and a hand reached in. She paused, staring up at him. "Really? Underwear?"

He shrugged. "A man can change."

She frowned, then stood. "You've gone and fallen in love, haven't you?"

He eyeballed her. "You know I'm not the love type."

"Yet you've done it anyway." She reached down and zipped up his fly. "While I enjoy our fun, I'm not about to betray another woman like my husband continually betrays me."

He buckled his belt. "That's very noble of you."

"You'd understand if you'd been cheated on." She sat in a chair by the window of the hotel suite, the bill footed by his cover, Shaws of London, offering spectacular views of the city. She lit a cigarette and took a drag, exhaling the toxic fumes. He didn't bother reminding her it was a non-smoking room.

He sat across from her.

"What's her name?"

"It doesn't matter. You know we don't use names. I don't know who your husband is. You don't know who my significant other is. I think it's best we keep it that way."

She took another drag. "Fine. Probably wise." She stood, lifting her dress seductively. He leaned back with a smirk.

"I thought we agreed we weren't doing this."

A Cheshire cat smile was the response as the hemline continued to rise, soon revealing she was as commando as she had expected him to be. She lifted a leg, placing her foot between his knees. "See anything you like?"

He had to look. His cover would. He smiled and reached out, removing the tiny memory card tucked into a garter.

She groaned in frustration, returning to her chair. "I was really looking forward to tonight. My husband is so useless in bed."

"Well, my girlfriend appreciates your self-control." He held up the memory card. "I understand you're providing this despite our quid pro quo agreement not being fulfilled tonight. What about in the future?"

She shrugged. "My husband will always be a philandering piece of garbage who seems to enjoy leaving classified material around for people to see. It makes him feel important. You'll hear from me again. And who knows?" She smirked. "Maybe things won't work out with your girlfriend, and we can return to our previous arrangement."

Kane chuckled. "Who knows?"

His CIA-customized TAG Heuer watch fired a coded electrical impulse into his wrist, letting him discreetly know he had a priority message from a non-Agency contact. Very few people had access to his private communication system, and if they were using this particular code, something was wrong with his friends.

Yet he had a mission.

"Would you care to have dinner?"

She dismissed the idea with a flick of her wrist. "No, I think I'm going to go and lose a bunch of my husband's money." He stood and extended a hand, helping her up. She leaned in and gave him a kiss, then patted his cheek. "She's a lucky woman, whoever she is."

He said nothing and escorted her to the door. She fit a hat in place, enough to hide her face from the cameras. After all, the wife of a Chinese Politburo member couldn't be seen coming out of an American insurance investigator's room.

"Until next time."

She patted his cheek again, and he opened the door. She stepped out, heading directly for the elevators with purpose and no hesitation. If she were spotted, it had to look as if nothing untoward had happened. Furtive glances, uncertain movements, led to suspicions.

He closed the door, locked it, then headed for the nightstand where his phone sat charging. He logged into his secure system and read the message from his former professor, James Acton.

His eyebrows shot up. "Holy shit!"

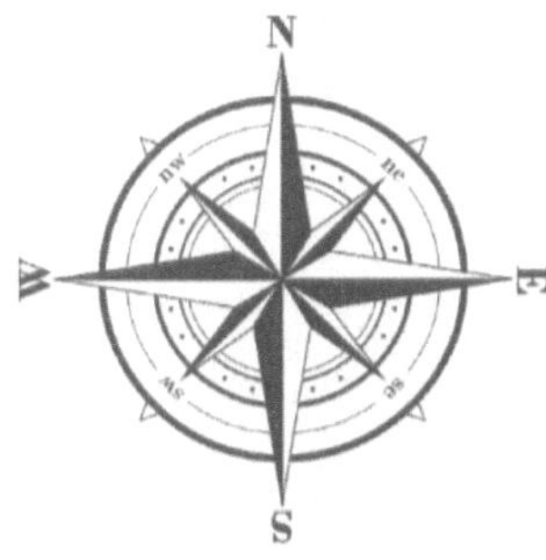

Dawson Residence, Lake in the Pines Apartments

Fayetteville, North Carolina

Command Sergeant Major Burt "Big Dog" Dawson belted out AC/DC's Thunderstruck as he lathered himself up in the shower, a classic rock station playing on the smart speaker in the bathroom. He was on leave, and now that he was married to Maggie, it meant there was always something to do, like today. They were up extremely early to go antiquing. And he loved it. He never thought he really would. He had always assumed he would die young and single. But after Maggie had inserted herself into his life, making her feelings known, he couldn't imagine being without her.

He wanted to have a family, grow old, spoil his grandkids, and die lying in bed, in each other's arms, peacefully in their sleep.

It was a fantasy, of course. It never happened. But fantasies could be comforting, and the alternative, unappealing.

His phone, sitting on the counter, rang. Maggie entered, naked as the day she was born. He stared through the glass with a grin as the drill sergeant took notice. She read the call display.

"It's Niner."

Dawson's eyes narrowed. "Niner? What the hell's he doing calling? He's in Italy. He's supposed to be on vacation."

"Do you want to take it?"

"Put it on speaker."

She swiped her thumb and tapped the display as he opened the door.

"Hey, buddy. You caught me in the shower."

"Sorry, BD, but we've got a situation."

Dawson, still covered in soap, turned off the water, recognizing the distress in his friend's voice. Maggie tossed him a towel as he stepped out. "What's going on?"

"Tankov and his buddies attacked the dig site. Mai Trinh's been shot and is on her way to the hospital. Vanessa, Angela, and Dr. Palmer have all been kidnapped. It's a real Charlie-Foxtrot. We need help."

Dawson turned to Maggie. "Find out where the colonel is."

Her eyes were filled with tears, but she rushed out into the hallway, her footfalls fading as she ran for her own phone.

"Are you and Atlas secure?"

"Yeah, we're fine. So is the professor. Tommy got clocked, but he's good."

"What about Mai? What's her condition?"

"Hard to say. She lost a lot of blood. I managed to pinch off the artery until the paramedics could take over. We clamped it, but I just don't know. It might be too late for her."

"Any leads on where they took our people?"

"Negative. All we know is they headed north.'

'The locals?'

"They're doing what they can, but you know Tankov. There's no way they were in the same vehicles for more than a few minutes."

"How long ago did this happen?"

"Not even fifteen minutes."

"Then they're still in Rome."

"Definitely."

"Why the hell would they come in shooting?"

"I don't know. The going theory, based on what they stole—some dead dude's skeleton—is that they think there's a clue on the body that could lead them to some lost treasure. That's just something I overheard the Doc saying."

"What do you need?"

"We need to find them. And if Mai dies—or a hair on our people's heads has been touched—I want to kill them all."

"I hear you, brother. I'm going to reach out to the colonel, see what we can do."

"You do that. The Doc's trying to make contact with Dylan. And Agent Reading's already reached out to his people at Interpol."

"Good. I'm going to let you go, and try to meet with the colonel. You keep me posted."

"Will do."

"And Niner?"

"Yeah?"

"We'll get her back for you. We'll get them all back."

"I'm going to hold you to that," said Niner, his voice cracking.

The beep of the call ending had Dawson back in the shower, rinsing off quickly as Maggie reappeared.

"The colonel's still at the office. Apparently, he never left. He's running an op."

"Good. Call him. Tell him I'm coming to see him, then give Red a shout. Tell him what's happened. Assemble the team here. And double-check my go bag. I have a feeling I'm going on vacation."

"Based upon the composition of the breastplate, I would place it in the fourth or fifth centuries AD. Certainly ancient Roman design."

"So?"

"The artwork on the breastplate is intricate, suggesting great care went into it. It's well worn—seen many battles."

"And? Is it him?"

"There's nothing on here to indicate his position. This suggests perhaps a family heirloom, handed down several generations. There was better armor available at the time, though this man preferred tradition. Symbolism."

"Yes, yes, yes. Fascinating. Is there any indication where the hell he hid the treasury?"

"Nothing that I can see."

The other man—the source of Tankov's expertise on the matter—growled in frustration. "He's not going to put it in plain sight. Take the damn thing off. Let's see what's underneath!"

"If you know what to do, then why the hell do you need me?"

"That's a good question."

Tankov held up a hand, calming his man. "We agreed. She does the examination."

Another growl and folded arms had the amateur archaeologist leaning back in a huff.

She carefully undid one of the straps, the other already torn away. She lifted the breastplate up, free of the skeleton it had clung to for over a thousand years, then turned it over.

And everyone gasped.

Deputy Director Morison's Office, CIA Headquarters

Langley, Virginia

"No direct involvement."

CIA Analyst Supervisor Chris Leroux wasn't surprised by his boss' answer. Deputy Director of CIA for Operations Leif Morrison was giving him more leeway than most would. The professors were a pain in the ass, but also a great help at times, and the fact two of the kidnap victims were the significant others of Delta operators made it personal. "Understood. No direct involvement." He shifted in his chair. "So, what does that actually mean?"

Morrison smirked. "Bend the rules, but don't break them. See if you can find them. Let the locals deal with it."

"Understood. What about Kane? He just finished his mission in Monte-Carlo. He wants to head in."

Morrison sighed, tossing his glasses on his desk and pinching the bridge of his nose. "If I say no, he's going to go anyway."

"Probably."

"Fine. Get him to Rome. Hopefully, by the time he gets there, we've already found them and the Italians have rescued them."

Leroux hesitated.

"What?"

"Well…Tankov's good. Knowing him, he could already be out of Rome. The Italians are refusing to ground their flights. They increased patrols and security at the airports and train stations, but they're refusing to lock down the city for this. They say it's too disruptive. Inspector General Giasson is trying to get them to change their minds, but right now, they seem to think Tankov and his crew have probably already made it out of the city, so inconveniencing millions of people would be a waste. Not to mention the fact, if Tankov's team gets cornered, they might kill the hostages."

"What do you think?"

"I think they're long gone, or about to be."

Morrison blasted air between his lips, leaning forward and resting his elbows on his desk. "Why can't there ever be a quiet day?" He checked his watch. "We're nowhere near lunch, and I already know this is going to be a nightmare." He sat up. "Fine. Get Kane to Rome as fast as you can. Divert him in the air if you have to. Get our local resources on it. See if they can shake anything loose. Use whatever birds we've got in the sky, but no re-tasking. See if you can trace them. Hack whatever systems you have to hack. Try to find them before Kane is boots-on-the-ground. Otherwise, he's liable to bulldoze his way through the city, and I don't need that kind of paperwork."

Leroux stood. "We're on it, Chief."

Morrison gestured toward the door. "Get out of here. And don't make me regret my decision."

"I'll try not to, Chief."

Morrison gave him a look. "Try hard."

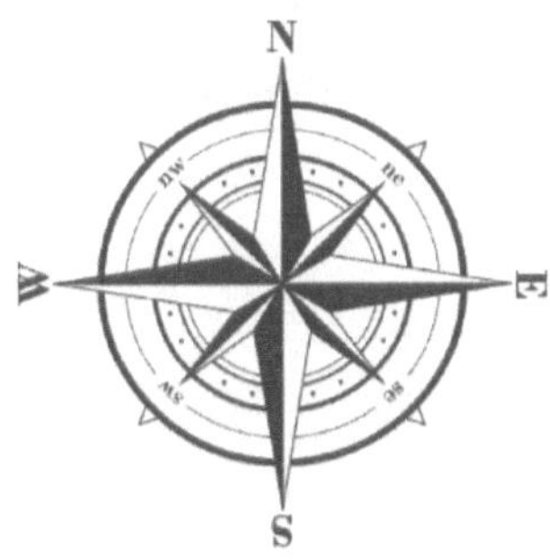

En route to San Giovanni Addolorata Hospital

Rome, Italy

Acton gripped the Oh Jesus handle as Atlas took a hard right in a commandeered Vatican vehicle, following the GPS directions to the hospital Mai had been taken to. Tommy was with her, transported in the back of the ambulance, and Acton was torn at the moment. Mai was fighting for her life, and was like a daughter to him. But his wife was in the hands of a madman, along with two women extremely important to the men with him now.

Men who had saved their lives on countless occasions.

But there wasn't much he could do but wait. He had made the calls, sent the messages. Now he had to trust the connections they had made over the years—the favors they had accumulated—would work their magic and find those taken from them.

For now, the best he could do was support Tommy in his hour of need.

His phone rang. It was Giasson. He took the call, putting it on speaker. "Hey, Mario. You're on speaker with Atlas and Niner. What can you tell me?"

"Nothing good, mon ami. We have four dead and six wounded—one critical—including your friend."

Acton squeezed his temples, closing his eyes. "How many were from your staff?"

A heavy sigh. "All the dead, plus two of the wounded."

It made sense. Decimus' body was on the Vatican side of the discovery.

"I'm so sorry to hear that, Mario."

"Thank you. Just so you know, I'm ceding the investigation over to the Italians. There's not much I can do. My primary concern for now is the fate of Laura and your friends."

"Have you heard anything?" The question had to be asked, though Acton already knew the answer—if Giasson had, he would have led with it.

"I'm afraid not. All I can tell you is they're not locking down the city. I just talked to the lead investigator, and she said they suspect Tankov and his men have already switched vehicles. They're trying to track them through traffic cameras now, but it's going to take time."

Acton fell back into his seat. "Too much time."

"That's what I fear, my friend."

"What are you going to do now?"

"I'm going to stay here. Act as liaison, then return to my office. You?"

"We're almost at the hospital. I'll be remaining with Tommy for now, until we find out what Mai's status is."

"She's in my prayers. And those of His Holiness."

"You've spoken with him?"

"Yes, I have."

"Pass on our condolences for the loss of his people."

"I shall, my friend, I shall. We'll talk soon."

"Okay. Talk to you soon."

The call ended and Atlas punched the steering wheel. "I can't believe there was no lockdown."

Niner, covered in Mai's blood, reached out and squeezed his buddy's shoulder from the passenger seat. "We knew they would switch vehicles the first chance they got. If we were in charge, we wouldn't do a lockdown either."

Atlas made another turn, his knuckles gripping the steering wheel tight, so tight, Acton feared for a moment the big man might actually tear it off.

"What are we going to do?" asked Acton.

The question was somewhat rhetorical. There wasn't much they could do.

Atlas eyed him in the rearview mirror. "We find them. We kill them. Tankov's crossed a line that can't be uncrossed."

Acton closed his eyes. "Let's just pray we can find them."

"Oh, we'll find them."

"Don't be so sure," said Niner. "They're civilians. And Laura's a Brit. They're nobodies as far as Washington is concerned."

"They're somebodies to us. And the powers that be have to know if they die because they didn't take action, I'm coming after them. Even if it means spending the rest of my days in Leavenworth."

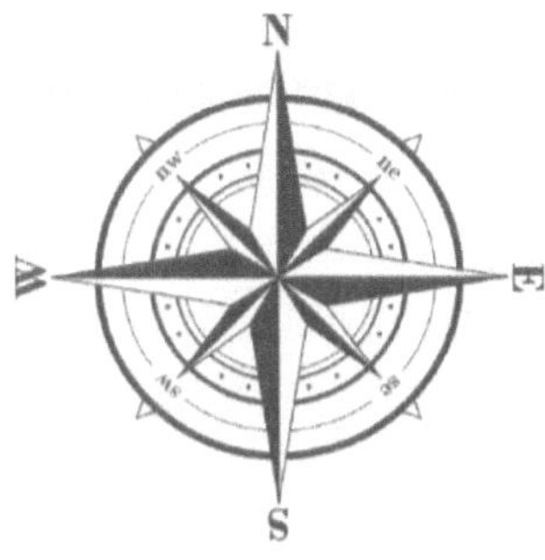

1st Special Forces Operational Detachment - Delta HQ

Fort Liberty, North Carolina

A.k.a. "The Unit"

"Make a hole!" shouted Dawson as he jogged down the hallway of the Unit, toward his CO's office. Everyone hugged the walls—even officers. He stepped into Clancy's outer office, usually manned by Maggie, finding her desk vacant.

"Come in, Sergeant Major," called Clancy from his inner sanctum, the door open.

Dawson collected himself, then stepped through the door to find Clancy behind his desk.

"Close it." Dawson shut the door, and Clancy indicated a chair. "Sit. Report."

Dawson did as ordered. "I received a phone call from Niner less than thirty minutes ago. There's been an attack at an archaeological dig site in Rome. He and Atlas, along with Vanessa and Angela, were there with Professors Acton and Palmer, and their friends Tommy Granger and Mai

Trinh. Alexie Tankov and his crew attacked the site using overwhelming and deadly force. Multiple fatalities. Multiple casualties—including Mai Trinh."

"What's her status?"

"Unknown. Last I heard, she's being transported to the hospital, but she had lost a lot of blood."

"Continue."

"The hostiles stole the remains of an ancient Roman general, apparently linked with some missing treasure. They left, but took Professor Palmer along with Angela and Vanessa. Their status is unknown."

Clancy cursed. "Unbelievable. I assume the locals are involved?"

"As far as I know, yes. My understanding is Agent Reading has been contacted, so Interpol is involved as well."

"We both know they're useless. They're just a liaison group. Most of the time, they don't even carry guns."

"Yeah, they're definitely not like they're portrayed in the movies."

"What are you about to ask from me?"

"I want in."

Clancy firmly dismissed the idea. "We can't get involved."

"Why the hell not? We *are* involved."

"No, *we* are not. Not as a Unit. Atlas and Niner are involved because it's their partners. You and the men are involved because they're your friends. But the US Army is not involved. The State Department is, but that's it."

"This is bullshit, sir. They were targeted because of who they are. Who *we* are."

"That may be, but they're not wives. They're girlfriends."

Dawson growled in frustration. "You know damn well that Atlas and Vanessa are talking marriage. And Niner's never been as crazy about anyone as he is about Angela. Those two are on the same path. I know that. You know that."

"But the Pentagon doesn't give a damn." Clancy held up a hand, cutting off Dawson before he said something he regretted. "You're on leave, right?"

"Yes, sir. The entire team is."

"I'll tell you what. *We* are not getting involved in this. But"—he held up a finger—"I couldn't give a damn what you and the guys do while you're on leave. I suggest a few of you take a much-needed vacation. I hear Italy's nice this time of year."

Dawson smiled as he rose. "Good idea, sir. I'll keep you posted."

Clancy shook his head. "I don't want to hear a thing from you until you're back."

Dawson snapped to attention. "Understood, sir." The colonel wanted plausible deniability, and he would get it. Dawson headed for the door.

"One more thing, Sergeant Major."

Dawson faced his commanding officer. "Sir?"

"I think it's time Tankov and his men were removed from any further participation in this little expriment we call life. Don't you?"

Dawson grunted. "You read my mind, sir."

Rome, Italy

Laura held the breastplate close, peering at the engraving on the interior. It was a map. There was no doubt about it.

"What is it?" asked Tankov, leaning in along with his amateur expert.

If they didn't know, she might play this to her advantage. "I'll tell you, but you have to set them free first." She jerked her chin toward her companions.

"Like I said before, this isn't a negotiation." Tankov aimed his weapon at Angela, the thumb no longer in her mouth, the desired effect taking hold. She whimpered, turning away. Vanessa wrapped her arms protectively around her friend. "What is it?"

Laura cursed to herself. There would be no negotiating here. No bargaining their way out of this. She had to keep them alive for as long as possible. If she told Tankov the full truth, they would be dead. "It's a map."

The other man reached out and grabbed the breastplate from her hand, staring at it, his eyes narrowing. He had no clue what he was looking at. She had leverage.

"Well?" asked Tankov.

The man shrugged. "It could be. It shouldn't be here. I've never seen engravings like this on the inside of a breastplate. Everything is done on the outside so people can see it. But I don't know what I'm looking at. It doesn't make any sense. It's just a line with a few other symbols on it."

Tankov pointed to the X at the end of that line. "X marks the spot, right?"

"You would think. But where is that spot? Where does this map start? There's nothing here to indicate that."

Tankov turned toward Laura. "You know, don't you?"

She nodded. "I do."

The gun was pressed against her forehead. "Tell us."

"Kill me, and you'll never know." She pointed at the breastplate. "If the legend is true, we're talking billions. Billions with a B. You'll get that retirement you always wanted."

Tankov and his men exchanged excited glances. This was all that motivated them—money. And they were all getting a little long in the tooth. It was clear to her they were seeking one final score. Something so big that, if they succeeded, they would never have to pull another trigger again.

And if she helped them succeed, she could be saving countless lives in the future.

But right now, the only lives she cared about were those of Vanessa and Angela. "I'll help you, but you have to let them go."

"I told you, this isn't a negotiation."

"It is now. You found what you were looking for—a map to the ultimate score. Billions in gold and jewels. You'll all be set for the rest of your lives. Live like kings. Change your faces. Do whatever you have to do. No one will ever know where you are or who you are. And I'm willing to help you, but only if you set them free."

Tankov eyed her. "I'll set one of them free."

"Not good enough."

"It's as good as it's going to get. Take it or leave it. I'll shoot them both and torture you until you tell me how to read this map. I don't really care. You've confirmed what I needed. The map is real. The treasure is real. And because we've never heard about it being found, it's still there. I'll get my payday one way or the other—with or without you. But I'm not without mercy." He flipped his weapon toward the two cowering women. "You pick."

Laura clenched her fists, her fingernails biting into her palms. "Don't make me pick," she whispered.

"Take her," said Vanessa.

Angela gasped. "No!"

Vanessa firmly rejected Angela's plea. "You're younger than me. And you didn't really know what you were getting into when you started dating him. I didn't either, but I've known for a long time. It should be you."

"Very well," said Tankov. "She'll be released when we're clear. Try anything, and she dies. Understood?" He directed the question at Laura.

"Yes. Understood."

"You better."

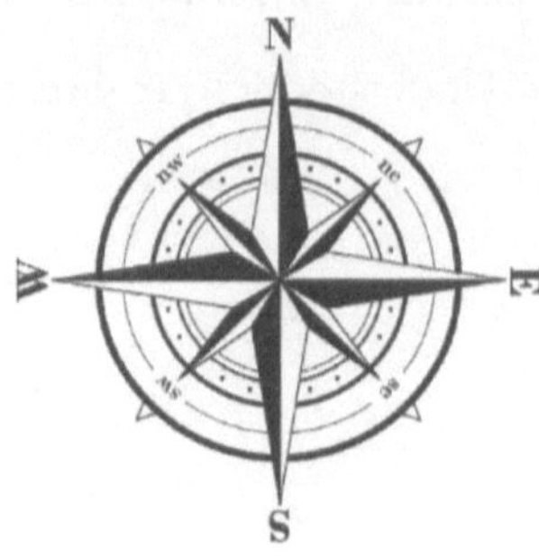

Dawson Residence, Lake in the Pines Apartments

Fayetteville, North Carolina

"Yeah, we're on our way. Should be in Rome in eight hours." Dawson checked his watch. "We'll probably be landing early evening."

"We'll make sure you're met."

Niner sounded exhausted.

"Any word on Mai?"

"She's in surgery now. At the moment, all I can say is she's still alive. She wasn't looking good."

"Understood."

"How many are coming?"

"Everybody's volunteered."

"And the colonel is okay with this?"

"Not at all. But like he said, 'I couldn't give a damn what you and the guys do while you're on leave.'"

"What are you doing for gear?"

"We can't come in full gear into the middle of Rome. The Italians will think we're invading, and with the way things are these days, probably best to avoid that. We're bringing full tactical gear on the plane, but we'll be wearing civilian cover."

"Weapons?"

"I reached out to Kane. He's arranged a special delivery for us."

"So, the CIA is involved?"

"Nope."

Niner chuckled. "Sometimes I wonder whose side that guy's on."

"Just thank God he's on our side today."

"Amen to that."

"I'm going to let you go. We're wheels up in thirty mikes."

"Copy that."

"Keep me posted on Mai."

"Will do."

Dawson ended the call and turned to the others gathered in his and Maggie's home, gear being sorted, each man with two bags except for those remaining behind.

The newest team member, Sergeant Gary "Angus" Tye, stood shaking his head in disbelief. "Is this really happening?"

Sergeant Will "Spock" Lightman cocked an eyebrow. "Somebody pinch the man. He thinks he's dreaming."

Sergeant Gerry "Jimmy Olsen" Hudson punched Angus on the shoulder.

"Ow!" yelped Angus, rubbing his arm. "He said pinch!"

"What are we, teenage girls? We don't pinch, we punch."

"Right. So let me get this straight. These professors are filthy rich?"

"Super filthy," clarified Jimmy.

"Fine, super filthy. And you guys have access to some secret bank account? And some contact who arranges things, no questions asked?"

"That about sums it up," confirmed Sergeant Zack "Wings" Hauser.

"That's unbelievable."

"We've been through a lot together."

"But I mean, they pay for everything?"

"Whatever's needed. Private jets. Hotels. Vehicles. Equipment. Anything we need."

"How often do you do this?"

"Not very. But there's been a few times we've had to go off the books and they footed the bill. Sometimes it's because we're going in to help them or their friends."

Master Sergeant Mike "Red" Belme finished the thought. "Sometimes, it's got nothing to do with them, and everything to do with us."

"Or someone important to us," murmured Spock.

Dawson sighed, remembering the circumstances surrounding Stucco's death, and that of Spock's wife. Jimmy reached over and squeezed the widower's shoulder. "They're stand-up people. The best. And even if Vanessa and Angela weren't involved, I know I'd be going, even if it had to be on my own dime."

The others agreed.

Angus folded his arms, leaning against the wall. "Well, I wish I was going."

Dawson reiterated the reasoning for his orders. "No. I need you and Jagger to remain behind, manning the phones, so to speak. Twelve-hour shifts. I need 24/7 coverage. You're going to be coordinating with us, Agent Reading, Kane, the Vatican, and anyone else we're pulling in here. We need up-to-the-second intel. Anybody gets wind of anything, I want to know. I don't want time being wasted as it makes its way through channels."

"Understood." Angus glanced around the room. "Where is Jagger?"

"Arranging a ride. You'll be setting up in an off-the-books ops center."

Angus cocked an eyebrow. "Oh? Where?"

"Can't tell you."

Angus' eyes narrowed. "You can't tell me? Why not?"

"Because even I don't know where the hell it is." Dawson forwarded a message to Angus' phone. "Those are your instructions. You'll be met by Kane's partner, Lee Fang. She'll be taking you to a classified location along with Jagger."

"She?"

"Like I said, Kane's partner."

"Partner, as in—"

Spock interrupted. "As in, you get any ideas, she's ex-Chinese Special Forces and will tear your throat out. And if *she* doesn't kill you, Dylan will."

Angus held up both hands in mock surrender. "Hey, I'm a gentleman. Jagger is the hound."

Red snorted. "He is that, but he's met Dylan. He knows not to mess with his woman."

Dawson zipped up his second bag. "Ready, gentlemen?"

"Yes, Sergeant Major!" echoed the room.

"Then let's go kill some Russians. They crossed the line this time. No mercy."

"No mercy!"

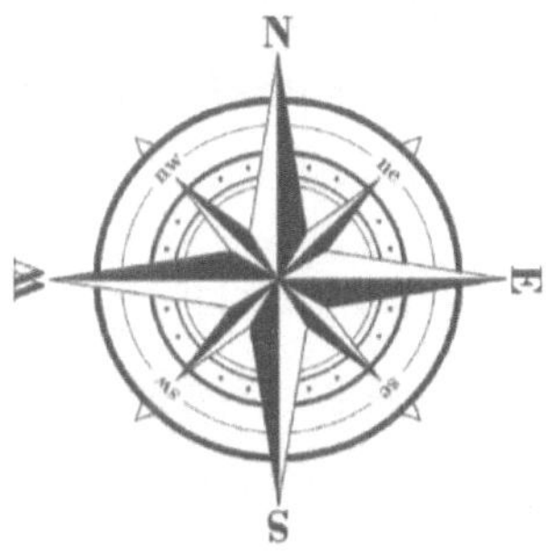

Ciampino–G.B. Pastine International Airport

Rome, Italy

Laura stepped out into the sunlight. Their instructions were clear. Don't make a scene. Just get on the plane, or everybody dies. She glanced back at Angela, still in the van, sobbing.

"I'm so sorry!"

Laura gave her a reassuring smile. "It's all right. Just tell James that I love him."

"Atlas too," said Vanessa. "Tell him I love him."

"I will!" cried Angela. "I will! I swear!"

The doors to the Sprinter slammed shut, and Tankov and the others led them to a private jet idling nearby, all wearing ball caps and sunglasses, no doubt to hide their identities from any prying eyes.

The first of Tankov's men boarded and Laura peered up at the sky, once again hoping against hope her face would be caught on a satellite, the footage reviewed by someone back home searching for them right now, because once they got on this plane, they might never be found.

Tankov's hand darted out, grabbing her by the hair on the top of her head, yanking it down. "Just what the hell were you doing?"

"Nothing. Just looking at the sun."

"Bullshit. I told you, no games!" He held a radio to his mouth, saying something in Russian. Two pops sounded from inside the van.

"No!" screamed Laura, struggling against Tankov's grip but failing, her shoulders slumping as the van pulled away and Vanessa screamed. Two of Tankov's men, now in civilian attire, grabbed Vanessa and hauled her up the steps and into the private jet.

Tankov's iron grip closed like a vise on her arm, his head on a swivel as he dragged her toward the jet as it powered up. Laura allowed him to load her onto the airplane, her fight gone. She should have listened to him. She shouldn't have played games. She should have just kept her head down, and Angela would be alive. She had gotten cocky, thinking she was getting away with something, but she had been wrong.

Horribly wrong.

And now Angela was dead.

Oh God, Niner, I'm so sorry!

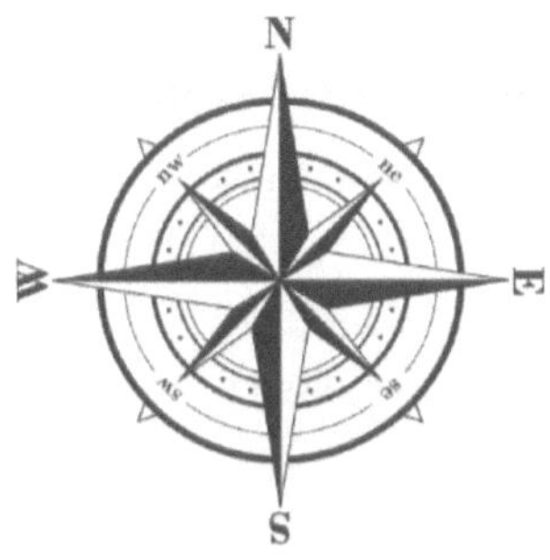

East of Leptis Magna, Tripolitania

Western Roman Empire

AD 431

The cries of men in battle, the clashing of swords, all had fallen silent over the past moments. Decimus stepped over the collapsed stone and cocked an ear.

"For the emperor!" shouted someone from the other side, the voice barely heard but loud enough to be recognized.

The young officer whose name he didn't know.

Then nothing.

He could only surmise the others were dead, and the brave warrior had sacrificed himself to assure the secret was preserved, to eliminate any urge to attempt escape.

"You will be remembered, my son."

"Brave man," said Tiberius.

"Yes, all brave men," agreed Decimus as he pushed off the rocks.

"A noble, yet necessary sacrifice."

A horn sounded in the distance, carried down the passageway, its pattern indicating those holding the entrance to the gorge would soon fall.

"They'll be here soon. We have little time. Let's get this over with," said Tiberius.

Decimus' personal guard turned to head for the entrance. He subtly nodded at Gaius who drew his sword and plunged it into the back of the nearest of his men. Decimus and Tiberius joined in the betrayal. The shocked soldiers never stood a chance—not a sword drawn in defense—against those they were sworn to protect and serve.

It took mere moments, and Decimus stood back, gasping for breath, his mouth swimming with bile at the sight before him.

One of the victims groaned and Gaius stepped over. "I'm sorry, my friend," he whispered before plunging the tip of his blade into the man's heart, ending his suffering—and his life.

And his chance of betraying the empire's secret.

Tiberius sheathed his sword then wiped the back of his hand across his brow, sweat and blood mixing. "Never in all my years did I think my own hand would take the lives of loyal servants of Rome."

Decimus closed his eyes for a moment. "Nor I, my friend, nor I. But this"—he opened his eyes, jabbing a finger at the pile of stone now hiding the treasury—"is too big a secret, too tempting for any man. Should just one of them have been captured by the enemy, they surely would have revealed its location under torture. Not for a moment do I believe these brave men would have ever come back for personal profit."

The horn sounded again.

There was little time and their work here wasn't done. Half a dozen bodies—slaughtered—all Roman. It would lead to questions if they were discovered.

Decimus turned to Gaius. "You said you found something during your exploration?"

"I did, Decimus. It should suit our needs."

"Good." He sighed. "Let's get this over with."

Gaius grabbed one of the bodies, tossing it over his shoulder, then another, gripping it by the belt, and headed deeper into the cave system. Decimus exchanged a look with Tiberius, then shrugged. He grabbed a body and slung it over his shoulder, then gripped the belt of another. He grunted.

"I can barely lift him." He let go. "I'm not the man I once was."

Tiberius grinned. "Were we ever?"

Decimus chuckled, then stopped himself. Respect. Reverence. Solemnity. That was the order of the moment. Frivolity had no place here. He retrieved a torch and followed Gaius deeper into the darkness. They didn't have to go far. They found the head of his personal guard standing at the edge of a narrow pit, both of the fallen comrades he had been carrying nowhere to be seen.

Decimus stepped closer to the edge and peered over into the blackest of blacks he had ever witnessed. "How deep is it?"

"I'm not sure, though I counted to almost five before I heard them hit bottom."

Decimus shrugged his load off his shoulder, and the man he had known for years fell silently into the darkness, a thud finally echoing from below.

"I'll get the others," said Gaius.

Tiberius entombed his burden. "It's unfortunate we couldn't give them a proper burial."

"It is, but there can be no evidence. When we return to Rome, they'll be remembered with honor for their sacrifice."

"Will how they died be revealed?"

Decimus frowned. "They died protecting Roman property from the barbarian hordes."

"I suppose that's one way of looking at it. Murdered by their commanding officers certainly doesn't sound as honorable."

Decimus tensed. His old friend was correct.

It was murder.

At least Tiberius and Gaius had the excuse that they were following orders. These men—willing to die to protect him—had done nothing wrong and hadn't even been given the option to sacrifice themselves honorably. Instead, he had betrayed them, leaving them with no chance to prepare their souls for what was to come. In battle, unexpected death could happen at any moment for a soldier of the empire. But this?

He would burn for eternity for what he had done, and what remained of his days would be tortured with guilt and shame. This wasn't who he was. This wasn't who he wanted to be.

But he had his orders, and the emperor's orders were absolute.

Footfalls and heavy breathing approached. Decimus held up the torch, extending it outward to light the darkened path. Gaius came into sight, his body dripping with sweat. Decimus stepped aside and the large man passed. He tipped forward, the body over his shoulder falling into the pit, then he grabbed the other he had been dragging and tossed him over the edge before standing at attention, his fist slapping against his chest.

"Farewell, brothers. May the earth rest lightly upon you. Rest in peace." Gaius faced Decimus, drawing his dagger and holding it out with both hands. "It would be an honor, Dominus, if you were to be the one."

Decimus took the dagger as it was offered, his stomach churning. "It would be my honor, my friend. You have served me well, as have your men for years. Your loyalty has never been questioned." He looked down, shame overwhelming him. "I swear to you—your sacrifice will never be forgotten. And I will personally make certain your family is taken care of."

Gaius bowed deeply. "Your words honor me, Dominus, and I thank you." He straightened himself and squared his shoulders. "For my comrades, for my commander, for my emperor, but most of all, for my empire, I give my life willingly." He removed his breastplate, tossing it into the pit below. He closed his eyes and gave a curt nod.

Decimus gripped the man's shoulder and squeezed. "Forgive me." He plunged the dagger into Gaius' chest, piercing his heart, then twisted. There was a sharp inhalation, and the man's eyes shot wide with the shock of the experience—not the event. A long sigh escaped, then his hips gave out, his knees buckled, and he collapsed backward, disappearing into the maw—swallowed by the earth, forever entombed with those who had served him.

Decimus closed his eyes at the thud below, then inhaled deeply, his chest swelling as he struggled for control. He cleaned the dagger on his uniform, then sheathed it, determined to give it to the man's son when he saw him.

He stepped back from the edge as Tiberius leaned forward, peering down below.

"An honorable man. Let's hope his sacrifice—all their sacrifices—was worth it." Tiberius faced Decimus. "It's only the two of us now, my friend."

A wave of shame swept through Decimus. "I'm afraid…that's one witness too many." His foot darted out, kicking Tiberius squarely in the chest. His friend's eyes widened in shock as he cried out, his hands reaching forward, gripping at the air—for anything to grab on to—but there was nothing.

Decimus closed his eyes at the echo of the final thud, and his shoulders slumped as a single tear rolled down his cheek. "Forgive me, my friend, but no one can know."

He tossed the torch into the pit, then felt his way back toward the entrance.

And a future he no longer wished to live.

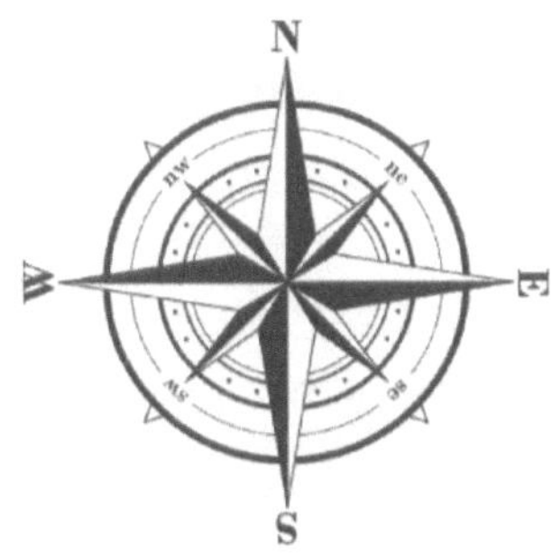

San Giovanni Addolorata Hospital

Rome, Italy

Present Day

Acton looked up as Niner emerged from a nearby bathroom, no longer covered head to toe in Mai's blood. The hotel had sent over a change of clothes, and the hospital had given him access to a shower. Everyone was extremely cooperative once Giasson had made a phone call confirming they were representatives of the Vatican.

They had been here for hours and had heard nothing. Perhaps that was good news, perhaps not. Niner was their expert in these matters, and had been gone for almost thirty minutes. Tommy worked furiously on his laptop in an attempt to keep his mind off things. The love of his life could be dying at the end of the hallway, and there was nothing he could do about it.

Acton stood, clasping his hands behind his head as he began pacing. He hated not being in control. It was so frustrating. He just wanted somebody to tell him what was going on. He wanted Laura and the others back, or at least word they were alive. They were completely in the dark, and it was driving him nuts.

"Still no word?" asked Niner as he approached.

Acton shook his head. "Nothing."

"Well, like I said, don't read too much into that. Even if everything goes perfectly, it was going to take hours anyway." Niner glanced over at Tommy, then lowered his voice. "What's the kid working on?"

Acton shrugged. "No idea, but as long as he's doing that, he's not worrying about her. How are you holding up?"

Niner sighed as Atlas joined them. "About the same as you, I guess."

"It's the not knowing that's killing me," rumbled Atlas. "Rescue or recovery? Until you know, you're just left wondering, imagining the worst."

Niner agreed. "One thing I know for sure is that however this goes down, revenge, I think, will be the order of the day."

Atlas folded his massive arms. "Tankov's gotta pay. They all do. They're a scourge that needs to be eliminated once and for all."

Acton was wholeheartedly in agreement. "Do we know how many of them there are?"

"Eight, according to the file I read," said Niner.

"Seven now," corrected Atlas, taking into account the one he eliminated with the battle ax earlier.

"Seven against two. I don't like those odds."

"Three." Acton tapped his chest. "I want in."

"Wouldn't have it any other way, Doc. Once the rest of the team arrives, that will even up the odds quite a bit."

Atlas grunted. "Odds mean nothing if you don't know where the hell the fight's supposed to be."

"We'll figure it out. And when we do—no mercy."

"No mercy."

Acton gripped Niner's shoulder, then Atlas'. "No mercy."

"Done!" announced Tommy from behind them.

Acton turned. "Done what?"

"I've got the footage of the attack."

Acton cocked an eyebrow. "Oh?"

"The cameras were still running. It captured everything. Extreme high resolution, remember? I just finished stitching everything together." Tommy reached into a duffel bag stuffed with gear he had Giasson's people retrieve from their disabled rental. He handed Acton a Virtual Reality headset. "Put it on. You'll want to sit down, though."

Acton sat and fit the headset into place.

"You guys can watch everything he's seeing on the laptop."

Atlas and Niner repositioned.

"Here you go, Professor."

The black was replaced with an image, and it took Acton a moment to reorient. It was so real, it was uncanny.

"Okay, you're in a freeze frame, standing in the center of the dig." A controller was placed in his hand. "Use your thumb—there's a little joystick there. Use it to move forward, backward, left or right. You can turn your head in any direction—up, down, sideways—and see everything."

Acton turned his head, his mouth agape. "This is amazing!" He pointed with his free hand. "That's us standing over there." He turned to his left and looked up to see a frozen Mai at the top of the ramp, Tommy several feet behind her. "Okay, I'm oriented." He drew a deep breath, preparing for what he was about to see. "Play it."

"Okay, here goes."

Everything suddenly came to life. Tommy climbing up the steps, Mai extending a hand, voices and sounds of the dig all around him. He desperately wanted to look over his shoulder to see Laura, but instead, he continued to focus on where the horror was about to begin.

Popping sounds. He recognized them instantly now—gunfire, everything still out of sight, Tommy and Mai no longer visible. Mai screamed, and Acton winced. Tommy shouted her name. Acton was sick to his stomach. He had experienced this moment before. But now? Knowing what everything he had heard meant? It was far worse than the actual events.

He saw himself running toward the ramp with Laura. The first of Tankov's men appeared. The ax whipped through the air, burying itself deep in Tankov's man's side. He collapsed off the edge of the ramp. More of the former Spetsnaz team swarmed into the dig and down the ramp as he and Laura fled for cover. He watched as they approached Decimus' final resting place, and winced once again at the callous disregard for the remains.

The breastplate was grabbed and yanked, one of the straps breaking away from the ribcage before it was stuffed into a large bag, everything else scooped up in rapid fashion.

Acton held up a finger. "Stop it."

Everything froze.

He didn't need to see what happened next. There was nothing to be seen. And some things weren't meant to be relived. But something had stood out. They had taken everything they could involving Decimus, but the first thing they had gone for was the breastplate. There were other artifacts there—weapons, other pieces of armor, but it was the breastplate they had gone for. Everything else seemed an afterthought.

They weren't there for Decimus. They were there for that out-of-place piece of armor, the one thing none of the other gladiators buried there had.

"Did you see something, Doc?" asked Niner to his left.

"Maybe. They seem to be after the breastplate. Everything else was just taken to be thorough. Can you zoom in on that?"

"You can," replied Tommy. "But let me back it up, first. Close your eyes."

Acton closed his eyes. There was a beep in his ears.

"Okay, you're good. You can open your eyes."

He opened them and was back to when Tankov and his men reached Decimus.

"Use your joystick to reposition yourself."

Acton pushed forward on the little stick, and the image advanced. He guided himself so he was standing right next to Tankov.

"Okay, play it."

Everything happened again, but this time, it was as if he was one of the players—right there in the thick of things. It was shockingly detailed, though there were gaps, filled with black, where Tankov's men were blocking what the cameras could see.

But he could see enough.

He could see the breastplate as it broke away from the ribcage and was shoved into the bag.

He gasped. "Wait a minute."

The image froze.

"What?"

"Back it up about two seconds."

The keyboard clicked and the image jumped.

"That's it. Hold it there. Is there any way for me to get lower?"

"Yeah, but let me do it." The image adjusted, and it was as if he was on his knees. "Is that better?"

"Perfect." Acton leaned forward, peering at the breastplate. It was now directly in front of him at an angle. "Advance it like…a quarter of a second." The breastplate swung in front of him, exposing the inside. "A few more milliseconds." It turned in front of him.

And he gasped.

"Holy shit! It's a map!"

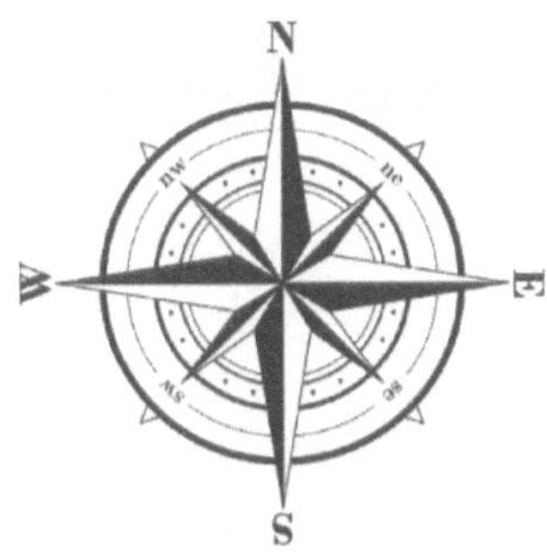

Kane's Off-The-Books Operations Center

Unknown Location

"Holy shit, this place is incredible!"

Angus had no idea where they were, though that was probably for the best. This couldn't be legal. There was no way. He didn't know who Dylan Kane was beyond the fact he was CIA and used to be a member of the Unit. But this appeared to be somebody who had gone rogue—or at least planned to.

The incredibly hot Lee Fang, who had given them a ride here while they wore hoods over their heads, gave them a brief tour of what appeared to be two shipping containers joined together side-by-side. From the outside, you would never know there was a fully powered facility tucked away in the middle of a storage yard filled with hundreds of containers.

"We've got sleeping facilities here on the right, full bathroom with shower, food stores and supplies for several months. Plus, the pièce de résistance." She led them into a room filled with computers and displays.

"Holy shit, this must cost a fortune!"

"Millions," agreed Sergeant Eugene "Jagger" Thomas. "I'm in the wrong business."

"Tell me about it." Angus turned to Fang. "So, is this boyfriend of yours crooked?"

Fang spun on him, glaring. "No!" She calmed down. "Everything is funded by his gambling winnings. Let's just say he's very good at reading people."

"So, he always knows when they're bluffing?"

"Exactly." She began flicking switches, the room springing to life. What was impressive a moment ago was even more so now. She took a seat, her fingers flying over the keyboard, and he found he couldn't tear his eyes off her.

She was stunning.

Jagger elbowed him and gave him a look. Angus inhaled sharply, then muttered, "I'm going to hit the head."

"Down the hall on your right." Fang stared at one of the displays. "Who's taking the first shift?"

"Dawson wants us twelve and twelve," replied Jagger.

Fang countermanded those orders. "Let's make it three shifts of eight. Nobody can sleep for twelve hours anyway. Which of you two want to rack out first?"

Jagger gestured at Angus. "You go first. Fang, you can show me how everything works."

"You got it." She turned in her chair to face Angus. "The quarters at the far end are mine and Dylan's. You two can use the closer one. Don't worry, there are two beds. You won't have to snuggle."

Jagger winked at Angus. "Sorry, dude. I know how you were looking forward to it."

Angus shrugged. "I was, but oh well, house rules." He headed for the bathroom, his bladder protesting, wondering just how long he would be holed up in the paranoid CIA operative's secret lair.

Operations Center 3, CIA Headquarters
Langley, Virginia

Leroux leaned back in his chair and stretched, closing his burning eyes. He spent way too much of his life staring at screens. Whether it was the three monitors spread across his station, the massive display arcing across the entire front of the state-of-the-art operations center, his phone, or just his TV at home, he was pretty sure almost every waking hour of his day was spent staring at something nature had never intended.

He would be blind by the time he was forty.

He turned in his chair, scanning the room filled with his team, almost all of them older than him. He was the youngest analyst supervisor in CIA history, and it had taken time to earn the respect of those with more years' experience. But he had. He confirmed what he suspected—most of those in their forties and fifties sported reading glasses. He could live with that, but there was no way he could get himself to stick contact lenses in his eyes.

Do people still do that?

For a while, his dad had, then gave it up, claiming it was vanity.

"Who gives a shit whether or not I wear glasses?"

He was sure people still wore them. They had to. It was just nobody talked about it. At least not in his circle. Then again, he was still young. Those his age that needed contact lenses had likely been wearing them for years and didn't talk about it. And he didn't really have older friends bitching about their eyesight. If he were to need glasses, maybe he would get the surgery, but then again, lasers zapping his eyeballs didn't sound much more appealing than sticking his fingers in there.

"I might have something," said Leroux's second-in-command, Senior Analyst Sonya Tong.

"What have you got?"

"A police intercept in Rome. Somebody's reporting a possible abduction at Ciampino Airport."

"Do we have any footage?"

"Not yet. I'm working on it."

"The intercept—what is it?"

"Emergency call. Their equivalent of nine-one-one. Sounds like a civilian."

"Let's hear it."

"It's in Italian."

Leroux cursed. "Of course it is. Transcript?"

She tapped at her keyboard then jerked her chin toward the main display. The transcript of the conversation in English appeared. Some of it was suspect—an icon at the top indicating it was an AI transcript, explaining why.

"Get a human on that."

"Already requested. Should have it cleaned up in a couple of minutes."

Leroux stood, clasping his hands behind his back as he read the transcript. Apparently, someone witnessed two women being hauled aboard a private jet.

Two women. Not three.

He cursed. If it was their people, there could only be one explanation. If one of them had gotten away, they would have heard something by now. It meant one of them was likely dead.

"Are we going to be able to get airport footage?"

"Still working on it."

He turned to Randy Child, the youngest of the group and their tech wunderkind. "Find out what planes left that airport around this time. Where they're going."

"You got it, boss."

Child went to work, and Leroux turned to Danny Packman, another analyst. "Check our satellite footage of the area. See if we got lucky."

"Yes, sir."

"I'm in!" announced Tong.

The room turned to see a security camera feed from inside the private terminal.

"This is the time the call was placed."

"I'm not seeing anything."

She pointed to the right of the screen. "Those are the windows to the outside."

"Looks like the tarmac. Zoom in there."

Tong executed his request, and he spotted a jet in the distance taking off.

"That could be them. Back it up."

She did, and he watched as everything played out in reverse. He spotted two women.

"Stop it there. See if you can clear that up. We need to identify them."

"The image quality's shit. That's as good as it's going to get."

One woman was clearly black, the other white.

"Check the info we have on Vanessa Moore and then have the computer determine her height based on the specs of that plane."

"On it." Tong furiously worked her station, then leaned back. "The height matches what we have."

Leroux folded his arms. "All right, that could be Vanessa Moore. And the other one?"

Again, Tong went to work. "It's got to be Professor Palmer. She's too tall to be Angela Henwood."

"But we can't be sure."

"No, we can't."

"I might be able to help with that," said Packman. "Check this out."

A satellite shot appeared. Packman tapped away at his keyboard, and the image zoomed in on the airport, then again, showing a freeze-frame with two men holding their presumed Vanessa Moore, another holding the possible Laura Palmer.

"Zoom in on the professor. Let's see if we can confirm it's her."

Child complied, and a moment later a near crystal-clear image appeared. There was no doubt it was her.

"Okay, good. Now confirm that's Vanessa Moore."

Again, no doubt.

"And that's Tankov with Palmer," said Child. "The computer confirmed it."

"All right, we found them. Get a tail number off that plane. Find out where the hell it's headed."

"Looks like Cairo, boss," replied Child.

Leroux cursed. "Why can't it ever be some place law-abiding?" He sighed. "Let's get that info to Fang. I'm going to go let the Chief know what's going on. And just in case, let Dylan know. He might want to change his destination." He headed for the door. "And don't forget, people, we're still looking for Angela Henwood. Find whatever vehicle dropped them off at the airport. See where it came from. See where it went if it isn't still there. I want to be able to tell Niner where his girlfriend is. Even if it's bad news."

International Airspace

"I can't believe she's dead," sobbed Vanessa as Laura held her, her own tears flowing.

This was her fault. It was all her fault. She should have just kept her head down, followed the instructions, but instead, she had been a fool, thinking she was smarter than Tankov, forgetting he was former Spetsnaz, former Special Forces. He knew full well there were eyes in the sky. It was why all of his men had worn ball caps when they stripped out of their gear.

They had given Vanessa one, but not her. The dead man's. They had eight changes of clothes, but Atlas had eliminated one of them, leaving one spare hat. It meant they hadn't planned on hostages. Vanessa and Angela weren't supposed to be there. Or, more accurately, Atlas and Niner weren't supposed to be there. They had to take them to keep them out of the equation.

She sighed heavily. "I'm so sorry."

Vanessa looked up at her. "For what?"

"I shouldn't have looked up."

Vanessa stared at her, puzzled. "What do you mean?"

Laura whispered in the woman's ear. "I was trying to get my face on a satellite so they could track us."

"Do you really think that's possible?"

"It's definitely possible, but only if a satellite happened to be going over the area at the time." Laura shrugged. "It's a definite possibility, but I wouldn't count on it."

"What are we going to do then?"

"Cooperate. Just do what they say. The longer we're alive, the more chance there is we could be rescued. We have to be smarter about this. Smarter than I've been."

Vanessa squeezed Laura's hand. "If you hadn't figured out the map, they would have killed us all. Stop blaming yourself. You couldn't have known they would do what they did. We need to—"

"I said no talking!" snapped Tankov from the front of the plane, huddled with the others. "Don't make me separate you."

Laura sat back in her seat, as did Vanessa, both saying nothing. The conversation up front resumed.

"We'll be landing in Tripoli in less than two hours," said Tankov.

"Is that wise?"

"Not much of a choice. If we land anywhere else, they'll blow us out of the sky. The visas were already arranged. We knew this was where we would likely end up. So, we go in under our planned covers. We'll be met at the airport by a government official whose palm has been heavily greased. We won't have any trouble." He glanced back at Laura. "Then we hope she can actually read that map."

"And if she can't?"

Tankov turned to the amateur expert. "Then you better hope you can. There's no damn way I'm leaving this desert without my retirement fund."

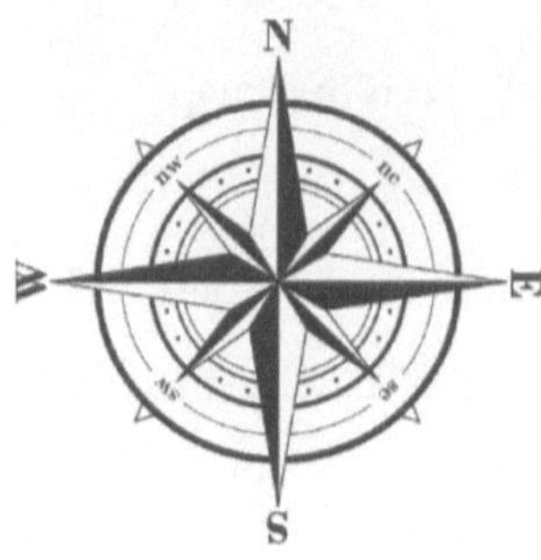

East of Leptis Magna, Tripolitania

Western Roman Empire

AD 431

With the last of his shameful acts still haunting him, Decimus quickly exited the cave, hitched the remaining horses together, then mounted his own. Leading them out of the gorge, he left no evidence behind of what had happened as the last desperate battle of those who remained echoed through the steep walls as their final stand was made.

It failed—but not before he had cleared the gorge.

He unhitched the horses from his, smacking the lead on the ass and sending it to the north. The others, tied in a row, followed. It would, hopefully, mislead the enemy that followed.

He peered into the sand—straight into the dark—and could see a faint trail cut ahead where the others had gone. Fortunately, a healthy wind was quickly obscuring it. He would have to hurry if he hoped to follow it, while at the same time praying it was erased before the enemy could do the same.

It took many hours to catch up to the rear of the convoy, the sun already high in the sky. The rear guard spotted him approaching and drew their weapons, not relaxing until one of them recognized him.

"Dominus! We feared the worst!"

Decimus came to a halt. "Report."

"Not much to report, Dominus. We've encountered none of the enemy and are making good time."

One leaned to his left, peering past Decimus and his horse. "Where are the others, Dominus? Where is the treasury?"

"I sent them northeast, toward Apollonia. There should be galleons there that can transport the treasury to Rome."

Another soldier, younger and with a loose tongue, appeared puzzled. "Then why didn't we all go?"

Decimus gave him a look, jerking his chin at the large convoy. "Do you realize how many ships it would take to carry all these people? The treasury can be loaded into the hold of a single ship. Thousands of people not only take up a lot of space but require a lot of provisions. Their journey was always by land. Our duty is to protect them while they make that journey."

"Yes, Dominus. Sorry, Dominus. I should have realized."

Decimus was in no mood to be cross with anyone—not after what he had done. "Not to worry, son. If no one asked questions, no one would ever learn the reason things are done."

The man bowed. "Thank you, Dominus."

Decimus stretched and yawned. He jerked a thumb over his shoulder. "I've seen no signs of pursuit. Though our brothers fought valiantly, I could hear their imminent defeat as I left. Keep an eye out. I fear our troubles may not yet be over."

"Yes, Dominus."

Decimus urged his horse forward, making for the head of the convoy. Cheers erupted as the soldiers and civilians spotted him. He smiled and waved, reassuring those terrified of their situation by exuding confidence. Yet he was sick. His stomach continued to protest what he had done. His chest ached, and the pressure his foot felt when it impacted his best friend's chest still pulsed.

He shouldn't have done it.

He could have trusted Tiberius.

He was a friend, a loyal subject—and he never would have had the opportunity to betray the emperor's trust unless captured, and even then, there were none stronger. He would never have submitted under torture.

His shoulders slumped, and he stared at the back of his horse's head as he continued forward. If Tiberius had been captured, it would have meant he would have been as well—for his friend would never have left his side.

What would happen if they were both killed? It was an interesting question. He was now the only one who knew the secret—who knew where the treasury had been hidden. What if something were to happen to him? The location of the massive hoard would die with him, lost forever.

All those deaths. All that sacrifice—for nothing.

And even if they escaped with their lives, the journey ahead would be long.

And this was a dangerous world.

He could be felled by an enemy, attacked by a thief, killed by a fall from his horse, or downed by some disease. Anything could happen. And he had a responsibility. But how could he keep a secret such as this? If he wrote it down, the risk of a map or journal entry being stolen was too great.

There had to be a way.

His personal servant, a slave named Masuna, hailed him with a broad smile. "Domine! It's so good to see you!"

Decimus smiled at the man who had served him since he was a boy. Masuna had been perhaps ten when his parents had been bought to serve the household. The mother and father were capable, and a bit of a curiosity—their ebony skin a status symbol. The more exotic the slave, the more prestige it brought to the household. Masuna was now a man—twenty years his junior—and had been at his side longer than anyone.

He was loyal, someone he could trust, for the young man had no ambition. No designs. No animosity.

"It is good to see you, Masuna. I'm happy you made it out. I wasn't sure."

"By the grace of your good planning, I did. Can I get you anything?"

Decimus waved him off. "Not now. I have to check on our status." He jerked his chin toward his personal carriage. "I'll be back soon. I must rest, then we have something to discuss."

"Yes, Domine."

Decimus surged forward, the cheers continuing, his smile spreading—genuinely—as a solution to his problem dawned on him.

It was perfect.

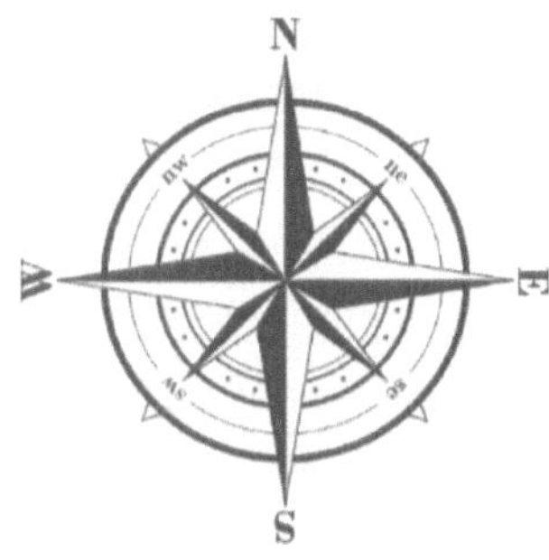

San Giovanni Addolorata Hospital

Rome, Italy

Present Day

The door to the waiting room opened and everyone shot to their feet as the surgeon working on Mai entered.

Tommy rushed forward. "Is she going to be all right? Is she okay?"

The surgeon smiled, though it wasn't much of a smile. "She's alive. We were able to remove the bullet and repair the damage. She lost a lot of blood before she even got here. At the moment, she's still unconscious."

"Will you be able to wake her up?" asked Niner.

The surgeon regarded him. "You're the one who clamped the artery?"

"Yes."

"Then you may well have saved her life. I'll be honest with you—it's touch and go right now. Fifty-fifty, I'd say. If she survives the night, then I suspect she will make it. The question is going to be, is there any permanent brain damage?"

Tommy gasped then bit down on his finger as he struggled to maintain control. "What are you saying? Like…she could be brain-dead?"

The surgeon dismissed the concern. "No. But there could be damage. We don't know yet. She lost a lot of blood, which means there was a period of time where her brain wasn't getting enough oxygen. She's young, she's strong, and thanks to your friend here, the blood loss wasn't as bad as it could have been. We won't really know until she wakes up."

"But she *will* wake up?"

"If she survives the night, I suspect she'll wake tomorrow. I suggest you all go back to your hotel. We'll call you."

"There's no way in hell that's happening," said Tommy. "I'm staying right here."

"Very well." The surgeon turned to the rest of them. "I'm afraid you all can't stay. Since the pandemic, she's only allowed to have one visitor at a time. Due to the situation, we've allowed you all to remain. But overnight? It's out of the question. Mr. Granger, you can stay since you're her fiancé. But I'm afraid the rest of you will have to go."

Acton didn't like it, but he understood. He had been in hospital waiting rooms pre-pandemic with huge families taking up space just to show they all equally loved their sick relative. The new rules were better, though he would have preferred two people being allowed to remain. Tommy needed support as well. "We understand, Doctor. And thank you."

The man bowed slightly. "Now, if you'll excuse me, I have a patient to check on. I'll let you know if anything changes with her condition."

"Thank you," mumbled Tommy.

Acton wrapped an arm around the young man's shoulders as they began shaking.

"I can't lose her."

Acton hugged him. "You're not going to. She survived the surgery. That was the biggest thing. Those were the odds she had to beat. Now let's let them do their job. Remember, this is Italy. It's a G7 country. The hospitals here are excellent. The doctors are among the best in the world. We're not in Egypt. We're not in Vietnam. We're in a modern facility with highly trained personnel. And you know her. She's a fighter. She's been through a hell of a lot in her life, and there's no way she's going to give up. Not before you two are hitched."

Tommy sniffed hard, then pushed away. Acton handed him a handkerchief and Tommy dabbed his eyes dry. "Sorry. You're right. I just—" He exhaled loudly. "I just can't imagine life without her."

"Then don't," rumbled Atlas. "Just focus on tomorrow. She'll be awake and you'll be able to talk to her. And like the doctor said, if she survives the night, then she'll probably survive. So just focus on tomorrow. The night will be over and she'll be alive. There's no other option."

"Is that how you two are getting through this?"

Niner folded his arms. "As far as I'm concerned, Angela is alive and well. So is Vanessa. So is the Doc's wife here. We're going to see them again, alive and well, and soon."

"You worry about Mai, we'll worry about the others. If you need anything, you just let us know," said Acton. "We're going to head back to the Vatican and meet with Mario. The moment you hear anything, you call. Understood?"

Tommy nodded and Acton gave him another hug then guided him back into his chair. The young man grabbed his laptop and buried himself in his work once again as they left the room.

"I would not want to be him," muttered Niner.

"Me neither." Atlas jabbed the down button for the elevators. "So, let's address the elephant in the room."

"What's that?" asked Acton.

"What next? You said you couldn't see where the map started, but Tankov doesn't have that problem. He's got the breastplate. He could see the whole damn thing."

"Would Professor Palmer be able to read the map?" asked Niner.

"Absolutely. The question is, would she?"

They boarded one of the elevators and Niner pressed the button for the ground floor. "Oh, she'll definitely read the map. She has no choice. If it was just her, maybe she might refuse or trick them or whatever. But with two other hostages? They'll just threaten to kill one of them. She'll read the map."

Acton frowned, forced to agree with Niner as the doors opened on the ground floor and they stepped out.

"So then, what do we do?" asked Atlas. "We don't know where to start."

"I wouldn't be so sure about that," said Acton as they headed for the doors.

Atlas eyed him. "What do you mean?"

"It's a fifteen-hundred-year-old map and we know the history. There's only one place it could possibly start."

"Where's that?"

"Ever been to Libya?"

Both Niner and Atlas responded, "Classified."

Kane's Off-The-Books Operations Center

Unknown Location

Angus entered the heart of the off-the-books operations center. He hadn't slept a wink. Too much was going on for his mind to settle. He tried all the tricks, but it didn't matter. He wanted to be out here, in the thick of things. He had to know what was going on. He was new to the Unit, but these were his brothers-in-arms, their families, their significant others. It meant they were his family now too. And one day, if he were lucky enough to find the right woman, and unlucky enough for something to happen to her, he would want all hands on deck doing everything they could to save her.

Rack time was bullshit.

Jagger glanced over his shoulder at him. "Shouldn't you be sleeping?"

"Could you?"

Jagger chuckled. "I suppose not. Have a seat."

"What's the latest?" asked Angus as he dropped into one of the free chairs.

"Langley caught Tankov, along with Professor Palmer and Vanessa, getting on a private jet at a terminal outside of Rome about forty-five minutes after the attack."

"Do we know where they're headed?"

"The flight plan says Cairo, but we just got a report that they've diverted."

"Where to?"

"Tripoli," replied Fang.

Angus clued in on something. "Wait a minute. You said the Professor and Vanessa. What about Angela?"

Jagger frowned. "No sign of her. But…." He tapped at one of the stations, then turned to the opposite wall where there was a large display. "Check this out."

They watched the hacked footage showing everyone getting on the airplane, but before they ascended the steps, something had Laura Palmer attempting to reach a nearby van.

"What do you think's going on?"

"Something's got her riled up. Watch it again. Watch Tankov."

The footage backed up, and Angus pointed. "He's saying something into his radio. And then she reacts."

"Exactly."

Angus cursed. "You don't think Angela was in that van and he ordered her killed?"

"Unfortunately, that seems to be the running theory."

Angus closed his eyes and sighed. "Does Niner know?"

"No."

"Are we keeping it that way?"

"Speculation doesn't help. He needs his head in the game. I talked to BD, and he said to keep it under our hats for now."

Angus pursed his lips for a moment, then blasted air through them. "I don't know if that's the right decision."

Fang left little doubt how she felt. "It isn't. If something happened to Dylan, I'd want to know. Even if I was on a mission. And this isn't a mission. This is all personal."

"It's a personal mission," Jagger said, disagreeing. "And a lot more important than anything the government might send us on. Vanessa and the professor are still out there. Those are our people. It doesn't get any more important than that."

Fang faced him. "No, it doesn't. What I mean is, if Niner knew, he'd be even more motivated to find those responsible and kill them."

"Or he could get himself killed because he's overcome with grief. And right now"—Angus jabbed a finger toward the screen—"we don't know what happened. We're making assumptions. And assumptions can kill."

"You think she's still alive?"

"No, I don't. But as long as there's any chance she is, I agree with BD. We keep it to ourselves. Let Niner focus on the mission, and in the meantime, let's find out where the hell that van went. Even if she's dead, Niner deserves a chance to bury her with dignity."

"Then let's hope Langley can find it," said Fang. "Because I've already lost it."

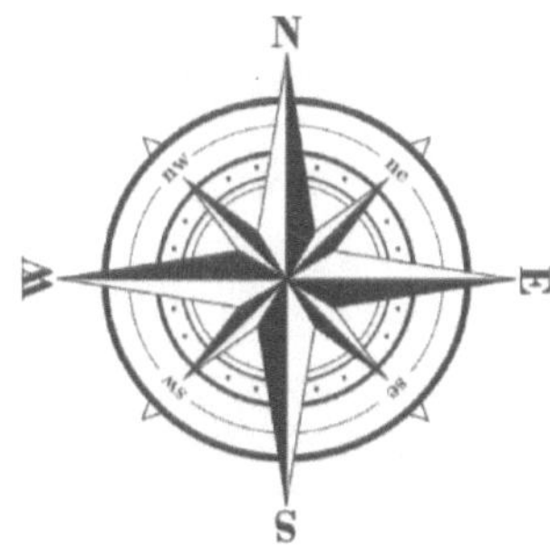

Rome, Western Roman Empire

AD 432

Rome.

Nothing compared to it. It wasn't just the architecture. The buildings. The streets. The sights most men couldn't imagine were possible. How does one describe the Colosseum to someone who had never seen a building with more than a second floor?

They would label you a liar. Or simply laugh and walk away.

But he had seen it. He had seen it all, and had traveled most of the world—and witnessed nothing comparable, save the pyramids of Egypt.

Yet it was one thing to build a pile of stones that reached into the sky. It was another thing entirely to build a massive building where thousands upon thousands of people could gather and witness events that demanded to be shared.

Sport had always been a part of his life—an important part. But there was nothing like the gladiator matches to get his heart pumping, to get him on his feet, cheering on his favorites, extending his thumb, pointed upward when he believed mercy was warranted, and downward when not.

It was a brutal sport—but an honorable one. There was a code. There were rules. And those that fought had respect, even if they didn't have their freedom.

Unfortunately, those were memories from his youth, since the matches had been banned for years. Today, the boyhood dreams of being a gladiator were behind him. His role as a leader in the Roman army was his reality, and he had been granted a great honor.

A Triumph.

A parade rarely seen these days.

The roar of the crowd lining either side of the road was exhilarating, but it was nothing compared to the smaller crowds that had greeted them in Alexandria. The journey had been long and arduous, but they had made it. All of them.

Except those sacrificed to preserve the empire's bounty.

He glanced over his right shoulder, where his second in command and friend, Tiberius, should be, his heart heavy. What he had done was a weight he would never shed. He had murdered his best friend, and could never forgive himself.

Earlier in the day, before the arranged pomp and circumstance, he had paid Tiberius' family a visit, personally delivering the news—and a lie.

"Your husband died on the field of battle, with honor. If it weren't for him, none of us would have survived."

It had brought them comfort. But it had made him sick to his stomach.

The steps of the Temple of Jupiter Optimus Maximus were just ahead. The emperor rose, his Tyrian purple toga distinct against the marble. Long banners hung high fluttered in the breeze, the spectacle something to behold. He was being hailed as the man who had saved the citizenry of Leptis Magna from the vicious hordes that would defy Roman superiority.

Deceit and incompetence were the excuses given for the fall of the city, its former governor's name already, when spoken, followed with a derisive spat. It wasn't the man's fault. The military commander had moved the bulk of the city's forces west to Oea, anticipating that was where the Vandals would attack. He had been wrong, but blame was placed on the governor. He wasn't held in high regard by the emperor's mother, and Rome's de facto leader, Augusta Galla Placidia, who now stood by her young son's side. But the true power, the military power, was wielded by the Magister Militum, Flavius Aetius, who stood on Emperor Valentinian III's opposite shoulder.

Flavius was a man Decimus knew well, and didn't trust as far as he could throw him.

He was in it for the power, for the glory, not the good of the empire, and under the leadership of these three, the empire continued to wane.

He feared one day it could collapse altogether.

He had yet to see the emperor in person since his return, though the mission report had gone on ahead long ago. Valentinian and his "advisors" were fully aware of the failure, though he had kept the location of the treasure to himself. Dispatches could be seen by anyone, even intercepted by the enemy. Giving the location of such vast wealth would be foolish.

He drew on the reins, bringing the four horses pulling his chariot to a halt, then locked the wheels in place. He stepped down, waving to the crowd as attendants took the reins and led his ride away.

As the procession behind him lined up in the massive square, the might of Rome on full display, the din of the crowd overwhelming, he thrust his shoulders back, raised his head high, his right hand clasping the hilt of his blade, his left hand clenched, then strode up the broad steps, his eye on the emperor the entire time.

The boy's smile suggested he was indeed pleased to see him. Decimus' eyes flit to the left, spotting his wife and children standing among the honored guests. He wanted to send them somewhere safe, just in case this went horribly wrong, but there was no way to refuse the emperor's invitation.

His family were honored guests.

Required guests.

Yet he had made plans. There were those here loyal to him, not the teenage emperor. Should things go awry, they would, hopefully, follow their orders, though nothing was certain—not here. Not in Rome.

He released the grip on his sword as he reached the top of the steps and smacked his fist against his breastplate as he took a knee.

"Ave Imperator, Dominus Noster. I, Comes Rei Militaris per Africam, Decimus Cornelius Vindex, stand before you having preserved the lives of your subjects, though at great cost. The treasure entrusted to me could not be safely returned without endangering all, and so, by my judgment, I hid it from the barbarians. The citizens are safe and under your protection once more. The treasury, though not here, is secure and shall remain so until you command otherwise. I beg your mercy, for I have chosen the lives of Romans over the spoils of war."

Valentinian smiled and extended a hand. "Rise, my friend, and honored citizen of Rome."

He rose, and Valentinian embraced him. The hug was gentle, ladylike, and, having nothing to compare it against, he couldn't say whether anything should be read into it. Was this how the boy greeted all, or was he simply an uncertain child who knew no better? Or was this simply a show, put on for the crowds, disguising his true feelings?

Yet why the parade if he were angry? It made no sense.

Valentinian held out a hand toward the crowd. "My friend, bask in the reverence your fellow citizens are demonstrating for you."

Decimus faced the crowd and Valentinian gripped his hand, raising it over their heads. The crowd, loud before, erupted with a fervor he had never experienced in all his days. Goosebumps erupted across his body, a distinct shiver betraying his excitement.

Valentinian turned his head toward him, obviously having felt him shake.

"It's intoxicating, isn't it?"

Decimus had to agree. "It is indeed."

"Don't get used to it, my friend. You've always been a military man. I would hate to see you become obsessed with power."

The words were delivered with a smile, but there was something behind the eyes. It was a warning. Decimus bowed his head slightly. "Not to worry, Imperator. The field of battle is all I've ever known, and it's where I'm happy to spend my final days in service to you and the empire."

"I'm happy to hear it." Valentinian lowered their hands, waved once more to the crowd, then turned. "Come with me. We have much to discuss."

Decimus followed his emperor inside, horns and drums sounding behind them, indicating the continuation of what was to be a day of celebration, rare gladiator fights capping off the festivities.

Heavy doors closed, and as they made their way deeper into the massive temple, a final set of doors shut, the last of the noise from outside cut off. They were in a smaller room now, though compared to most in the city, it was larger than the majority of residences. There was no natural light, everything lit by candles, torches, and lanterns.

Valentinian sat behind an ornate desk, and Decimus finally took notice of who was in the room—a handful of advisors standing behind the emperor, their faces grim for such a joyous day. On his left shoulder stood Augusta Placidia, on his right, Magister Militum Aetius, the real power behind the throne until the emperor was of age.

There were no chairs, save the emperor's, so Decimus stood in front of the desk, his hands clasped behind his back, and waited.

"You failed in your mission."

He was ready for this. "Imperator, that's not true. I—"

Valentinian raised a hand, cutting him off. "You were sent to retrieve the treasury. Is it here?"

"Well…no, Imperator, but I know exactly—"

"If it isn't here, then you failed."

"But I saved the citizens—"

"I don't give a damn about the citizens. I have millions of citizens. What are a few more thousand? And they lost everything. Now the empire must clothe and feed them and provide them shelter until they can reestablish themselves. All of that could have been paid for with the treasury you were sent to save and failed to."

"But, Imperator—"

Again, he was cut off, this time with a raised hand. It was clear Valentinian had planned this from the moment he had received his report, or more accurately, those standing behind him had. The decision had been made, and only one man could be blamed.

And it was to be him.

"You failed to mention in your official report that you abandoned your duty and instead sent the treasury north, under the protection of Tiberius Aemilius Severus. They never reached the port, which means now our enemies possess that which you were sent to retrieve."

Decimus said nothing. There was nothing he could say. The man was determined to punish someone.

"This dereliction of duty is unbecoming of a Roman soldier—let alone a Roman of your position. I'm disgusted with your conduct."

Decimus' chest tightened. It wasn't fear. At least not for himself.

It was for his family.

"Imperator, I realize I have failed you, and you have every right to be angry and to punish me. However, in consideration of my decades of service to the empire, I ask that you spare my family."

Valentinian scoffed. "What? So that your sons can come of age then seek vengeance? No. Let your punishment be a lesson to all. Abandon your mission, and not only is your life forfeit, but so is that of your family."

His fists clenched behind his back, but he maintained control. He could leap across the desk and break the boy's neck. There was no one in this room to stop him. Not the six old men standing behind their master, not Valentinian's mother, not his advisor, who would likely welcome the death.

They all had designs on the throne.

But that wasn't how he wanted to be remembered. And it would buy him only a brief reprieve. Killing the emperor would mean arrest. Brutal torture. For him and his family. Then death—in a most public and humiliating way.

He would rather die with honor. "What is to be my fate then?"

"Death. But I will at least make it merciful."

He could tell him where the treasury was hidden. It might, in fact, save his life, and that of his family. But only temporarily. It would take years for Rome to mount a strong enough expedition to retrieve what had been left behind, and the preparations for it would reveal the fact the hoard existed. There were only so many places it could have been hidden. It would be found before they could ever get there.

Perhaps he *had* failed.

He stepped forward, Valentinian flinching, those behind him retreating several steps. "I beseech you, Imperator, on behalf of my family. Let me speak to them. Order my sons to accept my fate. Exile them to a remote part of the empire if you must. But spare their lives."

Valentinian recovered from the unexpected movement and smirked. "My friend, the moment those doors closed"—he indicated with a wave of his hand the doors they had just stepped through—"your entire family was arrested, as well as anyone close to you. Their fates are sealed. There is nothing you can say or do to change that. Most, if not all, are already dead."

An involuntary inhalation revealed his shock to those in the room, much to the delight of Valentinian. "My wife? My children?"

"Are already dead. You have nothing left but what little honor you may still possess. Don't fight this, Decimus. It's over."

Decimus inhaled sharply, his chest swelling, his well-worn breastplate rubbing against his chiseled physique. "Then I have nothing to live for."

"No, you do not. The question now is, do you die with honor, with dignity, or as a coward begging for his life?"

Decimus glared at the boy. "I think you know. Where is it to take place?"

"At the games. You will be declared a traitor, then drawn and quartered for all of Rome to witness."

And then a thought occurred to him. "Imperator, may I make another suggestion?"

Mitiga International Airport

Tripoli, Italy

Present Day

Laura descended the steps of the private jet onto the shimmering tarmac, the concrete reflecting the heat of the early afternoon sun. Vanessa, unaccustomed to it, gasped, immediately pulling at her shirt, but Laura was used to it, what with her primary dig in Egypt's Lower Nubia. She had come to enjoy the heat, so alien to someone who had grown up in England, but only if she had relief available to her like an air-conditioned tent.

Living like this day in and day out would be unimaginable without it.

A man in a business suit approached them, and Tankov shook his hand. Two black SUVs pulled up and everyone climbed in, the drivers heading into the terminal, two of Tankov's men getting behind the wheels. The duffel bags with the Russians' gear and Decimus' remains were tossed inside, nothing said beyond the exchange of pleasantries.

Laura and Vanessa sat in the rear row with two of Tankov's men in the front, and Tankov in the middle row with the Libyan.

"That was rather easy," observed Tankov.

The Libyan shrugged. "Your contribution to the cause was generous. It allowed me to spread things around. As far as the record will show, your plane had mechanical difficulties so landed here with no passengers. How long do you anticipate being here?"

"Not very. One or two days, if everything goes according to plan."

"And if it doesn't?"

"Then it doesn't. I'll let you know."

"Understood."

They left the airport grounds and Laura peered out the window at Tripoli, looking a little rougher than the last time she had seen it—understandable, what with the civil wars.

The man jerked his chin toward them. "Who are they? Entertainment?"

Vanessa's jaw dropped and Laura reached out, surreptitiously squeezing the woman's thigh, indicating for her to bite her tongue.

"Something like that."

The man leered at them both. "Perhaps when this is over, you'll share."

Tankov chuckled, no doubt delighting in their discomfort. "Perhaps, but let's not get ahead of ourselves. You read my message. Can you get us into the ruins?"

"Absolutely, though I have to warn you, it's near the conflict zone. It could be dangerous."

Tankov jerked his chin toward the driver. "Utkin here says the rebels are nothing we can't handle."

Laura eyed the amateur archaeologist in the rearview mirror, a name finally put with the face.

"I wouldn't be so confident," said the Libyan. "Your Wagner group has certainly had trouble with them."

Utkin sneered a single word in Russian, and the passenger and Tankov laughed at what was obviously an insult.

"The equipment you sent ahead is waiting for you. Just follow the instructions in the GPS and we'll be there shortly."

"Good. I want to get underway without delay."

The Libyan dashed those hopes. "Not possible, I'm afraid."

Tankov eyed him. "What do you mean?"

"There's a special security operation taking place east of the city. They're stopping and searching everything."

"I thought we were bypassing the checkpoints regardless."

"We are, but whenever these operations take place, they send up drones to make sure nobody tries to bypass the roads. If we're spotted, they'll have helicopter gunships on us within minutes. It's best to be patient and wait for it to be over."

Tankov cursed. "And just how long will that be?"

"My sources inform me it'll be over in a couple of hours."

"And then?"

"And then nothing. It just goes back to normal—regular checkpoints. Give it about an hour to clear out and the traffic will be flowing freely.

Then you just have to worry about random checks, but that's why I'm with you. My government ID will get us through."

"But not now."

"No. Like I said, they're searching everything and everyone. The traffic will be backed up for hours, regardless, and you *will* be caught— unless you're lucky enough to be stuck in traffic until it reopens. So you see, my friend, there's no point in rushing things." The Libyan glanced at Laura. "Might I suggest a way to pass the time?"

Operations Center 3, CIA Headquarters

Langley, Virginia

Leroux stood, his hands clasped behind his back, as they all stared at the main display with a satellite feed showing the Russians' plane on the tarmac in Tripoli. Several portions were isolated, confirming it was Tankov's team, along with Laura Palmer and Vanessa Moore.

"Well, that's definitely them." Child spun in his chair as he stared up at the ceiling. "Professor Acton called that one."

"Well, like he said, there was only one place the map could start."

Child dropped his foot, his spin stopped. "Do you really think they're going to find this treasure?"

Leroux shrugged. "No idea. All that matters is that Tankov thinks they will. If it's as big as the briefing notes Sonya put together suggests, it's no wonder these guys are killing anyone that might get in their way. It could be in the billions."

"That's insane. What I would give for just a few million in the bank."

Packman chuckled. "Don't say that too loud. Security might just think you could be compromised."

Child regarded him. "Is that how it works? You just say you wish you won the lottery and boom—you're flagged?"

"Things are changing," said Leroux. "In all seriousness, I think we all have to be careful what we say, even if we're just joking. You've all seen how transcripts can be taken out of context." He returned his attention to the display. "Now, let's focus on the job. We got lucky with a bird overhead at the airport when they arrived, but for the moment, we have no clue where they are in the city—though we can assume where they're headed." He faced Tong. "What's the ETA on everyone?"

She peered at one of her screens. "Professor Acton's plane should be arriving in about ninety minutes. Kane's about fifteen minutes later."

"Delta?"

"Still hours out—they have to land in Rome first. A last-minute course correction with ten American males would just be too tempting to take a second look at."

Leroux grunted. "I guess so. But that might be a good thing. I'm sure they're going to want to leave some other people in Rome to try to find Miss Henwood. Any progress on that?"

"Not yet. Italian police found the van where we said it was, but no one was in it. Unfortunately, it was an extremely busy parking garage, so dozens of vehicles left within minutes of their arrival. We're tracking down everything but there's a lot. She could be in the fifth one we look at or the fiftieth."

"Then start with the fiftieth," muttered Child.

Tong gave him a dirty look.

Child held up his hands. "Sorry. You're right. No time for jokes." He leaned forward. "But I do have a serious question."

"What's that?" asked Leroux.

"Was there any blood in the van?"

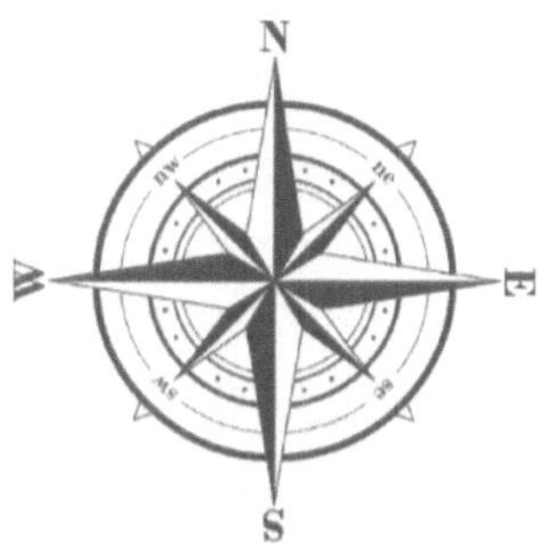

Mitiga International Airport

Tripoli, Italy

Acton stepped off the private jet and smiled broadly at an old colleague, Professor Faraj Ali Al-Mesmari, an archaeologist from the University of Benghazi, whom he had met at several conferences. Hugs and cheek kisses were exchanged.

"So good to see you again, Jim."

"And you, my friend. How's the family?"

"Good. Well, as good as can be expected in these troubled times, I suppose. Things are relatively peaceful here, so we're thankful for that. And your wife? I'm surprised she's not with you."

Acton hadn't told the man the truth—or at least not all of it. "Unfortunately, she couldn't be here. I'm sure she would have loved to see you again." He turned toward Atlas and Niner. "These are two friends of mine. Believe it or not, they're on vacation and happened to be there when we made the discovery in Rome. I thought it only fair that they got to see it through."

Introductions were made, Faraj's eyebrows rising at Atlas' ridiculously deep voice.

"It is exciting, isn't it? The final resting place of the lost Tripolitanian treasury."

"It is. But you've kept it quiet, right?"

"Absolutely! I haven't told a soul. Not even my wife. Though, I have no doubt she'll grill you over our late lunch."

Acton laughed. "I'm not sure we have time for that."

"Oh, you'll have to make time. She's been preparing since she heard you were coming. Not only would she disown me if I didn't invite you, but there's a security operation between here and Leptis Magna. There's absolutely no point in hitting the roads. You'll just be sitting, baking in the sun for hours."

Niner frowned, though couldn't express the true level of his disappointment without raising suspicions. "That's unfortunate."

Acton extended a hand toward the terminal. "How about we clear customs, and then go enjoy some of your wife's delicious food?"

Faraj grinned. "Wonderful idea. Wish I had thought of it myself."

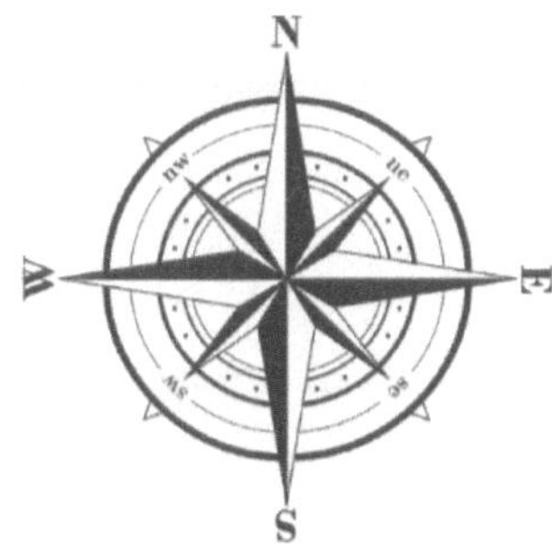

Unknown Location

Tripoli, Libya

"Don't touch me!" cried Vanessa.

Laura, her eyes glued to what the Russians were doing, spun toward Vanessa's pleas and found the Libyan—whom Tankov had called Tariq—pawing at the poor woman. "Get your hands off her or I'll break your neck!"

Tariq stood and leered at her. "A feisty one. I like that."

He approached, and Laura rose from her chair, hoofing him in the balls as hard as she could. The man groaned and collapsed to the floor, Tankov and the others laughing.

"I warned you." Tankov stepped over and hauled the letch to his feet, guiding him into a nearby chair. "If we had any, I'd say to ice your balls, but unfortunately, we don't even have electricity here." He turned to Laura. "Play nice now, or I just might have to kill your friend."

"Kill her, and you'll never get anything out of me."

"Don't be so sure. Pain is a powerful motivator."

"And you know as well as I do, that torture quite often only produces the answers the victim thinks you want, not the truth. I'll send you on a wild goose chase so far removed from where the treasure actually is, you'll never find it—and you'll never know I was lying." She jerked her chin toward Vanessa. "And if anyone lays a hand on her, the same goes. The only way you're getting your billions is if the two of us are alive and untouched."

"You still seem to be laboring under the incorrect assumption this is a negotiation. It isn't. But I'll tell you what—nobody will touch you in that way. *If* we find our treasure. If not, I'm going to sell both of you into the meat market—but not before you and I, and my friend here, have our fun. And as for torture, you misunderstand. I'm not going to torture you. I'm going to torture your friend. You're going to have to watch her in pain. I have no doubt about how strong you are when it comes to yourself. But I also know you're too good to just sit by while your friend is tortured when you could end her pain. So, like I said, not a negotiation. You do what we want, and I'll make sure you die painlessly."

Laura's chest tightened. "So, no matter what, you're killing us."

"I can't exactly have you running to your friends and revealing the truth now, can I?"

"If you kill us, our friends will never stop hunting you. You say you can change your face. That may be true, but there's always a trail. You *will* be found, and you *will* be killed. You know who you're dealing with. And besides, there's no need to kill us. Where the treasure is hidden is nowhere near civilization. You can just leave us there and we can take our chances."

Tankov regarded her. "I thought you said you didn't know where it was."

"I don't. But I can tell it's far enough away from Leptis Magna that it would take days on foot to get back. By then, you and your men will be long gone, already in the surgeon's chair for your new faces. Like I said, there's no need to kill us. Let me find you your retirement, then we go our separate ways."

Tankov scratched his chin. "I'll think about it." He poked a finger against her chest. "But you better be able to find it. Otherwise, you and your friend are in for a world of hurt."

"I'll find it. The markers are geological. They won't have changed. And if they have, then at least you'll have narrowed it down. You can go in later with the proper equipment and extract it."

Tankov leaned in menacingly. "You better hope that's not what ends up happening, because then you're dead, and I'll let my friend here enjoy himself before he kills you."

Ciampino–G.B. Pastine International Airport

Rome, Italy

Dawson stepped into the door of the Bombardier Global 8000 business jet, the fastest currently in production, capable of Mach 0.94. It had brought them here hours before a commercial flight could, the exceptional range the aircraft had allowing them to fly without any stops.

Yet despite that, it was still too late. Atlas and Niner were already in Tripoli with the professor, and Angela was supposedly dead, though that hadn't been confirmed yet. The latest update through Angus was that the CIA had tracked the Sprinter van from the airport to a nearby parking garage. The Italian police had hit the van and found it empty, but there had been blood. Testing was underway to see if it matched what was on record for Angela, though that would take time.

The question he had was, why had they taken her body?

It didn't make sense, and it gave him hope that maybe she was still alive. It was why he had ordered Niner be kept in the dark. They just didn't know what the hell was actually going on, and Niner needed to focus.

A truck pulled up beside the plane on the tarmac. The driver stepped out, and Dawson descended the stairs, his hand extended, a smile in place for the cameras. "Geronimo."

"Crazy Horse," replied the man.

The coded greeting confirmed this was Kane's contact, and Dawson relaxed.

"I've got everything you requested."

"Including our last-minute additions?"

"Yeah. Those were a bit of a surprise."

"For us too."

A fuel truck pulled up, the pilot already having arranged the next leg of their journey. In less than two hours, they would be where they needed to be.

"We need some baggage boys down here!" shouted Dawson into the airplane.

The rest of the team piled out, and the back of the truck was quickly emptied.

"Our rental?"

"One of my guys dropped it off at the front of the terminal. Keys are in the left driver's side wheel well. Everything you requested is in the trunk. Make sure your guys go through clean. This little exchange could draw attention."

"We should be fine. The Vatican has designated this a diplomatic flight."

The man's eyebrows shot up. "Really? How?"

Dawson smirked. "The less you know, the better."

"Yeah, I think so." A hand was extended. "Good luck."

"Thanks." Dawson shook the hand then boarded the plane. He turned to Red and Spock. "You guys set?"

Red nodded. "We're good."

"Get your asses out of here. Let me know when you find Tankov's missing man. I have a sneaky feeling you're going to find Angela with him, so don't go in guns a-blazing. Just in case."

Spock regarded him. "You still think she's alive?"

"I don't know what to think. You watched the video. It certainly looked to me like Professor Palmer thought something bad had happened in that van. And there was blood."

"But no body."

"Exactly. That doesn't make sense. Hauling a corpse around isn't easy. Let's just be careful."

"We will," said Red.

Spock faced the others. "Wish I was coming with you. God knows I love killing Russians. But Niner saved my life a few months back. If I can save Angela, maybe I can even the score and he'll stop humping my leg. For a little while, at least."

Red snorted. "I wouldn't count on it. Atlas has saved Niner's bacon God knows how many times, and he's still that boy's personal hump toy."

Spock rolled his eyes. "Forgot about that. I guess there's no hope."

Dawson agreed. "Nope. Now get the hell out of here. Let me know as soon as you're clear, then make immediate contact with Angus. See if they've got any leads on where she might have been taken."

Red nodded. "You can count on us. We'll find her and eliminate any hostiles so we don't have to deal with them anymore."

"Good. And if it happens to be painful, then so be it."

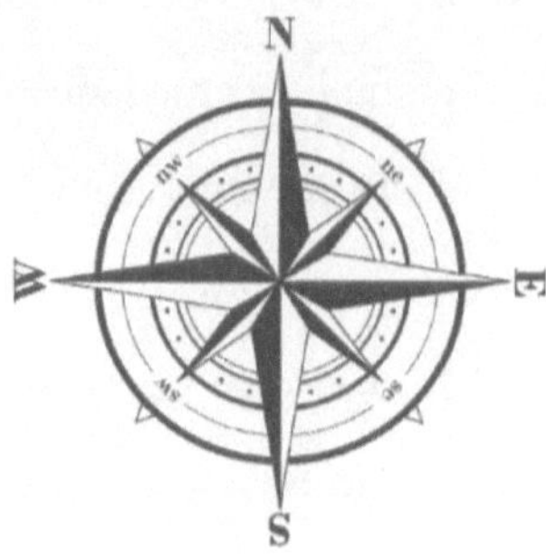

Operations Center 3, CIA Headquarters

Langley, Virginia

"We might have something."

Leroux turned toward Tong. "What have you got?"

She tapped at her station then gestured toward the main display. A security video appeared. "This guy left six and a half minutes after the Sprinter pulled into the parking garage. That's about the right amount of time for him to get to where they found it, transfer the body, then get out."

It was pretty thin, but he suspected she had more, and gave her a look. She smirked, then zoomed in on the suspect, revealing a ball cap and sunglasses.

"Okay, so we've got a guy who likes to wear his sunglasses indoors. Maybe he's just prepping for the afternoon sun."

She zoomed in closer, this time on the hat.

Leroux smiled, finally clueing in. "Show us the airport clip."

The screen split and on the right was a still from the airport. She zoomed in on the hat Tankov was wearing. White, blue, and red. A subtle Russian flag, identical to the one worn by their parking lot customer.

"Okay, let's assume that's him. Track him. See where he goes. And get that info to Angus so Red and Spock can run him down."

"On it."

"What about Delta?" he asked, turning to Packman.

"They're refueling. Once they're wheels up, they'll be about two hours out. They're gonna have to play catch-up. Everyone else will be heading for Leptis Magna and whatever pot of gold is at the end of this rainbow long before they land."

Leroux frowned. He was extremely limited with what he could do, relying on occasional flybys by various satellites on their assigned routes. He wasn't authorized to retask one or even deploy a drone. At the moment, the professor and his two Delta companions were unarmed, though Kane was armed to the teeth, pursuing Tankov and the hostages. But he was one man and his contact, against seven heavily armed, highly trained, former Spetsnaz.

Kane was good, but not that good.

Though he would never tell him that.

The only way they had a chance of rescuing the hostages alive was if they could get the Delta team inserted in time, and two hours' flight time, plus two hours of driving just to get to the ancient ruins, could prove too late.

He cursed to himself.

If this were a regular op, he could just have them inserted by a Black Hawk, right where he needed them. But this wasn't a regular op. And even if it became one, it was too late. They were committed with no possible way to adjust any of the critical variables affecting the success equation.

This could end very badly.

He folded his arms, staring at the screen. It already had ended badly. Mai was battling for her life, and Angela Henwood was likely dead. The blood types matched, though the DNA tests hadn't come back yet.

There were too many lives at stake, important to him or to people important to him.

And his damn hands were tied.

Autostrada A12

Rome, Italy

Red glanced at the latest update from Langley, sent to his phone via Angus. "Apparently, they're only a few klicks ahead of us," he said to Spock, handling the driving duties.

Spock pressed on the accelerator a little harder. They had to be careful. The last thing they needed was to draw attention and get pulled over for speeding, especially with all the weapons they had on them. Once they were identified, it could cause an international incident, and certainly a major headache for the colonel.

The good thing was that apparently the Russian had the same concerns, and was sticking to the speed limit. They weren't positive about their target's destination, though it was presumed to be a private airstrip where Langley had found a Hercules charter heading to Tunisia.

They had just received word that the Russians' plane that had brought them to Tripoli had already departed and was now en route to Italy. They would need a way out, and something to transport what could be a massive haul of extremely heavy loot.

They would need a transport aircraft.

The Hercules they had chartered would be more than capable, and it was a reasonable explanation as to why someone had been left behind. It wasn't to dispose of Angela's body, it was to arrange, and perhaps even pilot, the only means of escape.

Spock indicated ahead. "I think that's them."

They were hoping beyond hope Angela was in the car. If she was, none of the camera angles had spotted her, which meant she was in the trunk. And likely dead.

"Pit maneuver?"

Red dismissed the idea. "No."

"Then what do we do?"

"Nothing—for the moment. If we try to intercept at these speeds, we could end up causing an accident and killing Angela, if she's still alive in there. First, let's just confirm where they're going. See if our theory is right."

Mitiga International Airport

Tripoli, Italy

Kane cleared customs, speaking perfect Arabic under his Shaws of London cover, his visa arranged by the professor's extremely well-connected travel agent. It had him sailing through, though his single carry-on bag was thoroughly searched and scanned, his charming smile and demeanor of little use on these men hardened by civil war. Palms could have been greased, but it shouldn't have been necessary. He wasn't smuggling anything but himself in, and as far as the paperwork was concerned, he was legit.

Tripoli was desperate to have the outside world think it was business as usual, that commerce was open, despite all the evidence to the contrary. They weren't about to make life difficult for someone who might be here to spend large amounts of money, a reasonable assumption considering he had arrived solo on a private jet and was wearing a bespoke suit from Savile Row.

He stepped through the main doors of the terminal and spotted his local contact—known only to him as Mohammed—leaning against a dark blue SUV that had seen better days. He waved at him. Kane walked over and pleasantries were exchanged, nothing done to draw attention to themselves. His bag was loaded in the back, and they were soon underway. As soon as they cleared the airport—and any of its security cameras that might have been trained on them—Kane pulled out his phone.

He cursed. "No signal."

"Network's down again," explained Mohammed as he made a righthand turn. "It's been up and down for months."

Kane cursed again. "I didn't bring a satphone with me."

Mohammed glanced at him. "Good thing you didn't. Those things draw attention at customs. Don't worry, I've got one in the bag for you."

"Good. Status?"

"Your friends arrived less than an hour ago. They were picked up by a Professor Faraj Ali Al-Mesmari. I put a tracker on his vehicle. They're at his residence now. There's a security operation that's just wrapping up outside of the city, so they're probably waiting for that to clear."

Kane cocked an eyebrow. "Security op?"

"Nothing out of the ordinary. They do them a couple times a week. It's more to show they're still in control. They search everything and everyone on random highways in and out of the city. Sometimes they get lucky—find contraband, or somebody on the wanted list. Most of the truly bad people know how to avoid them."

"And you're sure it's wrapping up?"

"Yep."

"They actually announce that?"

"Nope, but I've got good contacts."

"All right. I'll assume they're as good as you think they are. Equipment?"

Mohammed jerked a thumb over his shoulder. "In the back. Everything you asked for. Enough for all of you, should it be necessary."

"What about Tankov?"

"According to the last update I got, satellite shows them loading two SUVs. They were met here by a local government official. Corrupt as hell. His name is Tariq Nasser Al-Kabir. If you get a chance, kill him for me. The fewer men like him we have in our country, the better the chance we have of actually coming out of this a free country."

Kane smirked. "If I get a chance, consider it done."

"Where do you want to go?"

"Let's get ourselves closer to Tankov. The mission is to rescue the hostages, not protect Professor Acton. My two friends that are already with him can handle that."

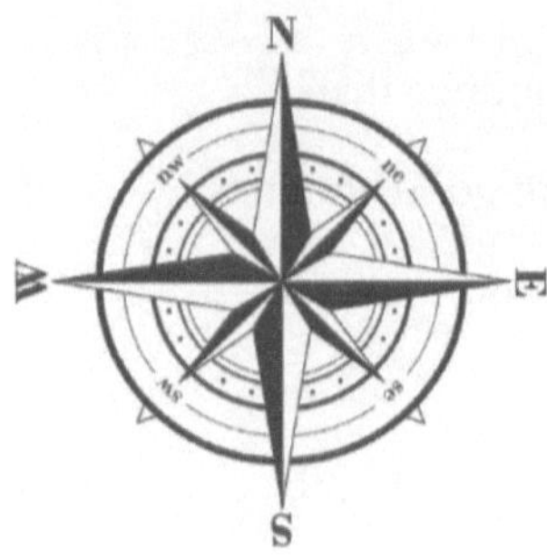

Autostrada A12

Rome, Italy

Spock lifted a finger off the steering wheel, pointing ahead. "I think that confirms it."

The Jeep Wrangler with their target exited the highway, taking the off-ramp that led to the airstrip where the suspected transport charter had been arranged by Tankov's team.

Red sent a text to Angus, still coordinating things as Spock followed their target, keeping a safe distance. So far, there had been no indication Tankov's man was aware he was being followed.

The possibility probably hadn't occurred to him.

Red checked his weapon, then holstered it, instead pulling out a taser. They needed this man alive, just in case Angela wasn't in the car. "Let's close the gap a bit. As soon as he opens his door, we hit him."

"You got it." Spock pressed the gas a little harder, and the gap closed. The Russian surged ahead, and they both cursed. "We've been made."

"Then balls to the wall. Let's get them."

Spock floored it. The Russian made a quick right onto the airport grounds. He hopped a curb, cutting through a large swath of grass, and Spock followed. "Something tells me he's not going through the terminal."

"Nope." Red debated shooting out the tires, but it was too risky. They were bouncing all over Hell's creation, and one stray bullet could kill Angela. But they were closing the gap—blazing the trail was always slower than following it. They rounded a building and Red gestured ahead at a civil-certified C-130E Hercules transport aircraft waiting on the tarmac, props already rotating, rear hatch open. "Sonofabitch!"

"You don't think—"

"I'm trying not to."

Spock cut left, spotting a slightly quicker route. He shoved the pedal to the floor as the Russian continued heading straight for the aircraft. Brake lights lit up and Spock chewed up the distance between them, but the Russian broke hard right and drove up the ramp, disappearing into the bowels of the aircraft.

Spock headed straight after him, but it was too late. The ramp began closing, and the plane started taxiing. He brought them to a halt, smashing his fist against the steering wheel. "What now?"

Red pointed to their left at two security patrol units racing toward them, lights flashing, sirens blaring. "Let's get the hell out of here. See if we can avoid the locals."

Spock cranked the wheel and hammered the gas, sending them back in the direction they had just come from. "What are we going to tell Niner?"

"I don't know. If she's alive, we can't get to her. At least not yet."

"And if she's not?"

"Then they'll toss her body into the Mediterranean."

Spock cursed, then inhaled sharply through his nose, holding his breath for a moment. "At least I got to bury Joanne. I can't imagine what it would've been like to not know."

Red squeezed the still-grieving widower's shoulder. "Don't worry, brother. It's not over yet. That plane has to land somewhere. Maybe we'll get lucky. Something tells me him driving onto that plane wasn't planned."

The Colosseum

Rome, Western Roman Empire

AD 432

Decimus had been greeted by cheers, his name chanted repeatedly the moment he was recognized striding into the mighty Colosseum by the capacity crowd of over 50,000. It had lasted until the emperor had finally risen and held up a hand to silence those gathered. It was only then that the charges against him were read. The punishment? The stripping of his citizenship—and that of his family—along with the death sentence, to be fulfilled in the arena in which he now stood.

The crowd had reacted with disbelief, though it didn't take long for it to turn against him. Boos, hisses, and jeers replaced the adulation of only moments ago. It didn't bother him, for technically, he was guilty of the charges. He had been tasked to retrieve and return the treasury and had instead chosen the safer course of action, hiding it away for later retrieval while saving the citizenry.

While he still maintained it was the wiser choice, the emperor, or more accurately, the emperor's advisors, clearly disagreed. He had never been given the chance to explain—and it had him thinking something else was going on. Perhaps the reaction of the crowd when he had first stepped out onto the sand was the real reason. He had become legend—and perhaps a threat to the emperor's grip on power.

As the crowd settled and his first opponent was named, his heart sank.

Invictus.

He was one of the greatest gladiators to have ever fought in the games, and dominated the underground circuit where gladiator fights now occurred since the near total ban. It appeared the emperor had no interest in prolonging his existence on this earth, instead content to have him slain quickly and eventually forgotten.

A footnote in history. A threat no more.

The crowd was once again in a frenzy, Invictus a hero to the masses, his name etched with reverence on many a wall by children dreaming of one day being a mighty gladiator.

His massive opponent approached, then bowed deeply. It was clear this man held him no ill will.

Decimus returned the gesture. "So, you are to be my executioner."

"Only should you best me in battle."

Decimus smirked. "So, you think I have a chance?"

"There's always a chance. And to be bested by the Hero of Leptis Magna would be an honor."

"The Hero of Leptis Magna?"

"That's what they're calling you. You saved thousands, choosing the citizenry over the treasury. You proved not only that you are honorable, but also a man of the people. You willingly sacrificed your own life to protect the innocent and the defenseless."

"They're saying all that, are they? No wonder the emperor wants me dead."

"Indeed." Invictus stepped closer, and if it weren't for their conversation, Decimus would have drawn his sword to defend against the menacing figure. "I bring word of your family."

Decimus tensed. "Good or bad?"

"Can there be any good news on a day such as this?"

"I suppose not. What word of them? What is their fate?"

"What their fate will be, ultimately, I cannot say. However, I can tell you that your wife and children managed to escape the temple—with the apparent help of many loyal to you."

"Where are they now?" asked Decimus, overcome with joy.

"That, I cannot say. All I know is I was told to inform you that, for the moment, they are safe, and are on their way out of the city."

Decimus' shoulders slumped in relief. "Thank the gods for that. At least—"

The surrounding chants had turned as the crowd grew impatient for blood, their insatiable thirst ever growing in this decadent city. "Fight! Fight! Fight!" was repeated, and Decimus shrugged, staring up at the massive warrior.

"I suppose we should give the crowd what they want."

"I suppose we should."

"Give me your best."

"I always do." Invictus lifted his left leg, bending it at the knee. "Though I must confess, my knee has been bothering me as of late."

Decimus regarded the man. "An interesting thing to tell your opponent."

"Indeed. But I have my reasons." Invictus drew his sword and Decimus did the same. "Let's give them a show, shall we? I grow weary of these battles which have no end in sight."

"But aren't we forgetting one thing?"

Invictus' eyes narrowed as they began circling each other. "And what is that?"

"Our salute to the emperor."

"Do you feel like saluting him?"

"Not at all."

"Then to hell with him." Invictus lunged, the crowd erupting. Decimus raised his sword to parry the blow and succeeded—but was knocked off his feet, the impact unimaginable, as if he had been struck by a charging bull, the mass behind the attack that of several men.

Invictus swung again at his now-prone opponent. Decimus rolled out of the way, and the blade slammed into the ground, sending sand spraying in all directions. He remembered what Invictus had said. It was clear to him this man no longer had the desire to fight. After all, he was a slave, and though worshipped by the crowds, when he left the arena, he had no freedom. He had no family. He had no one to love, to care for, to protect, to honor.

All he had was his owner—and his brothers who suffered the same fate, whom he could be asked to fight at any time.

The life of a gladiator was better than many slaves in the empire, though those serving in the homes of the rich and powerful were rarely asked to pick up a blade and fight to the death. These men—these proud warriors—knew they could die any day. And while the crowds thought they fought for honor and their emperor, their zeal on the field, often frenetic, was in fact self-preservation.

This man was tired of it.

Decimus had been aware of Invictus' prowess for years. What was it like to fight day in and day out for no other reason than to fatten the purse of your owner?

Decimus lashed out with his right foot, connecting with the colossus' knee. The tower of a man cried out in agony, collapsing. Decimus swung his sword as he rose, slicing through the warrior's wrist, his opponent's sword—and hand—falling to the ground.

Decimus rose, standing over the man, his sword pressed against the bare chest as it heaved. The crowd was on its feet in shock, and he peered over his shoulder at the emperor, on his feet as well—his mouth agape.

His mighty gladiator's defeat in mere seconds hadn't been the plan.

The crowd turned their attention to their leader to see what fate lay ahead for Invictus. The hand was raised into the air, a fist clenched, a thumb tilted to the side. Would the hand turn upward, indicating mercy—or down, indicating death?

If Decimus knew the boy, there was no doubt what the decision would be.

The thumb twisted, angling downward.

The crowd roared in shock, horror.

And delight.

Decimus returned his attention to the man who had given him at least a few more moments of life. "Why did you do it?"

"A life without hope, without a future, is not a life worth living."

"I understand, my friend. I shall pray for your soul, and God willing, we'll see each other again in the world that follows this."

"I look forward to it, and will save you a seat at my table." Invictus reached out with his remaining hand and gripped Decimus' calf. "May you die well, Dominus, Hero of Leptis Magna."

Decimus plunged the sword into the brave warrior's chest, twisting the blade. Invictus gasped from the jolt of pain, then sighed his last breath, a smile spreading, as if he had finally been released from the true pain suffered for far too many years.

Horns trumpeted and Decimus looked up from his silent prayer for the man's soul, his shoulders slumping as a dozen men entered the arena.

It appeared the emperor was determined to not give him a second chance.

He closed his eyes.

At least your wife and children are safe.

He pushed to his feet, arms held out to his sides—his shield in one hand, his sword dripping in the blood of a new friend in the other. He held his chin high and broadened his shoulders. The crowd erupted, his name chanted once again, and an enraged emperor pointed at him and shouted, his orders lost, though his intention clear.

One of the dozen sent to kill him once and for all sprinted from the group, and Decimus readied himself.

One at a time.

He just might prolong the emperor's misery.

"Bring it on."

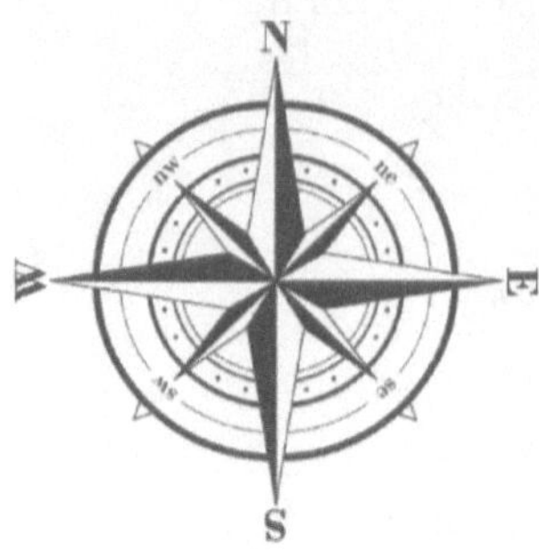

Tripoli, Libya
Present Day

Tankov climbed into the SUV with Tariq, Utkin behind the wheel, Kasparov in the passenger seat, and his two hostages in the rear row. He turned to Laura. "Leptis Magna. Positive?"

"No doubts."

He pulled out the breastplate from a duffel bag and held the back up. "Prove it to me."

She pointed to an etched square on the far left. "That's Leptis Magna."

"How do you know?"

She moved her finger slightly upward. "Because that's the coastline—the Mediterranean. And these"—she tapped four gaps in the sides of the square—"are the gates to the city. And you can see the line leaving the east gate, which would be in the direction of Alexandria, which is where they eventually arrived. And history tells us that the Vandals attacked from the west gate." She moved her finger slightly again, then tapped the square. "That's Leptis Magna. It's where the treasury was stored, it's where history records he retrieved it, and we know he headed east."

"So you're sure?"

"Absolutely. I'd bet your life on it."

Tankov chuckled. "Watch yourself, Professor. The only two lives in play today are yours and your friend's."

Utkin pulled away, having programmed their destination into the GPS.

"How long?"

"It says two hours, but who the hell knows if there are checkpoints?"

Tankov turned to Tariq. "What do you think?"

"At this time of day, traffic leaving the city will be lighter, and those manning the checkpoints will be exhausted after the security operation. They'll be pretty much just waving everyone through. It might take a little bit longer than two hours, but not much. We'll be there well before sundown."

"Good. If we're lucky, maybe we can get the hell out of here before daybreak."

Laura snickered, and Tankov turned to her.

"What's so funny?"

"You. You have no concept of what you're looking for. This is the treasury of the Western Roman Empire, for all of its possessions in North Africa with the exception of Alexandria. You've got two SUVs. Unless you intend to leave 99% of it behind, you're going to have to make a hell of a lot of trips, or arrange for some much bigger transportation than two passenger vehicles."

This at once excited and concerned him. If she were right and there was that much treasure, it indeed would be billions. But it did pose a problem. Multiple trips back and forth not only would take far too long, every trip raised the risk of being caught. And if he were to charter some transport trucks, those would be far more likely to be searched than an SUV.

He chewed his cheek for a moment before pulling out his satellite phone.

It was time to activate the backup plan.

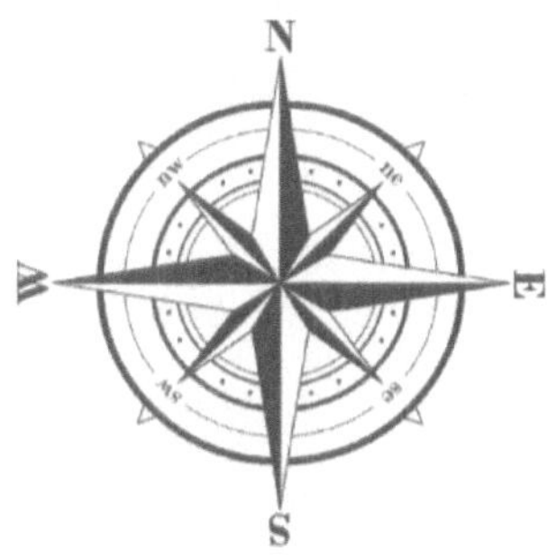

Al-Mesmari Residence

Tripoli, Libya

Acton sat back, stuffed to the gills. Faraj's wife was not only an exceptional cook but also a generous host. These were poor people, though better off than most in their country, and it certainly hadn't been in their plans or budget to feed three guests today. Yet to offer compensation would be an insult.

His phone started pinging, as did several others. He fished it out of his pocket as Faraj held up his own phone.

"Looks like the cellular network is back up."

"It goes down often?" asked Niner.

"It's down more than it's up. Very frustrating. You don't realize how much you rely on it until you don't have it."

Normally, Acton traveled with a satphone, but Mary had advised him not to bring one. Apparently, it was a red flag with Libyan customs. You needed special pre-arranged permission for them, and there hadn't been time for that kind of paperwork. They were lucky to have the visas.

Niner cleared his throat and held his phone up so Acton could see it. It was a message from Angus.

Tankov is on the move.

Acton rose. "I hate to eat and run, but I'm afraid we have to go."

Faraj checked his watch and sighed. "I suppose you're right. The traffic should be cleared by now." He stood and gave his wife a peck. "Thank you, dear."

"When will you be home?"

"Perhaps tomorrow. I'll try calling you as soon as I have word."

"You do that. And be careful. If you're not telling me where you're going, then I know it can't be safe."

He chuckled. "Don't worry, we'll be fine." He grinned at Acton. "Let's go find us a piece of lost history!"

Acton forced a smile. "Let's go!"

The Colosseum

Rome, Western Roman Empire

AD 432

Decimus prepared himself, his shield held high, his sword at the ready, his chest still heaving from the brief battle with Invictus. He was in shape—excellent shape—but a man in his forties wasn't meant for this. As the lone warrior sprinted toward him, sporting little but a loincloth and his weapon, Decimus noted the rippling muscles, the black skin, and a ferocious mask—one he recognized from previous games, usually worn by fodder meant to be slain by opponents the organizers desired to win.

Or by those who ran afoul of their masters and were fed to the lions.

This poor bastard was probably ordered to attack first and alone, to make things appear more sporting.

His opponent skidded to a halt and tore off his mask, and Decimus cried out in joy. "Masuna! What are you doing here?"

"They arrested me."

"When?"

"At the same time as they did you. They told me they'd feed me to the lions if I didn't participate. They wanted me—your loyal servant—to deliver the death blow when it came."

Decimus wryly regarded the man he considered his friend. "And do you intend to obey your orders?"

"Only one man can give me orders that I obey."

Decimus smiled. "You do realize that by defying them, should you survive, it won't be for long. And you'll likely die horribly."

Masuna took a position behind him, and they stood back-to-back as the others warily approached, the odds slightly evened, though only slightly. It was still eleven against two. They would lose, but at least he stood a chance of taking a few of them with him now that the likelihood of being stabbed in the back was reduced.

Decimus raised his sword and turned his head. "My friend, not that my word means anything anymore, but trust that these words, though they carry no weight, are honest in spirit. I hereby free you of your bond and obligation to my family. You are a freeman, and though you shall die here today, you die not a slave, but a freeman of Rome."

Masuna glanced at him. "Thank you for that honor. though I have one question."

"You better make it quick," said Decimus as the first challenger approached, flanked by several of his cohorts.

"If I am now a freeman, can I have a job? I suddenly have bills to pay."

Decimus laughed. This was one of the reasons he loved this young man as if he were a brother. "Consider it done." He swung. His blow was easily parried, but by the way the sword was held, he could tell this was an inexperienced opponent—the man's wrist broke, unaccustomed to the pressure. Decimus continued pushing down on the sword, spinning the blade and breaking his enemy's grip. The weapon spun through the air and Decimus swung around, slicing open his opponent's stomach.

A battle raged behind him and he fell back, closing the gap that had formed between them. It was essential they maintained their formation. "One down," he reported.

"Then make that two." Masuna grunted, his shoulder bumping into Decimus' back as he fended off an attack from behind.

Two advanced on him this time—one with a sword, another with a spear. His opponent probed with the tip of the long weapon, and he batted it away with his shield, advancing. He had never fought in battle with Masuna, but they had sparred on many an occasion and understood each other, his friend backing up with him, maintaining their distance.

Suddenly, Decimus charged his sword-bearing opponent, and the man's eyes bulged from behind his mask. Decimus feinted to the left, his enemy dodging in the opposite direction, when Decimus delivered a quick jab, the tip of the sword burying itself several inches into the man's chest. It wasn't enough to kill him, but it was enough to startle and weaken him.

The spear thrust toward him once again as Decimus withdrew his sword. He dropped to a knee, redirecting the parry over his head with his shield, then thrust forward once again, burying the blade in his wounded opponent's stomach, giving it a twist as he drew it free. He rose, pushing forward once again on the still-extended spear, and skewered his opponent with an upward thrust that pierced his heart.

Then he gasped in agony as something embedded itself in his side. He twisted his head to find a spear buried deep. He turned to see its deliverer standing back at a cowardly distance. He reached down and yanked it free, blood flowing freely.

He had lost, as predicted.

Yet he still had some fight in him.

"Are you all right?"

Decimus winced as he raised his implements of war once again. He charged the man who had delivered his fate, and the defenseless coward's eyes bulged as he turned to run. Decimus swung his sword, slicing the man's back open and his victim cried out in agony, collapsing to his knees.

Then another spear pierced Decimus' back. He reached around and pulled it free as well, but this was it. This was the one that would end his fight. He rolled onto his back and stared up at the sun, blocked a moment later by his trusted companion.

"Domine, you must get up!"

Decimus shook his head as the others surrounded them. "I'm sorry, my friend, but I'm done."

"There's still a chance. If you tell them where you hid the treasury, the emperor may yet spare your life."

Decimus dismissed the suggestion. He was too far gone as it was. There was no saving him. "No, my friend. It isn't my secret to reveal. Too many honorable men died preserving it to let a boy with no honor profit by it." He slapped his hand over his breastplate—given to him by his father when he was of age—and stared up at his friend of so many years as the last of his life force finally left him. "The secret dies with us, my friend."

And as the world faded to black, their executioners advanced, the final sounds those of the savage attack ending the life of his friend, and the only other person aware of where Rome's treasury had been hidden.

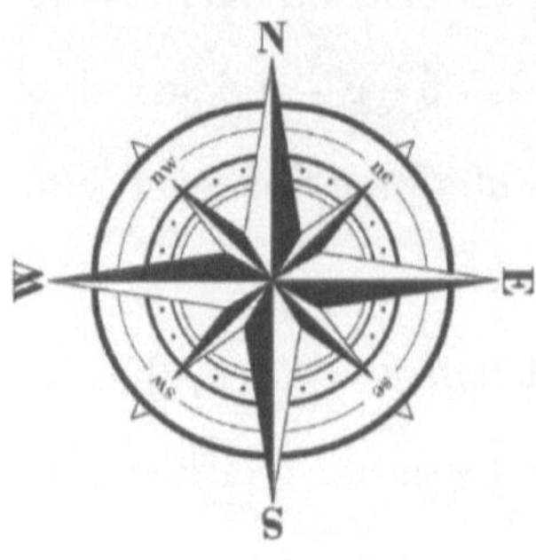

Leptis Magna Archaeological Site

Khoms, Libya

Present Day

"There they are," Utkin said, pointing ahead.

Everyone leaned toward the left side of the car, peering out the window at the impressive ruins, one of the most well-preserved sites on the Mediterranean. Thankfully, they had remained untouched during the civil wars, despite Gaddafi hiding weapons in the ruins, abusing them as archaeological shields.

But they had survived, and locals had actually guarded the site when the government couldn't, to prevent an ISIS-style looting or a Taliban-style destruction of the ruins.

Tankov turned toward Laura. "Where to now?"

"Go past them."

"What?"

"We don't need to go in. We know they left from the east gate. From there, according to the map, they headed southeast for six hours by cart."

Tankov regarded her. "How far is that?"

"Not very. We should be able to do it in less than an hour."

"Faster than that," said Utkin from the driver's seat.

Laura dismissed the arrogance. "No. We're going cross-country. They would have been on an old road. We have no idea what to expect. Break an axle, and you're screwed."

Tankov frowned. The woman was right. Even though the vehicles he had spec'd were meant for heading off-road, they still had their limitations. And they had time. The fact they were here unmolested meant the authorities either had no clue where they were, or hadn't found out in time. And with the current state of Libya, especially this region, no one would be sent after them. Not with hostages. If it took another hour or two to get to their destination, he didn't care.

Doing something foolish that left them stranded in the desert could ruin his plans.

He turned to Utkin. "Head southeast. Carefully." He returned his attention to the professor. "How will we know when we get there?"

"Get that laptop of yours out and start looking for a gorge southeast of here, about fifty kilometers. That's where you'll find your gold."

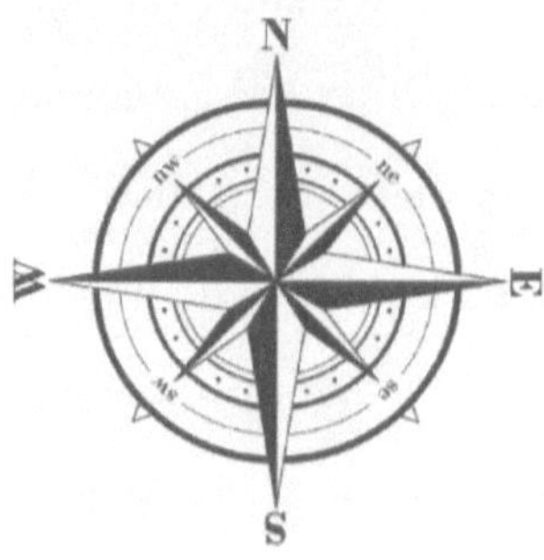

Kane's Off-The-Books Operations Center

Unknown Location

Angus leaned back in his chair, folding his arms. "Huh."

"What?" asked Jagger.

"Langley says they bypassed the ruins."

Jagger's eyes narrowed. "Why would they do that?"

Fang, proving remarkably astute, had the answer. "They know the treasure isn't there. That's where they took it from, so there's no point searching there. It's the starting point of the map they found on the inside of the breastplate."

Angus and Jagger exchanged looks. She was right. Why the hell it hadn't occurred to either of them was beyond him. Perhaps he was just too close to this and wasn't thinking straight. "If our people follow and they leave the road, they're not going to have cellphone coverage."

"And they don't have a satphone yet," added Jagger.

"Dylan does," replied Fang, gesturing toward Angus' station. "You better get this latest intel to him and the others before they lose comms."

"The last communication I had with Niner indicated their local contact was in the dark as to what was really going on. All he knew was they were on a treasure hunt. As soon as they say they've got to leave the road and meet up with someone else, it could raise questions."

"I don't think we have a choice. Remember, the mission isn't to find the treasure. The mission is to rescue the hostages. The sooner we get our people in position, the sooner that's going to happen."

Angus sighed, pulling his chair up to the keyboard. "I think we're going to have to unite them with Kane sooner rather than later. And once we do, we better hope this Professor Al-Mesmari remains on our side."

Leptis Magna Archaeological Site

Khoms, Libya

Faraj pulled them to the side of the road and everyone climbed out, staring at the ruins to their left.

Niner whistled. "Impressive."

Acton agreed. "Quite. I was able to tour them some years ago. It's an amazing find, extremely well preserved. Thank God they didn't get destroyed in the wars."

Faraj leaned against the hood, taking a long drink from his bottle of water. "I stood out here myself, protecting it from those damn heathens."

Acton regarded the man. "I didn't know that."

"It's not something I share. Not in written correspondence, anyway. In my youth, I was a member of one of the factions opposing Gaddafi, though, of course, no one knew it back then." He exhaled loudly. "You deal with all sorts of sordid characters, let me tell you. A lot of people who oppose the government only oppose it because it gets in the way of their criminal ventures. It's why I left all that nonsense and turned to academics." He jerked his chin toward the ruins. "Once you see something like that, you realize what you should be doing with your life."

Acton regarded the man for a moment, having learned something unexpected, then returned his attention to the impressive archaeological site in front of him. "I'm sorry you had to go through that."

Niner's phone chimed. He read the message then showed it to Atlas, and finally to Acton.

It was from Angus.

Tankov has gone off road. Heading southeast.

Acton said nothing. So far, Faraj had no idea why they were really there, and the longer he thought they were on a treasure hunt, the better. Acton slapped his colleague on the back. "We'll check that out later. Right now, I think we have more exciting things to pursue."

Faraj grinned. "I agree. Where to next?"

Acton held up his phone. "Let's follow the map, shall we?" He brought up the high-resolution image of the inside of the breastplate and zoomed in, then glanced up at the sun. "Looks like it's time to go off-road. Southeast."

"Then we're going to need a better vehicle. If I trash this thing, my wife will kill me."

En Route to the Gorge

Southeast of Leptis Magna, Libya

Everyone—friend and foe alike—focused on one thing. Finding the treasure. Each had their own motivations. For Laura, it was self-preservation—hers and Vanessa's. Tankov and his men? Greed. The corrupt Libyan? Probably the same. Tankov talked of retirement, the Libyan of escape. But there was also a part of her that just wanted to find it because she was an archaeologist. This was her job. Her life.

She loved it.

Solving ancient mysteries was thrilling, and this one could be huge. History-altering. The question of what had happened to the Tripolitanian treasury, a question asked by historians for over a thousand years, could about to be answered.

She worked Tankov's laptop, connected by satellite to her Smithsonian account. It gave her access to maps of the area, including declassified satellite images that could reveal ancient roadways and even entire cities invisible to the naked eye. "There it is. That's the road they would've taken. I knew I'd seen this before. It just didn't mean anything at the time." She pointed, tracing the road with her finger. "And look—it goes right through this gorge."

Tankov's eyes narrowed. "Why would they do that? Wouldn't that slow them down?"

"It would. But you have to remember how slow travel was back then. To get from the city to the gorge would take about six to eight hours by cart. That's a full day's travel. So, by going through the gorge, you'd have shelter from the elements. The wind here can be brutal. You travel for a day. You rest." She zoomed in on the gorge. "This is your destination. This is where you'll find your retirement fund."

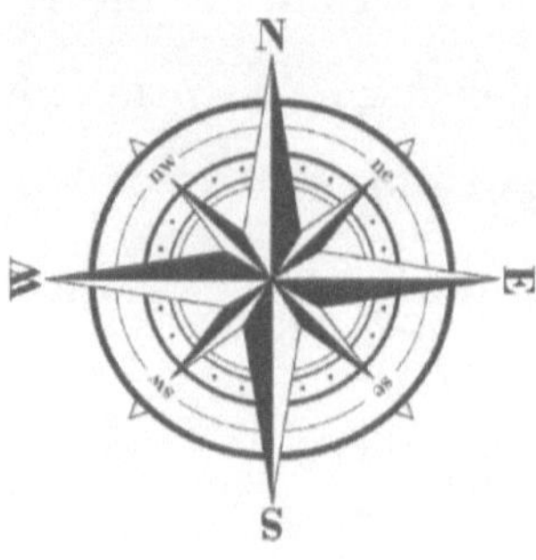

En Route to the Gorge

Southeast of Leptis Magna, Libya

Kane peered through his binoculars and squinted. He could barely see Tankov in the distance, but it didn't matter. Langley was feeding him updates through Angus, and now that he had satellite communications, there was little chance of losing them. It was better not to risk getting spotted. That could put Laura and Vanessa in danger.

The element of surprise was key here.

Langley had indicated there were six Russians and one Libyan he had to contend with. His contact was a CIA asset, but he had no idea how reliable the man was in a firefight. And he would have to be pretty damn good, considering six of their seven opponents were former Spetsnaz. Even he couldn't take that many out unless he was having a damn good day.

And they were having an equally bad one.

But not far behind him was Acton, good in a firefight, as well as Atlas and Niner, both exceptional. Three of the best in the world, plus one well-trained professor with a lot of experience under fire, and his unknown-quantity driver.

Against seven.

He liked those odds a hell of a lot better. He just wished Dawson and the rest of Bravo Team were here with them. That would shift the odds dramatically in their favor.

He lowered his binoculars and blinked a few times to readjust, then turned his head, something catching his eye. He raised the binoculars again but couldn't make anything out through the dust cloud to the south.

He called his ops center and the love of his life. Definitely-not-Angus answered. "This is Fang."

"Hey, babe, can you see what's south of us? I'm seeing a dust cloud."

"Negative. We're only getting text reports and the occasional satellite shot. I'm not seeing anything, but my last shot is almost ten minutes stale."

"Damn. I wish this was a real mission. Listen, contact Langley. See if they've got eyes on anything. I've got a sneaky suspicion trouble is on the way."

Operations Center 3, CIA Headquarters

Langley, Virginia

"He's right. Something is definitely there."

Leroux rose as Tong brought up the isolated portion of the satellite image, revealing half a dozen vehicles including two transport trucks, heading across open terrain toward Kane and the others.

"Are those technicals?" asked Child, leaning forward.

"Zoom in," ordered Leroux.

Tong adjusted the image, eliminating any doubt. These men were heavily armed.

"Who the hell are they?"

Tong shook her head. "I don't know. They're not flying any flags. Could be just a group of criminals."

Leroux folded his arms, staring at the image. "Heading directly for our people?"

"Are they? Or are they just out looking for random targets?"

He sighed, shaking his head. "I don't know. But I think it's time the professors and the others were armed. Get word to Kane. The game's about to change."

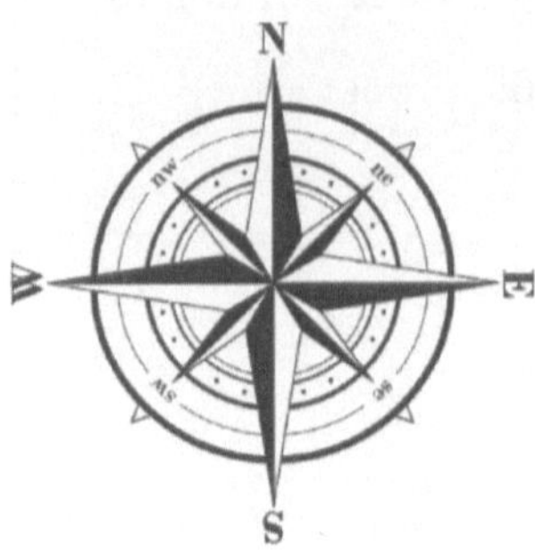

En Route to the Gorge

Southeast of Leptis Magna, Libya

Utkin pointed ahead. "There it is."

Tankov leaned forward and smiled. Even Laura couldn't resist. The gorge was ahead, the stretch of terrain slightly to their left. Utkin adjusted course, and they were soon at the forgotten geological formation, likely sliced through the landscape eons ago by an ancient waterway no longer there.

Utkin brought them to a stop. The ground ahead slowly descended into the gorge. It wasn't deep, though it was wide enough that an ancient roadway could indeed have passed through here, and according to the map, it was the final resting place of the Tripolitanian treasury.

Tankov twisted toward her. "Now what?"

She indicated the map. "According to this, there's a cave about four hundred meters inside. It's on the left, high up on the wall."

Utkin sneered at her in the rearview mirror. "Meters? It actually says that?"

"No, you dumbass. I'm converting from the Roman measurements that are indicated—two-hundred-fifty passūs, which is two paces heel to heel, from the gorge entrance."

Tankov chuckled. "Dumbass. I like that." He flicked his wrist. "You heard her—four hundred meters."

Utkin glared at her but pressed on the gas. They cautiously entered the gorge. Some stones had fallen over time, forcing Utkin to weave his way through, but nothing entirely blocked their way.

Laura kept her eyes peeled, staring up at the rock wall to their left, as did everyone else. She spotted a cave opening. It had to be what they were looking for. It was the right distance, and there was what appeared to be a walkway carved into the wall, though likely naturally formed, the stone shearing off at some point, leaving a ridge that could be used as a path.

Utkin slammed on the brakes, bringing them to a sudden halt. He pointed. "There!"

"Is that it?" asked Tankov, leaning forward.

She had no choice. She couldn't lie. She had to give the man his treasure and just pray she could convince him to let her and Vanessa live. "I think so."

En Route to the Gorge

Southeast of Leptis Magna, Libya

Kane leaned against the rear of their ride as Acton approached. He waved his hands in the air and the 4x4—which didn't match what they had left Professor Al-Mesmari's house in—skidded to a halt. The doors opened and Acton stepped out of the passenger side, smiling broadly.

"Hiya, Doc."

His old teacher laughed. "I was wondering when we'd run into you."

Faraj stood, his mouth agape. "You know this man?"

"Yes, he's a friend of ours."

Atlas and Niner approached, exchanging manly one-armed hugs.

"Good to see you, brother," boomed Atlas. "Please tell me you've got some toys for us."

Kane popped the rear hatch. "Oh, I definitely come bearing gifts."

Atlas and Niner attacked the duffel bags and began gearing up. Faraj shifted from one foot to the other, his head on a swivel. Something was clearly making the man uncomfortable. "What's going on here?"

Acton, shrugging into body armor, finally clued the man in. "I'm sorry to say we're not exactly on a treasure hunt."

The Gorge

Southeast of Leptis Magna, Libya

Tankov handed Laura a flashlight then gestured toward the cave entrance, a gaping maw of inky blackness carved into the cliff face. "This is your show, Professor."

She swallowed hard. She played the light along the entrance floor, then stepped forward, slowly, cautiously. The temperature difference was immediate, cool air washing over her, a stark contrast to the oppressive air behind her. She moved carefully, despite the impatient grumblings of the Russians behind her, counting off her steps, using the map as reference.

There was no precise way to measure where she was, but she hoped what she was seeking would be obvious, even after almost 1,600 years.

There was no evidence anyone had ever been here, though if they had, the signs could have long since vanished. It was clear water had washed through here on occasion, likely funneled from somewhere above during seasonal rains, the original ancient underground river now dry.

She swept her flashlight along the left-hand wall and her breath caught at a pile of stones. She stepped closer, raised the breastplate, and shined the flashlight across its interior surface then onto the rocks. "X marks the spot."

"This is it?" Tankov asked, stepping up beside her.

"It should be."

He indicated the rock pile. "But it's open. Wouldn't they have blocked it off?"

She had to agree. "I would have. Maybe they couldn't. Or maybe someone's already been here."

"That doesn't make any sense," Utkin muttered, scrambling forward. "There would've been word. You can't hide something that big. It would destabilize entire economies back then." He clambered up the pile and disappeared over the top. A moment later, his scream of frustration echoed down the passage.

"It's gone! It's gone!"

En Route to the Gorge

Southeast of Leptis Magna, Libya

Acton held a hand up to his eyes, peering out his window at a cloud of dust south of them. "What is that?"

Kane, riding in the passenger seat, glanced over. "The more accurate question is, who is that?"

"Okay, who is that?"

"No clue, but nobody friendly, according to Langley." Kane gestured ahead. "Let's get moving. The hostages have arrived at the gorge, we're presuming the same one your report said was on the map. We've lost visual on them, and I don't like the description of these guys." He held up his phone. "According to the latest update, they're not heading directly north anymore. They're adjusting course, following us."

Acton frowned. It was one thing to deal with the Russians, but if they also had to contend with one of the Libyan factions, rescuing Laura and Vanessa just got a lot more complicated.

The Gorge

Southeast of Leptis Magna, Libya

Laura stood back with Vanessa as the Russian team moved more of the loose stone out of the way, widening the gap that Utkin had wiggled his way through. He was still on the other side, cursing, mostly in Russian, though the occasional English slur made it through.

Tankov stepped back. "That's enough." He followed Utkin inside, and Laura couldn't resist. She scrambled over the rocks then came out the other side. Tankov extended a hand and she took it. He helped her down, then they both stood, staring at the scene in front of them.

"What do you think happened here, Professor?"

Her head slowly shook as she played her flashlight around the chamber. It was a good size, though, like Utkin had said, any treasure was gone. There were a few empty crates, remnants of others, and at least a dozen distinct skeletons, their body armor still in place. One man was leaning against the far wall, a blade buried in his stomach, what remained of his hands still gripping the hilt.

Not the blade.

He had delivered his own fatal blow.

"What's this?"

Utkin bent over in front of a soldier propped up against the wall. "There's something written on this."

Laura took a knee, first examining the remains. "He's high ranking." She took the tablet from Utkin, Latin writing etched into the surface.

"What's it say?" asked Tankov, kneeling beside her.

"It says, 'Should the traitor Decimus Cornelius Vindex return, know that I have taken the emperor's prize and hidden it where it will never be found. This is your punishment for your betrayal.'" She had to admit she was disappointed. She had wanted to find the treasure as much as Tankov had, though for polar opposite reasons.

"What does it mean?" asked a desperate Utkin.

"It means that's it. I'm sorry, but there's nothing here. It was obviously found."

Utkin shot to his feet and aimed his weapon directly at her. "Find it!"

"How? There's nothing here!"

"There must be a map!" Utkin tore the breastplate free from the remains and flipped it over, finding nothing. He rushed over to the nearest soldier, doing the same. Tankov joined in. Laura rose, slowly backing toward the entrance to the cavern, the desperation shown by her captors growing more concerning by the moment.

"Someone's coming!"

Acton gripped a handhold, everyone now packed into Kane's vehicle as they slowly advanced into the gorge. Langley had already confirmed this was where Laura and the others had gone. While part of him was excited at the prospect they might be about to find the lost Tripolitanian treasury, he was more concerned with safely rescuing Laura and Vanessa. Whether the treasure was there or not, this was the end of the map, which meant the end of his wife's usefulness.

Muhammad pointed ahead at Tankov's two SUVs. "There they are."

"Okay, this is far enough," said Kane.

But it was too late. Gunfire erupted, slamming into the engine compartment. Muhammad shoved it into reverse and hit the gas. The engine sputtered, then conked out.

"Everybody fall back!" ordered Kane.

Acton threw open his door and scrambled out, sprinting at a crouch toward a large rock just to his left. He hit the dirt and rolled as Atlas and Niner joined him, followed by the others. "Now what the hell do we do?"

Tankov peered through his binoculars from the safety of the cave entrance and cursed. He glanced over his shoulder at Laura. "It's your husband. How the hell did he find us?"

She shrugged. "Probably with the help of our friends. I told you, you can't kill us. If you do, they will find you, just like they did today. You have to let us go."

Tankov cursed again. The woman was right. The whole idea was one last big score. They would change their faces, change their identities, and disappear with hundreds of millions each to spend for the rest of their lives.

That was no longer possible. There was nothing here. The treasure was gone, and the fact the message was addressed directly to Decimus suggested it had been gone almost from the moment it had been left.

It made no sense. Who the hell had taken it, and why hadn't history recorded that it had? How does somebody steal that much money and not spend it, not draw attention to themselves?

He closed his eyes. Sixteen hundred years was a long time. Maybe it had been found, maybe it had been spent, maybe it had influenced history, but no one had questioned where the funds had come from, or if they had, those questions were lost to time.

He peered through the binoculars again. He recognized the two Delta members. If there were two here, more could be following. Hell, more could be here already, preparing to flank them. And it was possible the authorities could be on their way, the Libyans eager to look good to their former enemies.

He checked his watch. Time was tight, and he had little to waste on a gunfight he had no doubt he would win, but how many of his men might be lost? And more importantly, would he himself survive?

He turned to Laura. "Come here."

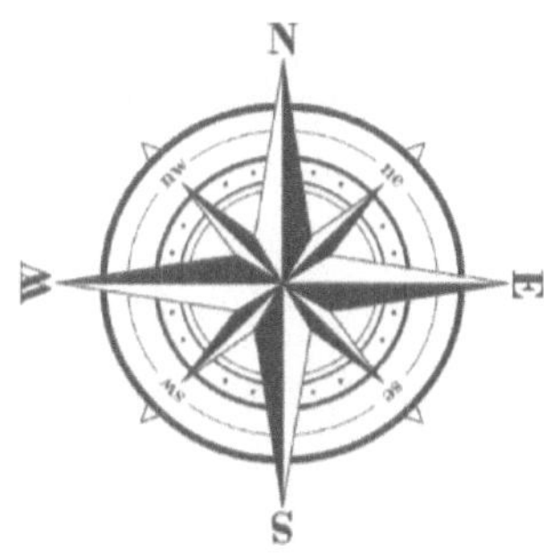

Operations Center 3, CIA Headquarters
Langley, Virginia

Tong threw a desperate hand toward the main display. "They're heading directly for the gorge!"

Leroux had to agree. Yet it was a hidden gorge in the middle of nowhere, not on any map, and only found because of satellite imagery.

"How do they know where it is?" asked Child. "How do they know they're there?"

Leroux folded his arms. "I don't know, but it's like they're tracking them."

"But how?"

"And why?" asked Tong. "There's no way they could know they're there. And there's no way they could know that gorge is there. And even if they did, it's just a gorge. Who gives a crap? There's no way they could possibly know there's anything of value there."

Child spun in his chair. "Maybe they think the targets might be worth taking as hostages. Hold them for ransom."

Leroux dismissed the suggestion. "No, that doesn't fit the facts. They were heading north before our people were even in sight. It's like they knew they were going to be in the area before they possibly could." He turned to Tong. "Get Kane on his satphone."

She tapped at her terminal, then frowned. "There's no reply. The gorge must be blocking the signal."

Leroux cursed, dropping into his chair. "We have to warn them somehow."

Tong faced him. "But how?"

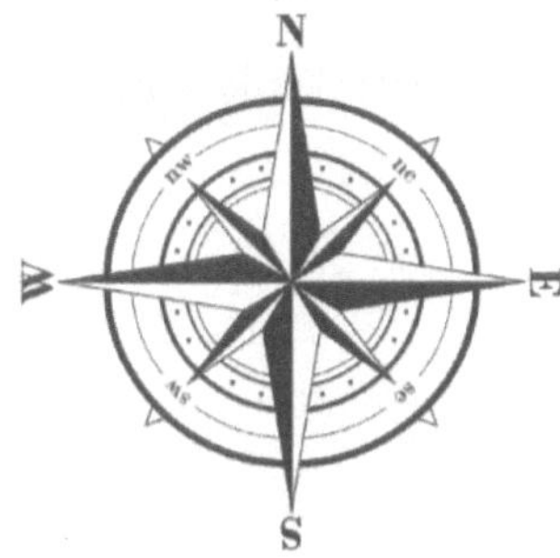

The Gorge

Southeast of Leptis Magna, Libya

Acton spotted Laura being pushed out of the cave entrance, Tankov behind her. "Hold your fire!" he shouted. "There they are!" The guns on their side fell silent, followed by Tankov's team. He rose, slinging his weapon, his hands held high. "I'll handle this."

Kane adjusted his position. "We'll cover you."

Acton stepped out from behind the rock then approached as Tankov descended a ledge along the cliff face, Laura and Vanessa behind him, leaving him to wonder where Angela was. He continued forward, stopping about halfway between their disabled ride and Tankov's shot-up SUVs.

The Russian stopped in front of him. "So, we meet again, Professor. How did you find us?"

"It's not very hard when you've got good friends. Did you find what you were looking for?"

"Unfortunately, no. Someone beat us to it."

Acton was at once disappointed and thrilled. The historical find hadn't been found, but at least Tankov had nothing to plunder. "What are we going to do here?"

"I think we're going to declare a truce. We give you your women, and we go. You don't follow."

"Fine. Where's Angela?"

A radio squawked behind him, and Acton turned to see Faraj rising and pulling the device out from under his robes. He held it closer to his ear.

"We're here," said a voice in Arabic.

He pressed the push-to-talk button. "Then join us."

Acton frowned. "What the hell is going on?"

Engines revved and several vehicles came into sight.

Faraj shrugged. "I'm sorry, my friend, but I'm afraid you won't be leaving here with your treasure. I need it to fund our cause and rebuild a country."

Acton raised his hands slightly as the heavily armed new arrivals poured out. He wasn't sure what to say, though he had a feeling telling the man there was no treasure might not be the wisest of moves. "Then take it. We don't want it anyway. We're here to rescue them."

Faraj shook his head. "I'm afraid that's not the deal I made with them. As far as they are concerned, you are infidels, stealing from the believers. I'm afraid you all have to die."

Tankov stepped forward. "Well, I hate to disappoint you, but there is no treasure. It was taken already."

Faraj's jaw dropped. "By whom? When?"

"No idea who, but it would appear shortly after Decimus hid it." Tankov sneered at him. "Looks like you lose." He raised his pistol and fired, putting a bullet in the traitor's head, then continued to squeeze the trigger as he fell back toward their trucks.

Acton tossed his assault rifle to Laura and pulled a pistol from behind his back. They both retreated toward the Russian's position, covering Vanessa. The rest slowly fell back, the Delta operators and the others using disciplined shots to whittle down the enemy while under heavy, undisciplined fire.

Acton turned to Tankov when he reached the Russian position. "How about we put aside our differences for a few minutes?"

Tankov grunted as he took aim. "Agreed."

Libyan Airspace

Dawson cursed at the latest update from Langley, turning to the others. "Looks like those hostiles Langley was tracking have entered the gorge. Our people are in trouble. There's no way in hell we're gonna be able to land as planned and make it there in time. That's hours of travel, and this could be over in the next few minutes."

Wings headed for the cockpit. "Plan B?"

"Plan B."

Gear was handed out as one large equipment bag was hauled to the side door. Jimmy and Sergeant Danny "Casey" Martin unpacked it as the plane adjusted course, dipping slightly to port. They were no longer heading for Tripoli.

Wings emerged from the cockpit.

"ETA?"

"Five minutes."

"He knows what to do?"

"He does, but he's not happy."

"Don't care. He's got a contingency built into his contract that'll pay him handsomely, so I think he'll get over it."

The whine from the plane's engines eased, the pilot killing as much speed as he could, a rapid descent starting. They had to get below 10,000 feet and 250 knots if they were to do what they planned.

Dawson stood, extending his arms to his sides. Sergeant Trip "Mickey" McDonald checked his equipment then turned, and Dawson did the same for him.

A Ramset gun fired and everyone turned. It pulsed three more times, then Casey gave a thumbs-up. "We're ready."

"Gear up."

Casey and Jimmy quickly donned their equipment, checking each other as everyone waited for the announcement from the pilot.

The overhead PA system gently gonged. "We're at eight-thousand feet, two-hundred-twenty knots. I can't go any slower without risking stalling out. Try not to rip apart my airframe. Two minutes to target."

Dawson gestured toward the door. "Open it. Everybody hang on." He gripped one of the seat backs and Jimmy pressed the button to open the door, an alarm warning of just how stupid this was.

"Overriding door," announced the pilot.

The door swung inward and the cabin immediately reacted, wind howling, anything loose whipping about. The jump rig Jimmy and Casey had installed was extended through the now open fuselage. Dawson stepped into the doorway. He would be first. He glanced over his shoulder at the others. "If I make it, you guys jump. If I don't, well, tell Maggie I love her. And I'm sorry."

Wings slapped him on the back. "Don't worry, buddy. She's already sorry."

Dawson gave him the finger as the pilot announced, "We're over the target."

Dawson stepped out, gripping the stabilizing bar. The force of the wind was shocking. He inched all the way out then pushed off, whipping past the fuselage, clear of the engines. Without the jump rig, it would have been a ridiculously short trip.

He breathed a sigh of relief as he cleared the jet wash and stabilized. The heads-up display on his helmet indicated where his target drop zone was, and he adjusted course. "This is Zero-One. I'm clear," he reported.

Now to survive the landing.

The Gorge

Southeast of Leptis Magna, Libya

Niner fell back to the Russian's position, squeezing off several rounds, taking out another of the enemy as he joined Atlas. "Where the hell's Angela?"

The big man shook his head. "Don't know. I didn't see her."

They continued falling back toward the second vehicle where Acton and Laura were with Vanessa. Niner kept firing, then reloaded. He stole a glance at Laura. "Where's Angela?"

Her eyes filled with tears. "I'm so sorry, but they killed her back in Rome."

The news hit him like a ton of bricks, his worst fear confirmed, and he dropped to his knees, his entire world destroyed, the gun battle around him forgotten, nothing but distant echoes. The only woman he had ever really loved was dead.

His life was over.

Somebody cried out to his left, snapping him out of his sorrow, and he sucked in a deep breath then smiled as one of the Russians collapsed to the ground, dead, a pit of rage flaring in his stomach.

They were all going to die.

Tankov cursed as Utkin dropped—dead. He roared in anger, standing and emptying his mag at the enemy. There were just too many of them, and his team had limited ammo. They hadn't planned on a firefight. This was supposed to be a quick in and out. Get the treasure, load it, leave. No one the wiser.

But now there was no treasure, his friends were dying around him, and he might not even make it out himself.

I guess I'm not getting that retirement after all.

Dawson pulled down on his toggles, flaring his chute, expertly sticking the landing. The jump had been a rough start, what with the unconventional exit from an aircraft definitely not designed for jumping, but once he had opened his chute, everything was routine.

A report over his comms from the flight crew indicated they had pulled the jump rig back inside and closed the door safely, and were returning to Rome rather than continue to Tripoli where they would have to answer questions as to why they had changed course. Those were questions better answered in a country where you could trust the legal system.

He spun around and pulled in his chute as the others landed around him. He shrugged out of the jump gear then bundled it up, tossing it to the ground and grabbing a rock to place on top of it. He didn't care if the authorities found the chutes. Right now, all he cared about was the gun battle he could hear echoing out of the gorge to his right.

He turned to his team. "Everyone good?"

Confirmations were the response.

"Then let's get the hell in there and save our people."

He advanced, the others spreading out on either side of him, forming a wedge, his Kane-supplied M4 raised. They had no idea what they were coming up on. Half a dozen enemy vehicles had been reported entering the gorge, including two transports. Were they filled with men, or were they there to transport this apparent treasure trove hidden somewhere within?

Either way, six vehicles meant a minimum of six hostiles, though more likely well over twenty. They would be outnumbered. But that didn't concern him. These wouldn't be highly trained soldiers, and they certainly wouldn't have equipment like his team had. His bigger concern was who he was also going up against. There could be another half-dozen Spetsnaz to contend with as well. They concerned him. They would be well-armed, extremely well-trained. This could end ugly.

Very ugly.

But Vanessa was in there. Professor Palmer was in there. Unfortunately, Angela wasn't. His heart ached for Niner, possibly still in the dark as to his loss. Yet was she dead? That wasn't the final word from Red's last report. They had no idea. Was she on that plane? Or had they dumped her body somewhere else? There were any number of possibilities, though he feared the worst. Tankov was acting differently this time, unconcerned with casualties more now than ever before.

He spotted something ahead and held up a fist, bringing everyone to a stop as he took a knee. He assessed the scene before him. The gorge was wide enough for the trucks to pass through, but only single file. They were all lined up, with none of the enemy immediately evident.

He rose and continued forward, then spotted two of the enemy using their doors as cover, though not firing. He signaled to Jimmy to take the one on the left and slung his rifle, drawing his blade instead. He advanced, then cupped his hand over the man's mouth and plunged his knife into his target's back, shoving the blade upward and twisting it, scrambling his vital organs.

He lowered him to the ground, all the while keeping an eye out for any sign those ahead were aware of what was happening, finding none. He took a quick tally. He could see six hostiles on his side firing in the opposite direction—obviously on his people and the Russians.

"This is Zero-One. I'm seeing six on my side, over."

Jimmy responded. "This is One-Zero. I've got five. Looks like quite a few are down, over."

"Copy that. Bravo Team, advance. Let's see if we can finish this nice and quick."

Casey and Mickey joined him, and everyone took aim, picking a target in their arc.

"Three, two, one—execute."

He squeezed the trigger, taking down his target, immediately adjusting his aim to the next one, firing again. He re-aimed, seeking a new target, but his side was secure. Gunfire continued, but it was no longer Kalashnikovs—the preferred weapon of their enemy. They were all coming from the Russian position. It was a mix of weapons, including M4s. It had to be Atlas, Niner, and Kane.

The two enemies must have united.

The enemy of my enemy is my friend.

"Hold your fire!" he shouted, and the opposing barrage settled slowly.

"Is that you, BD?" asked Atlas, his impossibly deep voice threatening an avalanche of stone in the narrow gorge.

"Affirmative! Hold your fire! We've eliminated the hostiles!"

The gunfire dwindled to nothing, and he tentatively rose, not trusting the Russians not to reengage. He spotted Atlas and Niner with the professors, Vanessa nearby, as well as Tankov. Bodies were scattered all about—most of them the Libyans, though a few of Tankov's men were down. He had no problem with that. He had intended to kill them all, regardless.

Something squawked in his comms, but he couldn't hear it. Very few would have access, so it could only be Langley. And if they were getting directly involved, something had to be about to go horribly wrong.

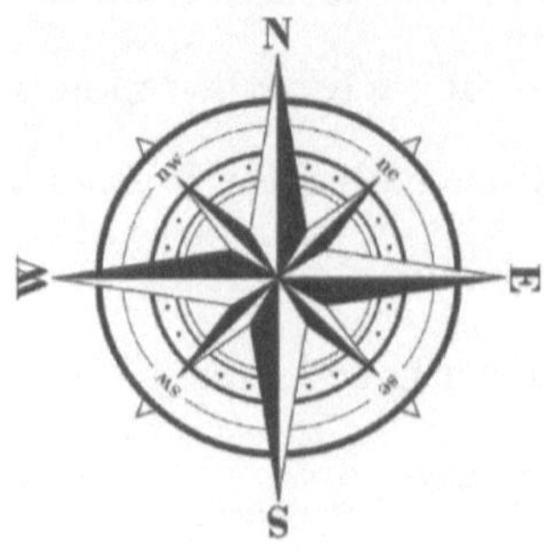

Operations Center 3, CIA Headquarters

Langley, Virginia

"This is Control Actual. Come in, over!" Again, there was no response, and Leroux punched the desk, everything on it rattling. "Are we even establishing a connection?"

Tong gestured at her display. "It's intermittent. The gorge is blocking everything. We can't even bounce a signal around in there. I'm not getting any type of response. And even if they were hearing anything, it's probably just a bunch of static."

"Sonofabitch. We need to get a signal to them somehow. They have to get the hell out of there before it's too late."

Tong faced him. "I don't know what we can do. Even if we deployed a drone, it would take too long to get there. And we don't have authorization."

Leroux cursed. "Keep trying them."

He stared at the display, his head shaking at what he saw. He had no idea what was going on inside that gorge. Was Delta heavily engaged with the enemy, or had they easily overwhelmed them like he suspected they would? Were Tankov's men now in a firefight with them? That concerned him more. Spetsnaz were tough. Though he had every confidence Delta was better, the problem was Tankov had hostages, which hampered what Dawson and the others could do.

"Control, this is Zero-Six. Do you read, over?"

Leroux breathed a relieved sigh and activated his headset. "Zero-Six, this is Control Actual. Do you read?"

"Affirmative, Control."

"You have to get out of there now. There's a large contingent of heavily armed hostiles heading in your direction. It looks like this Libyan group called for help. You've got dozens of vehicles headed your way, over."

"Copy that, Control. ETA?"

"Fifteen minutes."

"Copy that. I'll relay the message. Zero-Six, out."

Leroux slumped in his chair, yanking off his headset and tossing it on his station.

"Now what do we do?" asked Tong.

Child cut off his response. "Oh no."

Leroux turned his chair to look up at the young analyst, who pointed at the display. Leroux spun and cursed. The column of hostiles had split into two, heading to cover both ends of the gorge. If Dawson and his team didn't get out fast, there was no way in hell they would survive.

The Gorge

Southeast of Leptis Magna, Libya

Dawson lowered his weapon but kept it ready, just in case he had to respond. He slowly approached the defensive position set up by his people and the Russians. He relaxed a little when Tankov lowered his own rifle, motioning to the other two survivors of his team to do the same.

"How you guys doing?" he asked Atlas and Niner, but it was obvious from Niner's expression he had figured out what had happened to Angela.

"We're fine," responded Atlas. "But Angela—"

"Angela's dead!" gasped Niner, losing the control he had managed to keep during the firefight.

Atlas wrapped an arm around his friend, holding him against his chest as the fierce warrior, diminutive in comparison to his friend, released his grief. Dawson stepped forward and placed a comforting hand on the man's back, then spun along with everyone as Mickey sprinted onto the scene.

He held up his hands as he came to a halt. "I just spoke with Control."

"Report."

"Apparently there's a large contingent of hostiles heading our way. ETA fifteen minutes. But that was two minutes ago."

"How many?"

"Dozens of vehicles. Too much for us to take on. We have to get the hell out of here."

A plane engine roared and Dawson peered up to see a C-130E Hercules with civilian markings banking overhead.

"That's our ride," said Tankov. "You're welcome to join us if you like, as long as we go our separate ways when we land."

Dawson was inclined to just shoot the man and get on the plane, but there was no guarantee they would get on board without at least one of the Russians. He squeezed the back of Niner's neck. "Agreed."

"Then let's get the hell out of here."

Tankov turned and began sprinting toward the opposite end of the gorge. Both Russian SUVs were totaled and blocking the way. If they were leaving, they were leaving on foot, and they didn't have much time, because while the disabled rides would block anyone coming from the entrance to the gorge they had used, any good commander worth his salt would split his forces and attack from both directions.

They had to reach the plane in the next thirteen minutes.

Niner kept pace with Atlas—the big man far slower than him, though surprisingly light on his feet—as everyone ran for their lives. Literally. Acton and Laura had filled them in on everything as they made their escape, and it pissed him off.

Angela had died for nothing.

There was no treasure here. No reason for any of this. She was dead. He would never see her again. And right now, he didn't even know where her body was. As soon as they were on that plane, though, he was determined to find out.

Every single one of these Russians would be dead if he had any say in it.

They were a virus that kept flaring up, and far too many had lost their lives because of them. It was time they were wiped from the earth. And if he had to do it alone, so be it.

"There it is!" shouted someone ahead.

He looked up to see the path they were on slowly inclining upward. The Hercules' engines thundered, and it was clear the plane was on the ground. Everyone smiled in relief at the sight of the transport aircraft with its rear ramp down. Phones began pinging and beeping around him as satellite connectivity was reestablished—but no one bothered checking them. Everyone was focused on the ramp.

"There they are!"

Niner stole a glance to see the enemy approaching from the south. At least half a dozen vehicles were racing toward them, the dust kicked up behind them obscuring their numbers.

They were close.

Too close.

Vanessa tripped, yelping in fright, and Atlas skidded to a halt. He grabbed her and threw her over his shoulder in a fireman's carry. Niner pushed him, helping him regain speed, all the while keeping a wary eye on the approaching enemy.

Tankov reached the ramp first, and the rest quickly followed, and as the last set of boots cleared Libyan soil, the Russian shouted to the pilot. The engines revved up and the plane lurched forward. Tankov slapped the control switch, and the ramp began rising.

Everyone continued deeper into the aircraft, past a Jeep Wrangler and an ATV apparently meant to help transport whatever treasure they had found from its historic resting place into the hold of this modern transport. They all grabbed seats along the sides of the fuselage as the ramp door closed behind them, the red light turning green as the plane continued to gather speed.

Atlas held Vanessa tight.

Acton had his arm around Laura.

But for Niner, his beloved Angela…. He squeezed his eyes shut, the burn intense, and dropped his head between his knees as the plane lifted off.

He couldn't hold it in anymore.

He had to do something.

It was time for revenge.

He stood and grabbed a handhold, then drew his Glock, aiming it squarely at Tankov.

The Russian's hands shot up. "Hey, I thought we had a deal."

"You murdered my girlfriend."

One of Tankov's men reacted, raising his weapon. Atlas fired two shots into the man's chest. The only other surviving member of the Russian team reached for his HK and two more shots rang out. Out of the corner of his eye, Niner saw Dawson come into view, his weapon extended in front of him.

Tankov's hands rose a little higher. "Now listen, we had a deal."

Niner grabbed him and hauled him to his feet, and Atlas relieved him of his weapons. Niner pushed the piece of shit toward the rear of the plane then smacked the control button to open the ramp, his weapon trained on Tankov the entire time.

Tankov glanced back at the open cargo ramp, clearly nervous. "Listen, you don't understand. She's not—"

Niner didn't want to hear anything from this piece of garbage. They had agreed they would kill them all, and that was the plan he intended to stick with. He just didn't realize the price he would pay. His foot snapped out, connecting with the Russian's chest, sending him stumbling backward, his eyes bulging as he ran out of ramp, his scream fading quickly away.

Niner stepped to the edge and peered over it, spotting the Russian, his arms and legs flailing before he hit the ground thousands of feet below. Niner stepped back inside and smacked the button, the ramp slowly closing.

Dawson turned to Wings and Jimmy. "Secure the cockpit."

Wings nodded. "Mind if I fly?"

"Not at all."

"Where to?"

"Rome. Somebody probably wants their plane back, and I think we've overstayed our welcome here."

Niner collapsed onto a seat, and Atlas joined him, wrapping an arm around his friend. "I'm so sorry, brother."

Dawson checked his phone, and his eyebrow shot up. "Huh."

Niner looked up at him through tear-filled eyes. "What?"

"Latest update from Angus. Langley says they were able to track the Sprinter van from the airport to the parking garage, and then the Wrangler from the parking garage, right into the back of this aircraft. And there was never any sign of Angela."

Niner shrugged. "That just means they killed her somewhere else. Dumped the body."

Laura stood. "No, that's not possible. She was alive when we got out of the van."

Dawson turned to her. "Describe what happened."

"They caught me looking up, trying to get my face on a satellite. He said something like, 'I told you no games.' Then he said something into his radio, in Russian, then there were two popping sounds from inside the van. Then it pulled away a few seconds later. She was alive before that, in that van. So, if she was in the van when it left the airport, and the CIA tracked it all the way to the parking garage…"

"We have to assume they went over that entire place with a fine-toothed comb." Dawson wagged his phone. "Not to mention the previous report said he was only in there for a few minutes. He wouldn't have had much time to hide the body anywhere."

Niner gasped at the mention of Angela's body, and Dawson winced. "Sorry, brother. We have to assume he transferred her into the Wrangler."

Niner still wasn't seeing the point. "They could have had another vehicle parked there, and now she's stuffed in some trunk the Italians don't know about."

Acton shook his head. "No, that doesn't make sense. They never planned on hostages. There's no way they could have known you guys were there. And only one guy was ever leaving that airport. The rest of them were always taking the private jet to Libya."

Niner stared up at him. "What are you saying?"

Everyone turned to stare at the Wrangler at the rear of the plane.

Dawson hesitated and drew a breath. "Langley seems convinced Angela's in the Wrangler."

Niner shot to his feet and rushed to the rear of the plane, peering through the windows.

"She's…I don't see her."

Dawson rounded the other side and opened the door, poking his head inside. "Check the rear."

Niner stepped to the rear of the vehicle and grabbed the handle. He closed his eyes for a moment, taking a deep breath, preparing for the sight about to present itself. He pulled, swinging the tailgate to the side, then gasped, collapsing backward.

The strong hand of Atlas caught him, and Niner's shoulders shook. "I'm so sorry!" he cried. "I'm so sorry!"

He stepped forward and reached in, gently touching the only woman he had ever loved, now curled in a ball, blood staining her arm with little other evidence of what had killed her. She appeared so peaceful, as if she were simply sleeping. How many times had he seen her like this? How many times had he simply laid beside her, watching her sleep as he smiled, making plans for a future that would now never happen?

He gently worked his arm under her neck, his other under her knees, and lifted.

She moaned.

"Oh my God, she's alive! Help me!"

Dawson rushed forward and grabbed the latch for the glass, pushing it up and out of the way. Niner lifted her out.

Atlas was already ahead of him, pointing. "Clear that bench!"

Acton and Laura leaped into action, clearing off a makeshift bed, and Niner lay her gently on it. He checked her pulse. It was weak, but steady. He gently slapped her cheek. "Wake up, baby."

Nothing.

"Med kit!"

Mickey grabbed one and tore it open as he approached.

Niner gently slapped her cheek again, though this time a little bit harder. "Baby, wake up!"

She groaned.

Elation surged through him. "That's it, baby! Wake up!"

Her eyes fluttered open, and she smiled. "Where am I?"

"You wouldn't believe me if I told you." Tears and laughter were all he could manage as he hugged her, and she weakly returned the hug.

Acton patted him on the back as relief filled the cabin. "Well, I guess we know what Tankov was trying to say before you kicked him out."

Niner twisted his head up to see him. "What?"

"She's not dead."

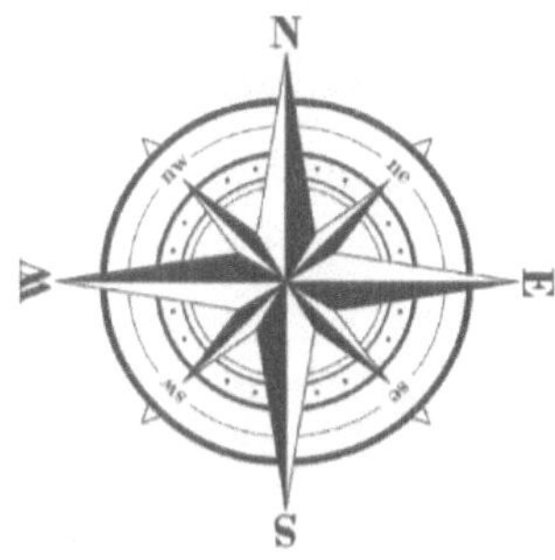

Giasson's Office

The Vatican

Acton sat in Giasson's office, Laura beside him, holding his hand. Bravo Team and Kane had gone their separate ways, getting back to US soil as quickly as possible deemed the prudent move. Tankov's man driving the Wrangler had thankfully put up a fight and was now burning with his comrades, the civilian charter pilot, held at gunpoint, now under investigation by the Italian authorities. Tankov and the threat he posed were now gone.

At least some good had come of this fiasco.

The Vatican Inspector General sat behind his desk, having just connected with Reading, and placed him on speaker. "You're on with Jim and Laura, mon ami."

Reading exploded. "'We're okay, talk to you soon!' That's all I get for hours?"

Acton cringed in his chair like an admonished schoolboy. "Sorry, buddy. A lot's been happening."

Reading calmed. Slightly. "Is Mai all right?"

"Yes," confirmed Laura. "We went and saw her at the hospital. She's awake. She's expected to make a full recovery. She had us scared, but she's a tough one."

"Well, thank God for that. When can she come home?"

"The doctors don't want her flying for another week, so we're going to stay here with her."

"That's good. What about Angela? What happened with her?"

"She's fine. She doesn't know much about what happened, except that as soon as the van doors closed, Tankov's man injected her with something to knock her out. Before she passed out, she felt him cut the palm of her hand. I guess they wanted to leave some blood behind to make us think she was dead. She woke up on the Herc on the way back., so, she's none the worse for wear."

"I think Niner had the worst of it," added Acton.

Reading grunted. "Yeah, I guess so." There was a burst of static. "Mario, my condolences on the loss of His Holiness."

Acton's chest tightened. It was a sad day at the Vatican. A sad day in Rome. A sad day for Catholics the world over. The Pope had died, finally succumbing to his illness, and Giasson was taking it hard. Acton hadn't seen him smile since they had arrived and the man greeted them at the airport.

"Thank you, my friend. These are challenging times. I believe God has a plan. Perhaps whoever is chosen next is the one who is needed now."

Acton sensed the man didn't want to talk about it anymore, so he changed the subject. "You'll be happy to know that Tankov and all of his men are dead."

"Good. Couldn't happen to a nicer group of people." Acton could almost hear Reading's smile. "So, there was no treasure?"

"There was, but it was gone," corrected Laura.

"Where is it?"

"No idea. And perhaps we'll never know. If it hasn't been found in sixteen hundred years, then maybe it won't be found for another sixteen hundred. All I know is I'm not going back to Libya to search for it."

"Assuming that's where it even is," said Acton. "Whoever left that tablet seemed confident it would never be found."

"And you think that was him in the chamber?" asked Giasson.

Laura leaned forward, the only one to have seen it. "I think so. I can't be certain, but he did appear to be holding the tablet, and he had markings that indicated he was a senior officer, so might have the balls to insult a man of Decimus' rank."

"Who do you think he was?"

"No idea. And unfortunately, all we can do is notify the Libyans where the chamber is, and they can send in an archaeological team if they think it's safe enough to do so."

"Hopefully one a little bit more trustworthy than the last one."

Acton frowned. "Yeah, that surprised me."

"Desperate times," murmured Giasson.

Acton inhaled, holding it for a moment. "So, how are things going there?"

"Good. Very good, in fact," replied Reading, a pep in his voice Acton hadn't heard in some time. "Listen. Remember that offer you guys made, about me living here?"

Acton smirked, exchanging a look with Laura. "Yeah?"

"Well, I might have a reason to take you up on it."

"You're going to finally retire?"

"Hell no! I'm going to request a transfer to DC."

"You can do that?"

"I have it on good authority that my boss would love to get rid of me."

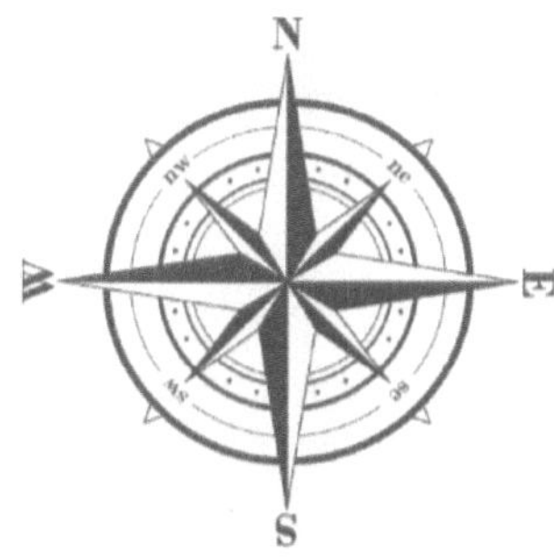

James/Moore Residence, Abbotts Park Apartments

Fayetteville, North Carolina

Atlas rose and headed for the door as Vanessa's phone rang. She grabbed it off the table. They had made it back a few days ago, the vacation obviously cut short. Angela was fine. They had stitched up her hand, and thanks to having been drugged most of the time, the psychological effects would hopefully be minimal. He was just thankful they were all alive, relatively unscathed.

He opened the door to find a man standing there. "Yes?"

"Vanessa Moore?"

Atlas eyeballed him. "Do I look like a Vanessa?"

The man took an involuntary step back, then chuckled. "Well, umm, no."

"Is that a question or an answer?"

"I've got a delivery for Vanessa Moore."

"That's my girlfriend."

"That's me!" called Vanessa, her footfalls hammering on the parquet flooring. "Yes, he's here…just a second. That's me."

A hand was held out, a set of keys dangling. "These are for you."

Vanessa took the keys and the man left. "Just a second, Professor. I'll put you on speaker."

Atlas didn't know what the hell was going on as Vanessa tapped her phone. "Okay, you're on speaker with me and Atlas."

"Did you get the delivery?" asked Laura.

"Yes." She looked at the keys in her hand. "But I don't understand. What's going on? What is this?"

"Go outside," said Acton.

"All right. Give us a moment."

Atlas slipped on his shoes, as did Vanessa, then they headed for the elevators. His phone rang. It was Niner. He wasn't sure what was going on, but the poor bastard was still blaming himself for what happened to Angela, and he couldn't leave him hanging. He took the call. "Hey, buddy. What's up?"

Instead of a morose best friend, he found a bundle of excitement. "You're not going to believe this! We just got an email from the nursing college. Angela's entire tuition has been paid in full!"

Atlas' eyes narrowed. "What? How? By who?"

"I think you know who. At least I assume it was them."

The doors opened and they stepped on. Atlas punched the button for the ground floor.

"Listen, buddy, I'm kind of in the middle of something. Let me call you back in a few."

"Okay. Talk to you soon."

Atlas ended the call.

"Was that Niner?" asked Acton.

"Yes, it was."

"We'll be calling them next."

"So, that was you?"

"Just a small token for what she went through."

"You guys know none of that was your fault, right?"

"And I'm sure Niner knows what happened to Angela wasn't his fault, but he still blames himself regardless."

Atlas sighed. "Yeah, you're right." The doors opened and they stepped out, heading for the lobby entrance. "So, just what are we supposed to—"

Vanessa interrupted him, crying out and rushing toward the doors. "Oh my God, oh my God, oh my God!"

Atlas jogged after her, his girlfriend and the phone conversation heading out the door. He caught up to her, but as he cleared the entrance, his mouth fell agape.

Parked in front of the apartment building was a brand-new food truck, Vanessa's logo painted on the side.

Vanessa hopped up and down, and had already made one full circuit around what was definitely not an old beater like what he had bought her.

He caught her. "Settle down, babe, breathe."

She squeezed her lips shut but couldn't stop hopping. The tears were flowing, her joy contagious.

"Docs, is this your doing?"

"No, it's your doing," replied Laura, her voice cracking with emotion. "You're wonderful people. All of you are. And you don't deserve what happened to you. This is just our little way of saying thank you."

"There's only one condition," added Acton.

"What's that?" asked Vanessa, still trembling.

"We eat for free."

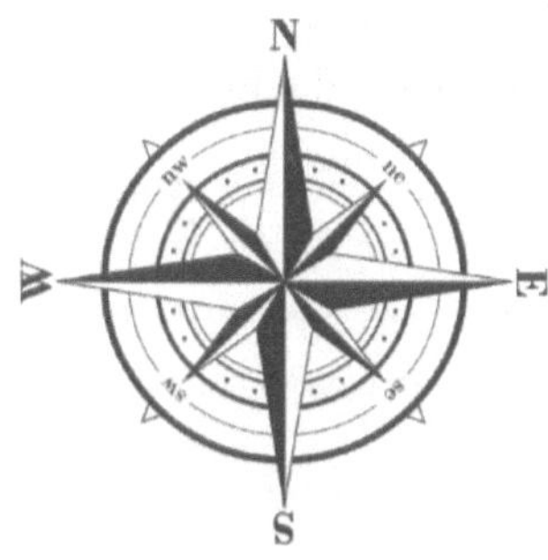

East of Leptis Magna, Tripolitania

Western Roman Empire

AD 431

Tiberius woke with a start, gasping in a breath that felt as if it were his first in far too long. It was pitch black around him, and it took him a moment to reorient.

He was in the pit.

More accurately, he was at the bottom of the pit. That bastard Decimus, his supposed friend, had left him here to die. Anger flared through him at the betrayal, the monumental betrayal. Why had he done it? Why had he thought he couldn't trust him?

He would never betray Decimus. He would never betray the emperor. And most importantly, he would never betray the empire. He was a good soldier, a good citizen, a good man.

Yet none of that had mattered.

He had served Decimus for over a decade, by his side in battle, in leadership, in brotherhood. He had even been there at the birth of his children and had cried on the man's shoulder when his own son had died in a tragic accident. They were like brothers. Closer than most blood.

Yet he had betrayed him, without warning, in the most cowardly of ways.

If he had just told him what was required, at least then he would have had a choice. And though he might not have readily sacrificed himself like Gaius had, he likely would have come to the same conclusion, allowing him to die with honor.

But now here he was, lying atop what he could only assume were the bodies of the personal guard, also betrayed, left to die.

He wished he had been stabbed in the heart. At least then he'd be dead. Now, he could be here for days before his suffering soul finally succumbed.

Or he could do something about it.

Like the soldier he was.

Lying here wallowing in self-pity wasn't what a man of his position would do. It was unbecoming.

He rolled off his back and onto his knees, cringing at what his hands touched in the pitch black. He stood and reached out for the walls, finding one side just to his left. He ran his hand along the surface— smooth, as if worn by water. It made sense, and it meant there were likely few, if any, handholds to climb his way out.

He stared up but saw nothing. He cocked an ear and heard nothing, though he could swear his own heartbeat echoed in the narrow confines.

And then he smiled.

He reached out and found the opposite wall.

These were indeed narrow confines.

He spread his feet. He could touch both sides. He confirmed he still possessed his dagger, then dropped to his knees, searching the bodies until he found another one. He jabbed it at the stone and it pierced slightly.

Good enough.

He stabbed his own blade into the opposite wall and began his long ascent. How long that would be, he had no clue. He had no idea how deep this pit was, and if there were no torches above, as he suspected, he would be met with equal darkness.

It had taken several counts from the time they had tossed the bodies inside before the thud of the bottom echoed. How far could that be? And he had survived the fall, another indicator Decimus should have killed him outright rather than surprise him.

Rage kept him going, kept him inching upward. His muscles screamed, his lungs burned. So many times he wanted to give up, but the thought of catching Decimus—of vengeance—kept him going.

He stabbed out with his right hand.

And found nothing.

The void surprised him and he almost fell, but before he slipped, he stabbed again. This time, he found something. But it was different. Something had changed. He couldn't see it, but he could sense it.

He had to take a chance.

He freed the tip of his dagger from the stone with his left hand, then swung—taking a leap of faith—and plunged the now-freed dagger into empty space with a downward thrust.

It connected.

Not against a wall, but a flat surface.

The cave floor.

He freed the dagger to his right, dug it in again, and smiled.

He swung his leg over and rolled onto his back, his chest heaving as he sucked in lungsful of air. His arms and legs were dead. But he was alive. He would survive.

And he would seek his revenge.

He rolled to his knees then stood, tentatively stepping forward, terrified he had lost track of where he was and might inadvertently fall back into the pit. There was no way he could do that climb again. That was a onetime effort.

He took another step. Solid ground. Then another. His left hand found the wall. He kept moving forward, half a pace at a time, and with each step, his confidence grew.

Then he saw a light.

The cave entrance.

He heard sounds below. Men shouting, horses whinnying. It was a language he had never encountered before. It had to be the Vandals. He crept forward and peered down. Scores of riders and men on foot charged through the gorge, their torches lighting the way, blinding them to anything more than a few paces beyond their circles of light. They shouldn't see him up here, but anything was possible.

He remained hidden as mixed feelings overwhelmed him. Part of him wanted them to catch up and slay Decimus, but the others were innocent. This was Decimus' betrayal alone.

Eventually, the enemy passed, and he spotted a torch burning on the ground below, likely dropped by one of the riders. He gingerly made his way down the cliff face, retrieved the torch, and headed back up, a new way of exacting revenge occurring to him.

He collected several other discarded torches and lit them, then stood in front of the rock face.

Smiling.

It would be a lot of work, but he was well aware that inside, the men had water and provisions on their persons. All he had to do was move enough stone to get inside.

Then the cause of Decimus' betrayal would be moved to where his so-called friend would never find it.

Into the depths of Hell, where he had been condemned to die.

THE END

ACKNOWLEDGMENTS

As I write this, I'm waiting to hear when my heart bypass surgery will be. It looks bad. I have seven blockages, including two that are 100%. As one cardiologist described the results of my angiogram: "Ugly cath."

The risks are high that things won't go well. Higher than I'd like, obviously. But they're higher that things will be fine. I'm trying to focus on that. It's hard to stay positive when your odds of being dead in a few weeks are as high as mine are.

I'm doing everything I can to improve those odds, and I'm optimistic even if I can't, I'll be in that majority that survive and thrive.

It will be a long haul to recovery, though I'm looking forward to it.

And should the worst happen? Then this is my last offering. I hope you enjoyed it, and I hope my legacy lives on, and more readers like you discover my writings and enjoy them in the future.

I'm lucky in that way, as my profession means I leave a legacy that can be remembered. Not everyone has that luxury, and I am blessed.

But I intend to survive this, recover, and write a hell of a lot more books over the coming years, and should I truly be blessed, decades.

I'm not ready to get off this ride.

Some of you know that I often name characters after people in my life. One of those is a good friend of many years, Mario Giasson. He's French-Canadian, not French Swiss, but is as bald as his fictional counterpart.

And he was a grandfather for three hours.

My heart breaks for my friend's loss, and as I told him after he discovered my news, should the worst happen, and there is a Heaven, I'll tell little Lili all about her granddad.

On another note, just as this book was ready to be released, the Pope died. I worked in a slight reference to this in the final Giasson scene. This was meant to honor the man, not offend the easily offended.

As usual, there are people to thank. My dad for all the research, Brent Richards for some weapons info, Gary Tye for some medical info (any mistakes are mine, and I unabashedly claim artistic license), and, as always, my late mother who will always be an angel on my shoulder as I write, as well as my family and friends for their continued support, and my fantastic proofreading team!

To those who have not already done so, please visit my website at www.jrobertkennedy.com, then sign up for the Insider's Club to be notified of new book releases. Your email address will never be shared or sold.

Thank you once again for reading.